Luke Jensen,
Bounty Hunter
Dead Shot

Luke Jensen,
Bounty Hunter
Dead Shot

William W. Johnstone
with J.A. Johnstone

WHEELER PUBLISHING
A part of Gale, Cengage Learning

Detroit • New York • San Francisco • New Haven, Conn • Waterville, Maine • London

GALE
CENGAGE Learning®

LIBRARY OF CONGRESS CATALOGING-IN-PUBLICATION DATA

Johnstone, William W.
  Luke Jensen, Bounty Hunter Dead Shot / By William W. Johnstone with J. A. Johnstone. — Large Print edition.
    pages cm. — (Wheeler Publishing Large Print Western)
  ISBN-13: 978-1-4104-6364-7 (softcover)
  ISBN-10: 1-4104-6364-8 (softcover)
  1. Bounty hunters—Fiction. 2. Large type books. I. Johnstone, J. A. II. Title.
PS3560.O415L86 2013
813'.54—dc23   2013030055

Published in 2013 by arrangement with Pinnacle Books, an imprint of Kensington Publishing Corp.

Printed in the United States of America
1 2 3 4 5   17 16 15 14 13

Luke Jensen, Bounty Hunter
Dead Shot

CHAPTER 1

Luke Jensen muttered, "Oh, hell," in disgust as a rapid whirring sound came from behind him. He knew what it was, having heard similar sounds many times in his life. A rattlesnake had been denned up in the rocks where he had taken cover, and the scaly creature was upset about being disturbed.

A bullet flew over Luke's head and splattered against the rocks. He had a venomous serpent behind him and an equally venomous human in front of him.

He crouched a little lower and looked over his shoulder. The snake had crawled out of a gap between the rocks and curled up at their base. It was big around as Luke's wrist and the diamondback pattern was etched vividly into its scales. Even though it was difficult to guess how long the snake might be since it was coiled to strike, Luke figured it would stretch out to six or seven feet, at least.

A blasted monster, in other words, and not something he wanted to share the hidey-hole with.

He was confident he could blast the head right off that serpentine body with a single shot, but the solid rock face was right behind the snake. There was a chance the slug would ricochet back into Luke's face . . . a good enough chance that he didn't want to risk it.

He sighed and drew the knife sheathed on his left hip. Reminding himself to keep his head down so Monroe Epps wouldn't put a bullet through it, he used his left hand to poke the Winchester's barrel at the rattler.

The snake uncoiled and struck with blinding speed. Luke swatted it aside with the rifle barrel, then brought his booted left foot down on the writhing body just behind the head. He was pretty fast. The knife flashed in the sun as he brought it down and severed the snake's head from its body with one swift, clean stroke.

He grimaced as he kicked the head back into the rocks. The snake's eyes were still open and its jaws opened and closed as it tried to bite the air. Its prehistoric brain hadn't realized yet that it was already dead.

Epps fired twice more, and the shots came so close to Luke's head that he ducked even lower. Starting out, capturing or killing Monroe Epps had been just a job to him, but he was starting to get irritated.

"Listen to me, Epps!" he called as the echoes of those last shots rolled away across the mostly flat and arid southern New Mexico landscape. "The reward dodgers on you say dead or alive, but I'd just as soon not kill you!"

"You lie, Jensen!" Epps screamed back at him. "I recognized you. Everybody knows you kill a lot more men than you ever bring in alive!"

"That's because they're always so damned stubborn," Luke replied. "They don't give me any choice. You can do better than that, Monroe. All you have to do is throw out all your guns and come out with your hands in the air."

Epps had forted up in a similar cluster of rocks on the other side of a broad, shallow draw, about twenty yards from Luke's position. The fugitive's horse had run off when Epps had been winged and knocked out of the saddle during their running fight awhile earlier. He wasn't hurt too badly.

Luke had watched the man scurry into the rocks, then had dismounted and sent his hammerheaded dun galloping back up the draw with a swat of his hat on its rump.

He wanted the horse well out of the line of fire. He had taken cover as Epps started shooting at him.

Monroe Epps had robbed close to a dozen banks in New Mexico Territory and western Texas. He wasn't a cold-blooded killer, the sort of mad dog outlaw who gunned down anybody who happened to get in his way, but he *had* killed a Texas Ranger and an El Paso city policeman during a couple of his escapes, so the Lone Star State wanted him pretty bad. Bad enough that there was a $5,000 bounty on his head.

Luke wanted that five grand. It was why he had gotten on Epps's trail and tracked him to that desolate landscape. It wasn't that he lacked a sense of justice or a desire for law and order. It was just that the money interested him more.

"Why would you want to give me more of a chance than all the other men you brung in dead?" Epps called.

"We're a good long ways from the nearest town," Luke replied, "and the weather's been pretty hot lately. If I have to kill you, there's a good chance you'll go to stinking before I can get you there and collect the reward. I have delicate sensibilities, you know."

Epps let out a bray of laughter. "That's

rich. A bounty hunter with delicate sensibilities. I guess you're just gonna have to let 'em be offended if you want to collect on me, because I ain't surrenderin', Jensen. No way in hell!"

Luke sighed again. "You're sure about that?"

"Damn sure!"

"In that case, I guess I'll just have to let a friend of mine give me a hand."

"A friend? I didn't see nobody ridin' with you whilst you was chasin' me!"

"You're about to meet him," Luke said. "I'm going to send him over there to introduce himself."

He turned and slid the rifle barrel under the thick, scaly body of the dead rattlesnake. It had finally stopped writhing around in its death throes. Grimacing again and being careful to keep the barrel in the middle of the snake's body so it was balanced and wouldn't slide off, Luke picked it up with the Winchester and took hold of the rifle with both hands.

Epps said, "I think the sun's made you go loco, Jensen! There ain't nobody —"

Luke swung the Winchester in a high arc with as much force as he could muster in his lean but powerful body. At the top of the arc, the snake flew free and sailed across the draw toward the rocks where Monroe Epps had taken cover.

The bank robber saw the huge rattler flying toward him and let out a startled, high-pitched yell. He started blazing away at the snake, trying to shoot it out of the air, never noticing that it didn't have a head anymore.

Luke dropped the rifle, burst out from behind the rocks, and raced toward Epps's position. He whipped his twin Remingtons from their cross-draw holsters as he charged the bank robber.

Epps realized what he was doing and screeched a curse at him, still shooting at the snake wildly, instinctively, as it dropped beside him. Luke heard the gun roar, but could tell that none of the shots were directed at him.

With the speed he had built up, he was able to bound atop one of the rocks and look down to where he could see Epps. The outlaw had shot the already dead snake to pieces and tried to wheel around and bring his gun to bear on Luke.

The Remington in Luke's right hand blasted and sent a slug tearing through Epps's left shoulder. Luke meant for the shot to go through his quarry's right shoulder, thus disabling his gun arm, but Epps had shifted to the side at the last second, just as Luke pulled the trigger.

Even so, the wound should have been enough to put him down, but Epps managed to stay on his feet. He held his gun and fired again, the slug sizzling past Luke's left ear. Luke figured the bank robber might be out of bullets after wasting so much lead on that rattler, but he couldn't afford to take that chance.

Both Remingtons erupted. The .36 caliber slugs struck Epps in the chest and hammered him back against the boulder behind him. He hung there for a couple seconds, his eyes wide with pain and his mouth opening and closing like a fish out of water. His gun slipped from his fingers and thudded to the ground. Epps pitched forward after it and landed facedown on the bloody shreds of the rattlesnake.

That seemed fitting to Luke. Both of them were low-down varmints who served no purpose, and the world was better off without them.

Just as Luke had predicted, the body of Monroe Epps started to get a little ripe before he reached the settlement of Rio Rojo late the next day. He had been lucky enough to find Epps's horse, so he'd lashed the bank robber's corpse over the saddle.

No way would he have shared his own mount with a dead man for that far.

If he hadn't found Epps's horse, he would have cut off the man's head like he had done with the snake, stuck it in a canvas sack, and left the rest of him for the buzzards and coyotes. The head would have been enough to let him collect the bounty. He had done that before when he had to, although he didn't like being forced to that grisly extreme.

It would have offended his delicate sensibilities, he had mused with a faint smile as he'd tied Epps's body over the saddle.

After more than a decade and a half as a bounty hunter, surviving in a violent land as he followed that ugly profession, he shouldn't have had any sensibilities left at all, let alone delicate ones. But to a certain extent it was true. He was a well-spoken man. He loved to read, especially the classics, and he appreciated a fine glass of brandy, along with a well-played piece of music.

Once a year or so, if he had the funds, he paid a visit to San Francisco so he could take in an opera, dine in the city's best restaurants, and enjoy the company and conversation of people who weren't thieves, killers, and ruffians.

He usually enjoyed the company of a few beautiful women, too, because despite the fact that he wasn't exactly handsome — far from it, in fact, with his craggy, deeply tanned face — the ladies seemed to find something about him attractive. He seldom lacked for pleasant feminine companionship during those visits to the city by the bay.

San Francisco was a long way off at the moment, although he thought briefly about it as he rode down the dusty main street of Rio Rojo, leading the dead outlaw's horse. Most of the buildings in the New Mexico Territory settlement were adobe, although some had been built of lumber brought in from the mountains to the north and east. A school stood at one end of the street, a church with a bell tower at the other. In between, a couple dozen businesses lined the street's three blocks. The residences were scattered haphazardly around the outer edges of the settlement.

Most important for Luke's purposes, Rio Rojo had an undertaker, a bank, a marshal's office, and a telegraph office. He planned to drop off the body of Monroe Epps at the undertaker's and then pay a visit to the local law. Once the marshal confirmed who Epps was and that there was a reward offered for him, he could send a wire to Texas and claim that reward for Luke. And then the bank could pay him. Simple as that.

Luke reined to a stop in front of the funeral parlor and dismounted. The sound of hammering drew him to the back of the building. As he expected, he found the proprietor building a coffin. The pieces of wood were varnished and decorated with fancy scrollwork depicting cherubs and flowers. Somebody important would be laid to rest in that coffin.

"Looks like you already have some business," Luke said to the man. "I've brought you another customer."

The undertaker was in his thirties, a dark-haired man with broad shoulders and brawny arms. He set down the hammer and said, "It'll have to wait awhile. I've got to finish this first. The funeral for one of the town's leading citizens is tomorrow morning."

"When did he die?" Luke asked.

"A couple hours ago. I've been working on this coffin for a while, though. We all knew it was just a matter of time."

"The fella I brought in has been dead since the middle of the day yesterday."

The undertaker frowned. "That might present a problem, all right. If you don't need a special-built coffin for your friend,

16

I've got a plain one already put together that might do."

"Plain is fine," Luke said. "And he's not my friend. You can stick him in anything and put him in the ground without any ceremony as far as I'm concerned . . . as long as it waits until after the marshal has taken a look at him and confirmed his identity."

The undertaker's frown deepened as he pursed his lips. "Like that, is it?"

"Like that," Luke replied with a nod.

"All right. You've got the body with you?"

"Out front, tied over the back of his horse."

"I hope you had the decency to wrap him up in a blanket or something."

"I did."

"Well, then, bring him on back here, I guess. Are you going to get the marshal now?"

"That's my next stop," Luke said.

"Fine. I'll send my boy on up to the cemetery to start digging a grave. Or does the deceased need to be laid to rest in consecrated ground?"

"I don't know anything about his religion, but I sure wouldn't waste anything sacred on him. Out back of Boot Hill is good enough for the likes of Monroe Epps."

"I never heard of the man, but I hate to hear anyone spoken of that way. How would you like it if someone said something like that about you, someday?"

Luke grimaced. "Mister, when my time comes they're liable to be saying a lot worse than that."

CHAPTER 2

Luke had expected the corpse to draw a crowd. Dead bodies usually did whenever he brought them into a town.

When he walked back around the building to the hitch rail where he had left the horses, he saw half a dozen people standing nearby. They didn't get too close, the stink saw to that, but they were near enough to satisfy their curiosity.

Only one man stood right beside the horses, and he had a tin star pinned to his vest.

The local badge-toter blew air through the walrus mustache that drooped over his mouth, jerked a thumb at the blanket-shrouded shape, and asked Luke, "This belong to you?"

"I suppose it does, until I get paid for it."

"Bounty hunter, eh? That don't surprise me. Who's under that blanket?"

"Monroe Epps," Luke said.

The lawman frowned. "That name's familiar."

"I'm sure you've seen it on wanted posters. The State of Texas has put a five thousand dollar bounty on his head." Luke reached inside the breast pocket of his black shirt that a layer of trail dust had turned gray and brought out a folded piece of paper. He held it out to the lawman and went on. "Here's one of the dodgers. You can compare the picture on it to the body."

He reached for a corner of the blanket to pull it back.

The lawman grimaced. "Not here. Let's at least take him around back." He inclined his head toward the bystanders, indicating that he didn't want to give them a show.

That was a little unusual, Luke thought. A lot of lawmen he had run across liked to put the corpses of dead outlaws on display for the public. Sometimes the undertakers even charged for taking a look. In those cases, though, it was usually the bodies of freshly slain owlhoots, which Monroe Epps definitely wasn't.

Luke untied the reins of Epps's horse from the hitch rail and led the animal to the rear yard.

The undertaker had resumed hammering on the fancy coffin. He stopped again as

20

Luke and the lawman appeared. "Marshal Dunbar."

"Howdy, Calvin," the marshal replied. He waved a stubby-fingered hand at the coffin sitting on the saw-horses. "That the box for old Lucius Vanderslice?"

"That's right. He called me in and gave me instructions for what he wanted about six weeks ago, after the doctor told him he didn't have much time left."

"Lucius was always one for bein' prepared, all right." Dunbar turned to Luke. "All right, let's have a look at that carcass."

Luke pulled the blanket back enough to reveal the bank robber's slack, pale face, even more unlovely to look at in death than it had been in life. He unfolded the reward poster he had taken from his pocket and held it up next to the dead man.

"Well, hell, it's hard to tell anything that way," Marshal Dunbar said. "The way he's loaded on that saddle, his head's hangin' upside down."

"Why don't you catch hold of his hair and lift his head up?" the undertaker suggested.

Luke sighed and turned the reward poster upside down, so that the picture of the man's face on it was oriented the same as the corpse's face.

"Oh," Dunbar said. "Yeah, that's him, all

21

right. No doubt about it. Epps was the name, you said?"

"Monroe Epps." Luke handed the poster to the lawman. "All the particulars are on there, including the charges and the place you need to wire to authorize the reward being paid to me."

"And just who might you be? I reckon I'll need to know that."

"The name is Luke Jensen."

Dunbar's eyes narrowed. "I think I've heard of you. Used to go by Luke Smith, didn't you?"

"That's right," Luke admitted.

"Why would you change your name?"

"It's a long story, Marshal, and one that has no bearing on our dealings here. So no offense, but if it's all the same to you, I'll leave both of you to your respective tasks. I want a bath and a shave and a place to stay, then a good meal."

"Bath house is down the block on your right. The Rio Rojo Hotel is across the street. It's the best place in town. It don't have a dinin' room, but Slade's Restaurant is in the next block and the food there is good. I reckon you'll need a livery stable for your horse."

"Yes, please."

"Dunbar's Livery."

Luke cocked an eyebrow.

"It belongs to my brother," the marshal went on, "and it's the only stable in town, so me bein' the law don't give it any sort of unfair advantage. What about Epps's horse?"

"Think your brother would pay enough for it to cover the expense of its late owner's burial?"

Dunbar studied the animal with a critical eye for a moment, then nodded. "More than likely. I'll see that Calvin gets paid."

"Thank you." Luke touched a finger to the brim of his black, flat-crowned hat. "That goes for both of you gentlemen."

"I'll send that wire right away," Dunbar said.

"I'm obliged to you, Marshal."

"Might get that bounty as soon as tomorrow," Dunbar went on. "Once you've been paid, won't be no reason for you to hang around Rio Rojo, will there?"

The question didn't surprise Luke. Most lawmen didn't like having a bounty hunter around. Neither did most of the other honest citizens, for that matter. Luke supposed he didn't blame them. He might be legally sanctioned, but he was still a killer.

"That's right, Marshal," he said, keeping his tone mild. "There won't be any reason for me not to move on."

Luke's first stop was the livery stable, where Marshal Dunbar's brother was more than happy to lead Luke's horse into a stall and promise to take good care of him. The marshal had failed to mention that he and his brother were twins, right down to the shaggy mustache each man sported.

"I reckon Cyrus sent you," the man said.

"That would be the marshal?"

"Yep. I'm Cyril."

"Cyrus and Cyril Dunbar."

"Yep."

"He mentioned a hotel and a bath house, too. Are they also owned by Dunbars?"

Cyril looked confused. He frowned and said, "What? No, old Mr. Vanderslice owned the hotel. Reckon his widow does now, since he passed away earlier today. And Felipe Ortiz runs the bath house and barber shop. Next closest one is all the way over in El Paso."

"I'm sure it'll be fine." Luke paid for his horse's keep for a night and left his saddle there, but took his saddlebags and Winchester with him. Behind him, Dunbar yelled for somebody named Hobie to rattle his hocks and fork down some more hay from the loft.

The usual red-and-white-striped pole led Luke to the bath house and barber shop, where the rotund and ebullient Felipe Ortiz welcomed his business, too. He had a fire burning under a huge pot of water big enough to cook a meal for a whole tribe of South Seas cannibals, Luke noted.

A hall that led from the back of the barber shop area had two cubicles partitioned off on either side of it, each with a tub in it. None of them were occupied at the moment, so Luke could have his pick, Felipe informed him. Luke replied that any of them would be all right, and with a spate of rapid Spanish directed at his sons, Felipe set them to filling the tub in the first room on the left. The little boys used buckets and had the tub almost full within minutes. Tendrils of steam rose wispily from the water's surface.

"I need a shave, too," Luke said.

"It will be attended to, señor," Felipe assured him. "You should bathe first."

Luke nodded and drew the curtain across the opening at the front of the little room. In addition to the tub, the room contained a bench and a stool. He leaned the Winchester in a corner, pulled the bench over next to the tub, took off his gun belt, and coiled it so the butts of the Remingtons were within easy reach when he placed it on the bench. His saddlebags went on the bench, too. One of the pouches held clean shirt, socks, and the bottom half of a pair of long underwear he intended to put on when he was finished with his bath, but he would have to don the dusty black trousers again.

When he was naked, he stepped into the tub. A chunk of soap and a brush sat on a shelf beside the tub, but Luke left them where they were for the moment. He was content to lie back and let the hot water soak away the aches and pains of long days on the trail.

He closed his eyes and let his mind drift, although a part of him remained alert. He had made too many enemies over the years to allow himself to relax completely unless he was in a place where he knew for sure he was safe. In the circles in which he traveled, men tended to settle old grudges with powder smoke and lead.

His thoughts went back to what Marshal Dunbar had said about him changing his name. That wasn't strictly true. When he had started calling himself Luke Jensen again, he had merely reclaimed his real name. Luke Smith had never been anything but an alias designed to conceal his true identity because of what he considered

26

some shameful events during the closing days of the War of Northern Aggression. Those days were long past and Luke had put them behind him, but he had continued to use the Luke Smith name out of habit, if nothing else.

Then he had run into his younger brother Kirby, who had another name, too — Smoke Jensen. Luke suspected that his brother had grown up to be the famous gunfighter known from one frontier to the other as probably the fastest man who had ever lived, but he had avoided a meeting until fate brought them back together.

Getting to know Smoke — fighting side by side with him — had convinced Luke that he ought to take the Jensen name again, but he didn't go out of his way to let folks know that he and Smoke were related. Smoke was a successful rancher in Colorado, a widely respected citizen. He didn't need people knowing that his brother followed a profession as sordid as bounty hunting.

Luke could have drifted off to sleep in the bathtub. The hot water felt that good. He didn't let himself do that, of course, and the part of his brain that remained vigilant knew right away when a soft footstep sounded just outside the curtained-off cubicle.

By the time someone pushed the curtain aside, Luke's eyes were open and one of the Remingtons was clutched in his right fist as he aimed it at the opening.

The young woman who stood there gasped in surprise. Her eyes widened as she took an involuntary step back. "Please, señor, do not shoot."

She didn't look like a threat. She was about eighteen, with smooth, honey-colored skin and masses of thick dark hair around a pretty face. The white blouse she wore rode low on bare shoulders and revealed the upper swells of her full breasts. She carried a basin in her hands.

"Who are you?" Luke asked. "What do you want?"

"I . . . I am Philomena," she said. "I have come to shave you. My papa —"

"You're Ortiz's daughter?"

"Sí, señor."

"So he has more than sons." Luke lowered the hammer on the Remington and slid the revolver back into its holster. "You can leave the basin and the razor. I'll take care of the shaving."

"But you have no mirror. You cannot see."

"Won't be the first time I've shaved without a mirror."

A stubborn look came over Philomena's

face. "I am excellent at shaving a man, señor. And my father sent me to do this. I must do as he says."

Luke had to wonder what sort of father would send his beautiful daughter into a small room with a naked man.

On the other hand, Philomena would be holding a razor to that man's throat, which would be enough to make most hombres behave themselves. If a fellow got out of line, all she had to do was press a little harder.

"I suppose it'll be all right," Luke said. "Where's the razor, anyway?"

Philomena set the basin of hot, soapy water on the bench and used a bare foot to drag the stool over closer to the tub. She smiled, reached into the top of her blouse, and took out a closed razor. "I like to warm it before I begin."

"I'll just bet you do," Luke muttered.

"Señor?"

"Nothing," he told her. "Go ahead."

She sat down, got a handful of soapsuds from the basin, and spread them on his face. Her slender, supple fingers worked the lather into his beard stubble with surprising strength.

"Lean your head back, señor," she said quietly. "It will be easier that way."

Luke did as she said. In that position, his eyes naturally closed again. What she was doing to him felt good. It wiped away all the stress of the long days he had spent trailing Monroe Epps.

She smelled good, too. A clean, healthy female scent. Not the perfume of the ladies he dallied with in San Francisco, to be sure, but just as appealing, especially since Philomena was right there and those ladies were hundreds of miles away.

He felt something brush his face and slit his eyes open to see that several thick strands of her raven-dark hair hung next to his cheek as she leaned over him. The blouse sagged enough to give him an unobstructed view of the valley between her golden breasts. He closed his eyes again and steeled himself not to react. He was old enough to be the girl's father, after all . . . but he was also human.

She began humming softly to herself as she took the razor and started scraping the stubble from his cheeks and throat. Her touch was smooth and sure. She hadn't been lying when she'd boasted that she was good at it.

Luke had a hunch she was good at other things, too, but he was determined not to find out about that. It just wouldn't be right.

Even a bounty hunter had *some* scruples.

"Señor?" she whispered, so close that he felt the warmth of her breath on his ear. "Señor, you are a very handsome *hombre*. I wish —"

Whatever she wished, Luke probably would have said no, but he didn't get the chance to. At that moment, another step sounded in the corridor, along with the jingle of a spur, and the curtain was suddenly swept aside, causing Philomena to cry out and jerk back from Luke. The razor in her hand nicked his neck as she did so, but the sting of the little cut was the least of his worries at the moment.

The stranger's face twisted in hate and anger as he thrust the twin barrels of a shotgun at Luke and screamed, "Time for you to die, bounty hunter!"

CHAPTER 3

Luke's reaction was instantaneous. His left hand shot out and grabbed Philomena's arm while his right flashed toward the basin of soapy water. He pulled Philomena into the tub with him as he grabbed the basin and sent it flying toward the would-be killer with a flick of his wrist.

Philomena's scream ended in a splash and a gurgle as she went face-first into the tub. Luke twisted aside and surged up from the water, partially shielding her body with his own.

The basin spinning toward the stranger's face caused him to flinch, pulling the shotgun's barrels out of direct line with Luke. But at that close range, the buckshot would spread enough to do considerable damage if the man triggered the weapon.

In the split second of grace that throwing the basin had given him, Luke snatched one of the Remingtons from its holster. He didn't aim, but fired from the hip, letting instinct guide his shot.

The bullet flew true, ripping into the man's left side and spinning him halfway around. Stubbornly, he stayed upright and tried to swing the shotgun back into line. Luke fired again, and put his shot right in the middle of the stranger's forehead. The slug bored on through the man's brain and exploded out the back of his skull in a grisly spray of blood and bone.

The man dropped the shotgun and fell to his knees, then toppled forward to land with his ruined head dangling over the edge of the tub. At that moment, Philomena emerged sputtering and choking from the water and found herself looking at the dead man's bullet-shattered skull from a distance of only a few inches. She started screaming again.

Felipe Ortiz rushed in brandishing an old cap-and-ball pistol and yelling in Spanish. Spotting his daughter in the tub and a naked Luke Jensen standing over her, he reacted normally and thrust the gun at Luke with both hands as he fired.

Luke didn't want to kill Ortiz. He dived to one side as the old pistol boomed. The ball missed him by several feet, hit the cubicle's rear wall, and blew a neat hole in it. He fell over the bench, rolled, and hooked a foot behind Ortiz's left ankle, sweeping the barber's legs out from under him.

Ortiz went over backward with an alarmed yell and bounced a little as his amply-padded rear end hit the floor.

"Papa, no!" Philomena cried. She kept shouting at her father in Spanish.

Luke understood the language fairly well, although the words flew out of her mouth so fast he missed some of them. But he knew she was telling Ortiz not to shoot anymore.

Finally she said in English, "The señor did nothing! It was this . . . this . . ." She looked down at the dead shotgunner again, and fainted dead away.

Luke grabbed her blouse to keep her face from sliding under the water.

The barber shop door slammed open and heavy footsteps charged back to the bathing area. Marshal Cyrus Dunbar came to a startled stop and looked around to see Ortiz sitting on the floor, a dead man draped over the edge of the bathtub with blood leaking from his head turning the water red, and a passed-out Philomena sagging in the tub while Luke, naked as a jaybird, held her up.

"Good Lord! I must be seein' things!" Dunbar squinted and looked away from Luke. "Things I don't want to be seein'."

"I assure you, Marshal, there's a reasonable explanation for all of this," Luke said.

"You mean besides me bein' loco?"

"Yes, and if you'll take Señor Ortiz and his daughter out of here and let me get dressed, I'll tell you all about it."

"What about, uh . . ." Dunbar gestured vaguely at the dead man.

"He won't be going anywhere or bothering anyone else."

"Fine, fine," Dunbar muttered. "Felipe, go back out front and take that old horse pistol with you."

Philomena started moaning and moving around as she came to, and the marshal added, "Señorita, let me give you a hand."

While Dunbar helped the groggy and soaking wet Philomena climb out of the tub, Luke picked up his hat and held it in front of him so that he was no longer completely exposed.

Dunbar put his arm around Philomena's shoulders and steered her toward her father, who had gotten to his feet but still looked completely confused. Dunbar looked back at Luke and snapped, "Is there gonna be a dead body involved every time I run into you, Jensen?"

"I hope not, Marshal. I sincerely hope not."

Luke hadn't gotten the chance to scrub off all the trail dust, but the idea of getting back into the tub after so much of the dead man's blood and brains had leaked into it didn't hold any appeal. He used the rough towel hanging on a nail driven into the wall to dry off and then got dressed. At least some of his clothes were clean, he told himself.

He left the body where it was and went out into the barber shop. Night was settling down over Rio Rojo, he saw through the big window in the front of the shop.

Dunbar and Ortiz were waiting for him, but Philomena was gone. Luke supposed her father had sent her home. He said, "The first thing I want you to know, Señor Ortiz, is that I did nothing to dishonor your daughter. I give you my word."

"What was she doing in there?" Ortiz asked with a glare.

"Shaving me." Luke touched a finger to the little nick on his throat. The drop of blood from it had scabbed over. "She said you sent her in there to do it, that it was her job."

"Dios mio!" Ortiz threw his hands in the

air. "That girl! I have told her such things are not decent, but she watches and when she sees a man who appeals to her — as so many do! — she sneaks in to flirt with them. She has the . . . the heat in her blood . . . like her mama. A good thing for a man when his wife is like that, but not so good when it is his daughter!"

"What about the dead hombre?" Dunbar asked heavily.

Luke shrugged. "He came in, pointed a shotgun at me, and yelled that it was time for me to die."

"And you took exception to that."

"It seemed like the appropriate reaction."

Dunbar's eyes narrowed. "You must be pretty handy with a gun if you were able to stop him from killin' you when he already had a greener ready to cut loose."

"I was lucky." Luke explained about throwing the basin at the stranger. "That gave me just enough time to get my hand on a gun."

"And that's all you needed, wasn't it?" Dunbar held up a hand. "Never mind. Who was he, and why did he want you dead?"

"Your guess is as good as mine, Marshal."

"You mean you don't know him?" Dunbar sounded like he had a hard time believing that.

"I never saw him before," Luke said. "He knew who I am, though. He called me a bounty hunter. He said it like an obscenity."

"To some folks I reckon it is," Dunbar muttered. "Let's go take a better look at him."

Ortiz crossed himself and said, "Not me. I just want him out of my place, Marshal."

"As soon as I can, I'll tell Calvin to fetch his wagon," Dunbar said. "Come on, Jensen."

They trooped back to the cubicle. Dunbar took hold of the corpse's shoulders and pulled him away from the tub. The body rolled loosely onto its back. The man's face was set in a permanent grimace, etched there by the bullet that had left the black, red-rimmed hole in the center of his forehead. "You sure you don't know him?"

Luke studied the dead man for a long moment, mentally comparing the face to the drawings on hundreds of wanted posters he had memorized. It wasn't an unusual face, sort of foxlike and bordering on ugly, with a weak chin and straggly hair the color of straw. The man wore range clothes that had seen better days. In addition to the shotgun, he packed a .44 revolver in a holster strapped to his waist.

"He looks like a thousand other drifting

hardcases, Marshal," Luke finally said. "I don't know him, but I feel confident that he was wanted. He must have seen me come into town, recognized me as a bounty hunter, and figured it would be in his best interest to kill me before I recognized him and came after him." Luke shook his head. "His high opinion of his own notoriety got him killed. I wouldn't have known him if I'd bumped into him on the street."

"Well, I don't guess anybody can blame you for shootin' him. He was gunnin' for you, no matter what the reason, and if he'd pulled those triggers he likely would've killed poor Philomena, too. So I reckon you saved her life." Dunbar paused. "You really weren't up to anything with the gal when this gent busted in?"

"I swear I wasn't, Marshal. She was giving me a shave, that's all."

Dunbar grunted. "You're lucky ol' Felipe ain't a better shot. You can't blame him for jumpin' to the wrong conclusion when he went rushin' in."

"Even with a dead man halfway in the tub, too?" Luke asked.

"I don't imagine he saw much of anything just then except his daughter and a naked gringo old enough to be her daddy."

"No, I suppose not," Luke said with a

sigh. "Don't worry, Marshal, I don't bear any ill will toward Señor Ortiz for taking a shot at me. These things happen."

Dunbar gave him a skeptical look. "It seems like they do around you, anyway."

Since Luke's shave had gotten interrupted, Ortiz finished it in the barber chair once Calvin the undertaker had shown up to haul away the corpse. Ortiz tried to apologize for the misunderstanding, but Luke assured him that everything was all right. Ortiz told him that the bath and the shave were on the house, considering the circumstances, but Luke insisted on paying and added a nice tip to the sum.

With that taken care of, he took his Winchester and saddlebags and walked across to the Rio Rojo Hotel, newly owned by the Widow Vanderslice. It was a two-story adobe building with a red tile roof and a balcony with decorative wrought iron railings along the second floor. Plants in pots hung from chains attached to that balcony where it formed a roof over the first floor gallery. The warm yellow glow of lamplight filled many of the windows.

As Luke signed the registration book for the clerk at the desk in the lobby, he commented, "I was sorry to hear about the owner's passing."

The young man nodded and pushed up the pair of spectacles that had slid down his nose. "Yes, Mr. Vanderslice was a good man to work for. He was one of the first American settlers in Rio Rojo, you know. But he's been sick for quite a while, so his death came as no surprise. Still, it's a sad day, Mr. . . . Jensen, is it?"

"That's right," Luke said.

The clerk's eyes narrowed in thought. "You're the man who brought in that dead outlaw earlier."

Luke nodded. "I am."

"I heard some shots a little while ago. Did you have anything to do with that?"

Luke didn't see any point in lying. The whole story would be all over town in no time, anyway. He knew how quickly gossip spread in little settlements like Rio Rojo. "A fellow tried to kill me. I discouraged him — permanently."

"There won't be anything like that happening here in the hotel, will there?" the clerk asked nervously.

"I doubt it."

"But you're not sure?"

"Nothing is certain in this life," Luke said. "If you'd prefer, I can seek other accommodations."

"No, that won't be necessary," the clerk said with a wan smile. "We'll just hope for the best."

"I always do."

The clerk gave him the key to room eight. "To your left at the top of the stairs."

Luke carried up his gear. It was a good enough room, clean and with a bed that looked comfortable, along with a woven rug on the floor. The single window opened onto the balcony and overlooked the street. He didn't care much for that. People had climbed onto balconies and taken shots at him through windows in other towns. But he figured the odds of somebody else in Rio Rojo being after him were pretty small, so he decided not to do anything about it at the moment.

He thought he might make a pallet on the floor on the other side of the bed when he got back from supper and heap some pillows and blankets under the covers to make it look like a man was sleeping there, just in case.

Marshal Dunbar had recommended Slade's Restaurant in the next block. Luke was there eating a decent steak a little while later when the lawman came in, looked around the room, spotted him, and started toward him.

"Avery at the hotel said you got a room and then left again but didn't take your things with you, so I figured you'd gone to eat," Dunbar said without any preamble. "I went through all the wanted posters in my desk, but I didn't find that hombre with the shotgun. If he really is wanted, I don't have paper on him, so I don't reckon you can claim a reward on him."

"I'll kill a man for free any time he's trying to blast me with a shotgun," Luke said dryly.

Dunbar grunted. "Yeah, I reckon that makes sense." He pulled out one of the vacant chairs at the table and sat down without being invited. "I sent that telegram to the Rangers in Texas. Don't really expect to hear back from 'em until in the mornin', though. How much of a reward did you say you was due for that fella Epps?"

"Five thousand."

"Our bank ought to be able to cover that. I'm sure you've noticed that Rio Rojo ain't very big. But we're sittin' right between some prime ranchin' country to the north and some good producin' silver mines to the south, so the bank does pretty well for itself. Has to keep considerable cash on hand for payrolls and such-like. Not to mention the occasional bounty."

43

"Have you ever had to pay one out before?" Luke asked in idle curiosity.

"No, can't say as we have. But there's got to be a first time for everything, don't there?" Dunbar laughed, but he didn't really sound amused. "Hell, you might even get through a day without bein' shot at."

"It could happen. But I don't think I'm going to hold my breath waiting for it."

CHAPTER 4

Luke still felt vaguely unsatisfied when he was finished with his meal, even though the food was good. The marshal had left after commenting that it would be nice if nobody else got killed tonight. Luke had agreed with that sentiment, but hadn't made any promises.

Pausing on the street outside the restaurant, he fished a cigar out of his pocket and struck a match to light it. When he had puffed the cheroot to life, he shook out the match and dropped it in the dust at his feet.

The cigar was good, but it didn't take care of the restlessness inside him. That left only two possibilities — a drink or a woman.

Fortunately, there was a good chance both cravings might be satisfied at the same place, he thought as he looked up and down the street and his gaze came to rest on an adobe building with the word *Cantina* painted above its arched entrance. He moseyed in that direction, smoking the cheroot as he ambled along the street.

The door to the cantina was open, allowing music and smoke to drift out into the night. The music came from the strings of a guitar being plucked by an expert musician. The smoke was a mixture of tobacco and the sweeter odor of hemp.

With the cigar clenched between his teeth, Luke went through the little alcove at the entrance and pushed past a beaded curtain into the cantina's main room. Unlike many such establishments he had visited, it had a real plank floor instead of hard-packed dirt. Candles had been stuck in the necks of empty wine bottles standing on several of the tables. The bar ran along the back of the room.

In a rear corner near it, sat the guitar player. An old man, he stared straight ahead, and his milky eyes told Luke that he was blind. His fingers were bent and gnarled with age, but that didn't stop them from moving over the guitar strings faster than the eye could follow as he coaxed lovely strains of music from the instrument.

The cantina was fairly busy, with a dozen men drinking at the bar and at least that many at the tables scattered around the room. Luke scanned their faces, but didn't spot anyone familiar. A number of the men glanced at him and he saw recognition in their eyes, but it probably came from watching him bring in the body of Monroe Epps a couple hours earlier.

No one reacted violently to his entrance, and that was the only thing that really mattered to him. Any time he stepped into a new place, especially a saloon or a cantina, he had to be ready for the possibility that somebody might recognize him and slap leather. Danger went with the job.

It was possible none of the men in the cantina paid much attention to him because they were all busy watching the woman dancing to the music of the old, blind guitar player. She wore a dark red blouse even more low-cut than the one Philomena had worn. Several bracelets around each slender wrist clicked together as she swayed her arms above her head. Her long skirt lifted and swirled to the movement of her muscular brown legs. Waves of thick dark hair tumbled all the way down her back.

She was darker skinned than Philomena, with more Indian blood mixed with the Spanish. The most important difference as far as Luke was concerned, though, was she was a full-grown and full-blown woman, while Philomena was still a girl.

She twirled and spun toward him, and her lithe, agile movements suddenly faltered for an instant as their eyes met. The break in her rhythm was so tiny most of the spectators in the cantina didn't notice, although Luke did. The dancer twisted away and began clapping her hands over her head as she worked her way back toward the guitar player.

Luke walked across the room to the bar, where a lean man with a pockmarked face stood on the other side of the hardwood and asked, "Drink, señor?" The man's left ear was missing its lower half.

The severity of the scar told Luke that someone had carved it off with a knife.

"Cerveza," he said. Some instinct told him he would be wise to keep his wits about him, so it was smart to stick to beer.

He had learned to listen to his instincts.

The bartender drew a glass of beer and pushed it across the bar. Luke tossed down a coin to pay for it, then picked up the glass and half turned to watch the dancer as he sipped the warm, bitter brew.

"Her name is Magdalena," the bartender said. "And do not waste your breath asking if her time is for sale. She goes only with those she chooses. Anyone else risks danger even by approaching her."

"Is that so?" Luke asked wryly.

The bartender touched his mutilated left ear. "I grew too bold with her one night and she gave me this. I watched her night after night from behind this bar, and my blood grew so enflamed that I was willing to risk the danger."

"Do you still feel that way?"

"Sometimes . . . but then I remember the cold fire of her steel."

"I'll keep that in mind." Luke sipped the beer and watched Magdalena dance.

When the old man stopped playing, she gave a defiant toss of her long, midnight hair to bring the dance to a conclusion. Men whooped and applauded. Her face was expressionless, as if she didn't hear any of the acclaim. She was not exactly beautiful, Luke thought, but any man who looked at her would have a hard time looking away, and not just because of her lush body.

He wasn't surprised when she came straight toward him, pacing across the room like one of the great cats that roamed the mountains south of the border. He had seen something flicker in her eyes during that brief moment they had shared. Disappointed noises came from some of the men in the room, as if they had been hoping she would choose them.

One of the customers, a burly man with a jutting beard who looked like he might be a miner or a bullwhacker, started to his feet and reached for her as Magdalena walked past the table where he sat. "Wait just a damned minute."

Luke would have stepped in to teach the man a lesson in manners, but he didn't have to. Before the man could touch her, she whirled around and her hand lashed out. The man jerked his hand back, yelping in pain. Bright red blood welled from a cut on the back of his hand.

Magdalena turned and walked away as if nothing had happened.

Luke caught a glimpse of the little knife in her hand, but then it disappeared and he couldn't tell what she did with it.

The wounded man sank back onto his chair, muttering as he nursed his bleeding hand. His friends at the table with him laughed, and one of them offered a bandanna to tie up the injury.

Magdalena walked up to Luke and asked in English, "Do I know you?"

"I doubt it. I've never been in Rio Rojo before today."

"Perhaps in another life, then. I feel strongly that we have been together before."

He shrugged. "It may be true. There are

50

many mysteries in life."

"And many things that are true, like what happens between a man and a woman."

"Perhaps the greatest truth of all," Luke said.

She put a hand on his arm. "Will you come with me?"

"A man would be a fool not to. But you have a certain . . . reputation."

Amusement flashed in her eyes. "Did that fool of a bartender tell you I cut off his ear?"

"He mentioned it," Luke admitted. "And I've seen for myself your skill with a blade."

"Do not worry, señor. I will not cut off anything that belongs to you." Her lips curved in a sly smile. "Unless, of course, you disappoint me."

"I'll do my best not to," Luke promised with a smile of his own.

What with one thing and another, it was long after midnight before Luke got back to his room in the Rio Rojo Hotel. The lobby was empty, and he saw no sign of the clerk. Avery, that was the man's name, Luke recalled idly.

He went upstairs, drew one of the Remingtons, and used his other hand to unlock the door as he stood to one side of it, just in case somebody was waiting on the other side to fire a shotgun through the panel at the first rattle of a key in the lock.

Nothing of the sort happened. The room was empty. Working by the starlight that came through the window, Luke made the covers look like someone was sleeping under them, then bedded down on the floor as he had planned. The mattress would have been softer and more comfortable, but the floor was better than a lot of places he had slept.

The restlessness inside him had been stilled. Tomorrow he would collect the reward he had coming for Monroe Epps and ride out of Rio Rojo in search of his next quarry. He would take with him fond memories of Magdalena . . . for a while, anyway.

Luke dozed off quickly and was still sound asleep when the sun rose and a new day began in the settlement.

Gunner Kelly knew the Rio Rojo bank opened promptly at nine o'clock every morning. He had been in the settlement for a week, keeping an eye on the place until Dog Eater got there. The Apache had shown up the night before, so there was no point in waiting any longer to go on about their business.

The two of them stood on the porch in

front of the general store and watched the bank manager unlock the door of the building across the street. The bank was the only building in town made of brick. It was supposed to make people think their money was safe inside, but that was the furthest thing from the truth.

Kelly took off his battered old brown hat and ran his fingers through his red hair. His skin was so fair it never tanned, just blistered whenever he stayed out in the sun too long. "We wait until the manager has time to unlock the safe so he can take out some cash for the drawers in the tellers' cages."

Dog Eater grunted.

"Then we go in before he can close the safe again. That way we don't have to waste time forcing him to open it. I know how long it takes for him to get the money out. I watched through the window the other day and counted it off in my head." Those numbers were already ticking over in Kelly's brain.

When he'd gone to school as a kid, he had always had trouble with reading and writing, but numbers came as natural to him as riding a horse and shooting a gun. Everybody had their own strengths, he liked to tell himself, and he knew how to put his to good use.

"The tellers won't give us any trouble," he went on. "I'm gonna pistol-whip the manager right away, so he won't, either. We should be out of there in five minutes."

Dog Eater grunted again. He was short and stocky like most Apache men, although he had a habit of carrying himself sort of stooped over and was taller when he straightened up. He had a Navajo blanket wrapped around his body, concealing the faded blue shirt, the buckskin leggings, the breechcloth, the double gun belt, and the crossed bandoliers of ammunition he wore. He looked harmless, which was exactly how he wanted to look.

Kelly wore range clothes and could have been mistaken for a drifting cowboy. The only thing about him that stood out, other than his pasty face, was the pearl-handled Colt on his hip.

The gun was his pride and joy, and he was good with it. Good enough that he had killed three men back in his native Missouri and earned the nickname Gunner before he was twenty years old. During the past five years, while embarking on a career of outlawry, he had killed half a dozen more. And not lost one second of sleep over it, either.

"There's one of the tellers," he said to Dog Eater. "And here comes the other one.

We'll give it a couple more minutes. . . ."

The time seemed to pass slowly to Kelly as tension grew inside him. He wasn't scared, just ready to get on with it.

Dog Eater said, "Now?"

And Kelly replied, "Now." He started across the street with an easy, confident stride. Dog Eater shuffled along a couple steps behind him.

When they walked into the bank the manager mistook them for the first customers of the day, or at least that's what he assumed *Kelly* was. His gaze flicked over Dog Eater and then ignored him, except for a fleeting grimace of distaste. He smiled at Kelly from the teller's cage where he was putting money in the drawer and said, "We'll be right with you, friend."

Kelly walked up to the cage and drew his gun. "You'll take care of us now."

Behind him, Dog Eater shrugged the Navajo blanket aside and raised both pistols. He covered the stunned tellers while Kelly leveled his revolver at the bank manager.

"Come on out of there and you won't get hurt," Kelly said.

"I . . . I . . ."

"I didn't say for you to talk. Just do what you're told or I'll kill you." Kelly paused for a second to give his next words the proper dramatic weight. "I'm Gunner Kelly, so you know I'll do it."

The bank manager's eyes widened in fear. Kelly had a reputation, all right. He and his Indian partner had robbed close to a score of banks in New Mexico, Arizona, Colorado, and Utah. Kelly was so contemptuous of the law — apparently with good reason — that he never tried to conceal his identity. He announced it every time he and Dog Eater pulled a job.

"D-don't shoot me, Mr. Kelly," the manager said as he raised his hands and came out from behind the counter. "Please. I have a wife —"

"That's your problem," Kelly said. "Mine is relieving you of all the money in this bank."

"There's really not that much —"

"You shouldn't lie to me." Kelly struck without warning, slamming the pistol in his hand against the man's head. The bank manager went down like a poleaxed steer.

Dog Eater pulled a canvas sack from under his shirt and tossed it onto the counter. He grunted as he glared at the tellers.

"What he means is that you boys should start filling up that sack," Kelly said. "Get everything in your cash drawers, and then all the money in the safe, too. Make it fast. If somebody comes in before we're finished, there's liable to be shooting. And we'll make sure you boys catch the first bullets."

The tellers didn't waste any time. The sack was bulging with greenbacks in a matter of minutes. Dog Eater holstered one of his Colts and took the loot. He started to back toward the door.

"I don't have to tell you what'll happen if you raise a ruckus before we're well away from here," Kelly warned the tellers. "You just tend to your boss there and make sure he's all right. That way everybody gets to live."

Kelly backed through the door after Dog Eater. The two of them turned and walked quickly toward their horses tied nearby, but not quickly enough to draw attention.

It might have worked if a hearse pulled by a team of six black horses hadn't rounded a nearby corner just then, carrying Lucius Vanderslice's body to the church for his funeral. The buggy right behind the hearse had Mrs. Aurora Vanderslice in it and was being driven by Marshal Cyrus Dunbar, who knew right away what was going on when he saw two men backing out of the bank, one of them carrying a full canvas sack.

"Son of a —" Dunbar exclaimed. He dropped the reins and clawed at the spot on his hip where his gun usually was. But he hadn't figured he would need it at a funeral, so he hadn't worn it.

He had his badge pinned to his coat, though, and that was all Kelly needed to see. He turned, flame lancing from the muzzle of his fancy Colt as he opened fire on the lawman.

CHAPTER 5

The Widow Vanderslice screamed as Kelly's bullet slammed into Dunbar and drove him heavily against her. The marshal was hit hard, but had the presence of mind to shield the elderly woman's body with his own. He pressed a hand to the hole in his side where blood was leaking out.

Since there was no point in trying not to attract attention anymore, Kelly and Dog Eater raced toward their horses as several more buggies came along the street. Quite a few pedestrians marched in the funeral procession, as well. Kelly had heard talk the day before about some important man in town dying, but he hadn't expected the funeral to be so early in the morning.

On the other hand, it got pretty hot in southern New Mexico Territory that time of year, so it made sense they'd want to get the old geezer planted while it was still cool. He should have thought of that, Kelly told himself bitterly.

But there wasn't time for self-recrimination. He shoved those thoughts away and opened fire on the crowd, aiming a little high. Dog Eater followed suit, spraying lead just over the heads of the towns-people. They yelled and screamed and scattered like a flock of spooked chickens.

None of the men returned the fire — too much confusion in the street — and there were womenfolk to protect. Kelly and Dog Eater reached their horses without anybody making an attempt to stop them.

They jerked the reins free from the hitch rail, then swung up into their saddles. With an efficient twist of his wrist, the Apache tied the money sack's drawstring around his saddle horn. Kelly sent another shot screaming into the crowd as he wheeled his horse.

A young man dashed toward the bank robbers, intent on grabbing Kelly and pulling him out of the saddle. The outlaw swung the gun toward the kid and pulled the trigger. The hammer fell on an empty chamber.

Kelly cursed. He pulled his right foot out of the stirrup and kicked the young man in the chest as he lunged at him. The kid flew backward and landed in a dusty sprawl.

Dog Eater urged his horse into a gallop and raced past Kelly as he headed toward the edge of town. Kelly booted his mount into a run and leaned forward in the saddle to make himself a smaller target in case any of the townsmen decided to take a potshot at him.

The sound of gunfire roused Luke from sleep. He groaned as he lifted his head. He hadn't had much to drink the night before, so he wasn't hungover, but the time he had spent with Magdalena had been exhausting . . . in a good way, of course. But still, he wasn't as young as he used to be.

The shooting was in the street somewhere. It wasn't any of his business. He was tempted to roll over and go back to sleep.

Then he heard the screaming, and knew he wouldn't be able to do that. He sighed and climbed to his feet, wearing only the bottom half of that set of long underwear. He drew one of the Remingtons from its holster where the gun rig lay coiled on a chair. As he slid up the pane in the room's lone window and threw a leg over the sill and onto the balcony, he heard hoofbeats drumming in the street. Two men were riding past the hotel.

Kelly didn't hear any guns go off behind him, but as he and Dog Eater rode past the hotel, a man with a gun in his hand stepped out onto the second floor balcony. Kelly glanced up and saw him. The man had a craggy, hard-planed face, a thin black mustache, and slightly curly black hair.

He had a good shot at Kelly, too, and Kelly's gun was empty.

All it took was a glance for Luke to recognize them. He had never laid eyes on them in the flesh, but had seen plenty of reward posters for Gunner Kelly and his Apache partner Dog Eater. The lumpy canvas sack tied to Dog Eater's saddle horn was more than evidence for Luke to feel certain the sack was stuffed full of money the two men had just stolen from the Rio Rojo bank.

He lifted his gun, but before he could draw a bead, Dog Eater opened fire on him. The first shot screamed past Luke's right ear and thudded into the wall behind him. He felt the hot breath of the second slug against his left ear. Dog Eater had him bracketed, and Luke felt confident the next shot would hit him right between the eyes.

He flung himself backward through the open window, and that quick reaction was all that saved his life as Dog Eater triggered again and the bullet sizzled through the space where Luke's head had been an instant earlier.

Diving out of the line of fire, Luke wound up sprawled on the floor inside the window with his legs hanging out. By the time he recovered from that awkward position and looked out the window again, he caught just a glimpse of the two riders disappearing around a corner.

He bit back a curse. Kelly and Dog Eater would be long gone before he could get dressed and have his horse ready to ride. From the looks of the confusion Luke had seen in the street, nobody was going to be mounting a posse any time soon, either.

It appeared the bank robbers had made a clean getaway.

For now, Luke told himself. *Only for now.*

He pulled on his clothes, buckled his gun belt around his hips, and hurried downstairs. The clerk's eyes seemed big around as saucers as he said, "My God! Did you hear all that shooting?"

"I heard it," Luke replied. He went out to check on the aftermath of the robbery.

Now that Kelly and Dog Eater were gone and lead had stopped flying around, people were emerging from the buildings where they had taken cover and converging on the vehicles that had stopped in the middle of the street.

Luke recognized a familiar figure in the first buggy and headed in that direction.

An elderly woman in a black hat and mourning dress perched on the seat, crying as she tugged on the sleeve of the man next to her. "You have to go after them, Marshal. They've ruined poor Lucius's funeral. You have to go after them!"

Marshal Cyrus Dunbar didn't say anything. His face was pale, and he was holding himself like he was hurt.

As Luke came up to the buggy, he saw blood trickling over the fingers of Dunbar's hands. "Madam, I believe the marshal has been shot." His voice was loud and urgent enough to break through her hysteria.

"But poor Lucius —"

Luke figured she was the widow of the late Mr. Vanderslice. He didn't want to be rude to her, but he said, "Your husband is beyond harm, ma'am. The same can't be said for the marshal here."

"I'm shot," Dunbar croaked. "But it ain't too bad. I got to raise a posse and go after those varmints."

Luke lifted Dunbar's hands and saw the hole in the lawman's coat where the bullet had gone in. He pulled the coat and shirt aside to get a better look at the wound. The bullet had penetrated Dunbar's body, but the wound wasn't much more than a deep graze. Messy, but probably not life-threatening. Dunbar would be off his feet for a while because of it, though.

Rapid footsteps pounded up beside the buggy. Luke glanced over and saw the undertaker, Calvin, who announced, "I've brought the doc."

Luke was glad to step back. He had patched up plenty of gunshot wounds in his time, including some he had suffered, but he was better at inflicting damage than repairing it. He let the spare, white-haired physician take over.

He asked Calvin, "Does the marshal have a deputy?"

Cyril Dunbar, the liveryman who was Marshal Dunbar's twin brother, stepped forward from the gathering crowd. "I helped out Cy whenever he needed a hand. I ain't exactly what you'd call a lawman, though."

A young man who was rubbing his chest edged forward and said, "Mr. Dunbar —"

"Now hush up, Hobie, you ain't no deputy, either. And that was a damned fool stunt you pulled, runnin' out there to try to stop those fellas. You're lucky that one just kicked you and didn't kill you. I saw him point his gun at you and pull the trigger. You'd be dead now if he hadn't run outta bullets when he did."

"But you know your brother promised he'd take me on as a deputy one of these days, at least part-time," Hobie protested. "He said I could work for you as a hostler durin' the day and he'd make me night deputy."

Cyril Dunbar snorted. "And when would you have slept if he'd done that?"

Luke didn't see that the wrangling was accomplishing anything. The end result was that Rio Rojo didn't have any real law except Cyrus Dunbar, and the marshal wasn't going to be chasing any outlaws for a while.

That left it up to him. Gunner Kelly and Dog Eater each had a price on his head, and Luke wasn't going to pass up a chance to collect those bounties.

First, though, he had business to finish. He turned back to the buggy and asked the doctor, "How's he doing?"

"He's passed out from loss of blood," the doctor replied, "but I think he's going to be all right."

Luke nodded. He had wanted to ask Dunbar a question, but supposed he would have to handle things himself.

Calvin had helped the Widow Vanderslice out of the buggy and was awkwardly patting her on the back while she leaned against him and sobbed. He said, "We're gonna have to go on with the funeral, Doc."

"Don't let me stop you," the doctor replied. "I'll take Cyrus down to my house in this buggy. You can load Mrs. Vanderslice in one of the others and continue with the service and the burial."

Luke left them to sort out the details and walked down the street to the telegraph office. He found the telegrapher standing on the porch, watching the commotion in the street.

"The marshal sent a telegram to Texas yesterday afternoon," Luke said to the man. "Has a reply come in yet?"

The telegrapher frowned. "I can't hardly tell you that, mister. It's against the rules."

"But Marshal Dunbar sent the telegram on my behalf," Luke argued. "I'm Luke Jensen. The telegram was to confirm that I'm entitled to collect a reward on an outlaw named Monroe Epps."

"I know who you are, Mr. Jensen. I reckon just about every body in Rio Rojo knows you're the bounty hunter. But I still can't reveal the contents of a message intended for somebody else."

"Then you *have* gotten a reply from Texas."

"I didn't say — Ah, hell. I guess I can tell you that a reply came in for the marshal a little while ago. I was going to give it to him as soon as Mr. Vanderslice's funeral was over. Do you know if the marshal is gonna be all right?"

"He should be."

"Tell you what. I'll get the telegram, and we'll go down to Doc Pritchard's place. If the marshal's awake, I'll ask him if it's all right to give the wire to you."

Luke was tempted to go inside the office and rummage around until he found the telegram, but supposed he could go along with the plan the telegrapher suggested. He was very aware of the fact that Kelly and Dog Eater were getting farther away with every passing minute, though.

The man went in the office and came back out a moment later. The funeral procession had gotten underway again and was approaching the church at the other end of town.

"I'm a little surprised that the bank and the telegraph office and all the other businesses are open this morning," Luke commented as he and the telegrapher walked toward the doctor's house. "If this fellow Vanderslice was as important as everybody seems to think he was, I would have thought the whole town would close down for the funeral."

"Mr. Vanderslice wouldn't have wanted that, especially for the bank to close. He owned it, you know."

Luke shook his head. "No, I didn't know that. I thought he owned the hotel."

"Oh, yeah, that, too. And the general store. He really was an important man. Not to speak ill of the dead, but he liked to squeeze every dollar he could out of his businesses. His widow's like that, too. She's a real skinfl— I mean, she's very thrifty and a canny businesswoman."

Luke chuckled. "I get your drift, my friend. She probably gave orders for all the businesses to stay open."

"I'm sure she did."

They reached the whitewashed frame house where the doctor's office and residence were located. When they went inside they found Marshal Cyrus Dunbar sitting up in a bed while Dr. Pritchard wound bandages around his midsection. The marshal's brother was there, too.

"Jensen!" Dunbar said when he saw Luke. "I should've known you'd have something to do with me gettin' shot."

"Not at all, Marshal. I'm innocent of that charge. I was sound asleep when the shooting started. I did try to stop the robbers as they galloped out of town, but all I got for my trouble was to come uncomfortably close to having a bullet part my hair."

Dunbar grunted, then winced as the doctor pulled the bandages tighter. "Bullet hole or no bullet hole, I still got to breathe, Doc."

To Luke, he went on. "You got a look at the varmints?"

"Gunner Kelly and Dog Eater," Luke told him. "I've never crossed trails with them before, but I've seen posters on them."

"Yeah, so have I. Everything happened so fast out there on the street I never had a chance to take a good look at them, but I know bank robbers when I see 'em. The Indian had a bag full of money." Dunbar frowned at the telegrapher. "Hank, what are you doin' here?"

"Got a reply to that message you sent yesterday, Marshal. Mr. Jensen here wanted to take a look at it, but I told him I couldn't let him do that without your say-so."

"Give it here." Dunbar held out his hand.

The telegrapher handed him the yellow telegraph flimsy he had brought along from the office.

"Where the hell are my spectacles?" Dunbar asked as he squinted at the piece of paper in his hand.

70

Luke tried to suppress the growing feelings of impatience and frustration inside him.

The doctor handed Dunbar a pair of glasses. The marshal settled them on his nose, peered intently at the telegram for a moment, and then looked up at Luke. "Looks like you get your reward, Jensen. This authorizes the bank to pay it out to you. Only . . . wasn't the bank just robbed?"

Luke's eyes widened in the realization that Dunbar was right. He knew he should have thought of that earlier. The time he had spent with Magdalena must have taken more of him than he had thought.

Dunbar went on. "Cyril, consider yourself deputized again. Go with Jensen to the bank and find out just how bad things are." He held out the telegram. "Take this with you."

"All right, Cyrus. Take good care of him, Doc."

Luke was seething inside as he and Cyril headed for the bank. The street was mostly empty, although knots of people stood here and there in front of the buildings, still talking about the excitement that had gripped the town earlier. When Luke and Cyril reached the bank, they found the front door locked.

Cyril banged a fist on it, and a minute

71

later one of the tellers came to open it. He looked pretty shaken. "Mr. Bellford told us the bank was closed for the time being."

"Well, I'm the law for the time being," Cyril said, "and I got to talk to him. My brother sent me to find out just how bad things are."

"Bad," the teller said. "Really bad." He stepped back to let them into the bank.

Bellford, the manager, sat at a desk with his face in his hands. He had a bloody lump on his head where one of the robbers had pistol-whipped him. He looked up with a bleak expression as Luke and Cyril approached him.

"Cyril, how's your brother?" Bellford asked. "I heard he was shot."

"Doc Pritchard thinks he'll be all right. You look like you're hurt, too, Ed."

Bellford shook his head. "This is nothing. What really hurts is that the robbers cleaned us out."

Luke took the telegram from Cyril's hand and set it on the desk in front of the bank manager. "This wire authorizes you to pay me a five thousand dollar reward on behalf of the State of Texas."

Bellford stared at him for a couple seconds, then started to laugh. "Mister, I told you they cleaned us out. I couldn't pay you a *five dollar* reward right now! You're just downright out of luck!"

CHAPTER 6

Losing his temper wasn't going to do any good, and Luke knew it. Despite that, he couldn't stop himself from picking up the telegram and crumpling it in his hand. He threw it on the floor, turned, and stalked out of the bank.

He had planned to go after Gunner Kelly and Dog Eater, anyway. Now he had even more reason to do so. He couldn't collect what he was owed for Monroe Epps unless he recovered the stolen money.

Luke headed for the stable. He had left Cyril Dunbar behind at the bank, but that didn't matter. He was used to saddling his own horse.

When he walked in, Hobie, the young hostler, paused in mucking out one of the stalls. "What can I do for you, Mr. Jensen?"

"Not a thing," Luke snapped. "I'm taking my horse. Your boss and I should be square on the bill."

"Yes, sir, I know. Are you goin' after those outlaws?"

"Damn right I am." Luke went into the stall where his horse was stabled, pulled the saddle blanket off the partition between stalls, and threw it over the horse's back.

"I'd be glad to do that for you," Hobie offered. "Isn't your gear still over at the hotel? Let me saddle up for you, and it'll save you a little time."

The suggestion actually made sense, Luke realized. He had been so mad at potentially losing the reward for Epps, he hadn't been able to think straight for a moment. He nodded. "Thanks, Hobie. I'm obliged to you."

"I'm glad to do it. I'd like to be a bounty hunter myself, someday."

Luke looked at the skinny, gangling young hostler with his mop of brown hair and thought Hobie looked about as much like a bounty hunter as President Grover Cleveland did. But he didn't see any point in saying that, so he just gave the young man a curt nod and headed for the hotel to get his saddlebags and rifle.

The desk clerk wanted to talk, too. The whole town was still buzzing about the robbery and the marshal's shooting. Luke brushed aside Avery's questions and went upstairs to get his gear from his room.

When he came down to the lobby again, he was surprised to see the Widow Vanderslice standing beside the desk with the bank manager, Bellford. It was obvious that she was waiting for him. "Mr. Jensen, I want to talk to you."

Luke had his saddlebags thrown over his right shoulder and his Winchester in his left hand. He didn't want anything slowing him down, but his upbringing wouldn't allow him to be rude to any woman, let alone one who was mourning her husband. He took his hat off and told her, "Ma'am, I'm sorry for your loss."

She was dry-eyed and looked stern and angry, especially in that black getup. "If you're talking about my late husband Lucius, then I appreciate your condolences, Mr. Jensen. If you're talking about the money those scoundrels stole out of my bank, I've come to make you an offer."

"Actually, ma'am, I thought you would still be at the funeral."

"Once I calmed down from having Marshal Dunbar shot while he was right beside me, I realized that Lucius wouldn't want me to neglect our business. I told Calvin Dobbs the service would have to be postponed for a short time, and I came to find you."

"Me, ma'am?" Luke said with a frown.

"I realize that you're a . . . bounty hunter." She couldn't quite keep a tone of disapproval out of her voice. "At the same time, with Cyrus Dunbar laid up, you're the closest thing Rio Rojo has to a representative of law and order at the moment. You're also the only man in this town who's qualified to go after those bank robbers."

"That's exactly what I intend to do, Mrs. Vanderslice. My horse is being saddled right now —"

"I understand you were going to collect a five thousand dollar reward from my bank." Mrs. Vanderslice paused. "I'll see that five thousand, and raise five thousand. That's the correct parlance, isn't it?"

Luke's frown deepened. "For what, ma'am?"

"If you go after those outlaws and bring back the money they stole, I'll see to it that you receive not only the reward that's already owed to you, but I'll also pay you an additional reward of five thousand dollars. That's ten thousand, over and above whatever you might collect for those two men."

Luke understood and nodded. "That's

very generous. I was going after them, anyway, but an extra five grand certainly doesn't hurt."

"In situations like this, the rewards are usually paid whether the fugitives are brought in dead or alive, correct?"

"That is correct," Luke admitted.

The widow's blue eyes were cold and hard as chips of ice as she said, "Then I'll simply ask this as a favor to an old woman, Mr. Jensen . . . bring them back dead."

After picking up his horse at the livery stable and some supplies at the general store, Luke rode to the edge of town where the bank robbers had galloped out of Rio Rojo. Picking up their trail wasn't difficult for his experienced eyes. He had tracked fugitives in all sorts of places, under all sorts of conditions. Gunner Kelly and Dog Eater had been in a hurry to get out of town, so they hadn't worried about concealing their tracks.

That wouldn't hold true later on. Once they had put some distance between themselves and the settlement, they would slow down and start trying to cover their trail.

Because of that, Luke knew it was liable to be a long chase. He was prepared. Mrs. Vanderslice had written a note for him to give to the manager of the general store, telling him to let Luke have whatever supplies he needed at no charge. If he was successful in his quest, she had said, she would take the cost of the supplies out of what she owed him later on.

Luke smiled faintly as he thought about that provision in the deal. He wouldn't want to do any horse trading with Mrs. Aurora Vanderslice. He had a hunch he would come out on the losing end of any such negotiations.

If he lost out on the deal, though, it would be because he was dead, so he didn't figure he needed to worry about anything as piddling as the cost of a few supplies.

The temperature rose as midday approached. Luke continued following the trail westward as it led into a wide stretch of salt flats that shone a dazzling white in the sunlight. The ground had been baked so hard by the sun that it didn't take tracks easily. The sign left by the fleeing outlaws was a lot more sparse. He had to concentrate harder in order to not lose the trail.

Despite that concentration, he was still alert to things around him, and a sudden prickling of the skin on the back of his neck warned him that someone was watching him. He reined in and hipped around in the saddle to look behind him.

Nothing but the salt flats and the gently rolling hills to the east where Rio Rojo was located met his gaze. As far as he could see, nobody was back there.

But his instincts said otherwise. Having learned to trust them, his eyes narrowed as he thought about what that might mean.

Someone could have followed him from the settlement. It was also possible that Kelly and Dog Eater, or at least one of them, had peeled off and lay in wait to let any pursuit pass by. Then they could follow and bushwhack anybody who was trying to trail them.

Such an attack didn't seem imminent to Luke. For one thing, there wasn't enough cover to try something like that. But he was sure that somebody was behind him, so he was going to remain doubly vigilant.

When the time came, maybe he would set up an ambush of his own.

A little later, he came across an area where the ground was slightly softer. Kelly and his Apache partner either hadn't noticed the change or were so confident they were going to get away they hadn't gone to the trouble to avoid it. They had ridden straight across that stretch. Luke had no trouble making out the tracks of both horses.

He knew they belonged to the mounts being ridden by the bank robbers. He had studied the tracks enough to recognize the little nicks and irregularities in the prints those horseshoes made.

That meant if someone was following him, as he was still convinced was true, it wasn't Gunner Kelly or Dog Eater. Those two outlaws were still ahead of him.

Knowing that made Luke even more curious about who might be trailing him. He had a pretty good idea, but would deal with that problem when the time came.

Meanwhile, he had some bank robbers to catch.

The afternoon passed slowly. From time to time, Luke came across horse droppings and dismounted to take a closer look so he could get a better idea how far ahead of him his quarry was.

Kelly and Dog Eater had had about an hour's lead on him when he started out from Rio Rojo. They seemed to be maintaining that.

Luke's horse was fairly fresh after spending the night in Cyril Dunbar's livery stable, but Luke had been on the move quite a bit in the past few weeks so the animal didn't have deep reserves of strength and stamina.

He didn't know what condition the outlaws' horses were in, but it stood to reason that Kelly and Dog Eater would have made sure they had well-rested mounts before they robbed the bank.

During one of his stops, Luke looked up at the sky. The afternoon was fairly well advanced and the chances of him catching up to the outlaws before nightfall were pretty slim. Almost nonexistent, in fact, he judged. He would have to stop once it got dark because he wouldn't be able to follow the trail by starlight.

Kelly and the Apache, on the other hand, could push on if they wanted to. Eventually, they would have to stop and let their horses rest for several hours, but even taking that into consideration, by morning they would have widened their lead.

It was a setback, Luke thought, but not an insurmountable one. It would have been nice to catch up to them, but when he had ridden out on their trail, it was with the knowledge that the chase might take days or even weeks.

A stubborn persistence was one of the best qualities a bounty hunter could have.

The real worry was that Kelly and Dog Eater might manage to get their hands on fresh horses. If that happened, they could stretch out their lead even more.

There were a few isolated ranches spread out around there, Luke recalled with a frown as he continued riding west. The two men might be able to make a trade. If not, they wouldn't hesitate to take whatever they wanted and kill anybody who tried to stop them.

The sun dipped lower and lower as he left the salt flats behind, finally touching the horizon in front of him. He knew it wouldn't take long for darkness to descend over the rugged landscape. He started looking for a good place to make camp while the fiery orb slid the rest of the way below the curve of the earth.

He found a shallow dip where enough water had collected in the past to nourish a little grass and a couple scrubby mesquite trees, although no moisture was to be found at the moment. He picketed and unsaddled the horse, poured some water from one of his canteens into his hat so it could drink, then left the animal to graze.

Taking a folding shovel from his gear, he dug a fire pit deep enough to conceal the flames of the small blaze he built of mesquite twigs. He figured Kelly and Dog Eater would assume someone was on their trail, but there was no point in confirming that and telling them exactly where he was.

He boiled a pot of coffee and fried some bacon. After he had washed down his meager supper with a couple cups of Arbuckle's, he sat and mused as he peered into the darkness and let the fire burn down. He craved a cigar, but more than once he had aimed a gun just above the glowing coal of an unwary owlhoot's cheroot. He didn't want to provide a similar target for some unknown enemy.

When he saw a little flash of light in the distance, he thought he had imagined it. But it came again and then again. On the third time the light caught and held, it grew stronger. Luke's eyes narrowed as he studied the glow.

Something was on fire about a mile away from him. He remembered those ranches he'd been considering earlier. It was possible Kelly and Dog Eater had stopped at one of the spreads, enjoyed the hospitality of the settlers, and tried to make a horse trade.

It was also possible they had just ridden in, gunned down the rancher and his family, and taken what they wanted, setting the place on fire as they left.

Either way, the knowledge that his quarry might be that close drove Luke to his feet.

"Sorry about this, fella," he told his horse as he started saddling up again. "I know you were ready to eat your fill of this grass and get some rest. Maybe you still can before the night's over."

Once he had everything packed and the horse ready to ride, he headed for the still-visible light. Something was definitely burning and that was a bad sign.

When he got close enough to make out the actual flames, he saw that a long, low ranch house was on fire. The roof and the insides were burning, but the adobe walls prevented the fire from spreading to the barn and corrals off to one side. Lit up by the flames from the house, Luke could see the spread was a small one, the sort of outfit a man would run alone or with his wife.

Luke reined in about fifty yards from the burning ranch house and raised his voice, shouting, "Hello! Is anybody here? Hello!"

There was no reply, and he didn't see anybody moving around the house. It hadn't set itself on fire, he thought. Kelly and Dog Eater could have touched off the blaze and then moved on. He would see if he could find any sign they might have left, but first, make sure no one needed help.

He turned toward the barn and rode up to the open double doors. He called, "Is anybody in there?"

He got an answer right away, in the form of a spurt of orange flame from the muzzle of a gun as a bullet whipped past his ear.

CHAPTER 7

Luke jerked his horse aside and yelled, "Hold your fire, damn it! I'm a friend!"

He didn't know that for sure. It might have been Kelly or Dog Eater who took that shot at him. He heeled the horse into a run toward the corner of the barn as he drew one of the Remingtons.

Luke kicked his feet free of the stirrups and dropped to the ground as his mount reached the corner. He let the horse run on into the darkness as he pressed his back against the rough wall and drew his other gun. Watching the barn doors, he listened intently.

At first, all he could hear was the roaring crackle of flames from the house. Then what he thought was a muffled cough came from inside the barn. The gunman was still there.

Luke began edging toward the doors. He heard another cough, followed by some muttered words. After a moment, he realized they were half-incoherent curses. The man inside the barn sounded like he wasn't in very good shape. He might have been drunk, but more likely he was hurt.

"Damn outlaws," the man slurred. "G'damn owlhooss . . . Show yourselves again . . . Kill you for what you done . . . send you both to hell . . ."

Luke's eyes narrowed. The man in the barn was cursing two men. Gunner Kelly and Dog Eater seemed pretty likely. The man probably was the owner of the ranch. The bank robbers could have wounded him, stolen some horses, and left him in the barn to die.

But he wasn't dead yet. When Luke had ridden up, the man could have mistaken him for one of the outlaws returning, especially if he was wounded and in bad shape. But why was the house on fire? Were Kelly and the Apache responsible for that, too?

The basic theory made sense, Luke decided, so he risked calling out again to the man in the barn. "Hey! Mister! I'm not one of the men who did this. I'm on their trail. Like I told you, I'm a friend!"

"Why?" the man called back.

Luke realized the question wasn't exactly directed at him when the man went on.

"Why'd you have to do it? We give you ever'thing you asked for . . . Why'd you have to do that to Martha?"

That anguished question made Luke frown. In his profession, he had seen so much ugliness, so many examples of utter depravity, that he realized there were no depths of horror to which human beings could sink when they chose to. He had learned to steel himself to that fact.

But reminders of it still affected him. He heard the agonized grief in the man's voice and realized the poor fellow was suffering from that as much as from any physical injury the outlaws had inflicted on him. In that state, it was unlikely Luke would be able to get through to him.

He wanted to help the man if he could, might be able to patch up a bullet wound even if he couldn't do anything else. And he wanted to know how long ago Kelly and Dog Eater had been there. He had to at least try to get that information out of the man in the barn.

Luke pouched both irons. The man's muttering seemed to be getting weaker, he thought as he listened for a moment longer.

Then he took a deep breath and exploded into action, driving hard around the edge of the door and going into the barn low and fast.

He knew he would be silhouetted for a second against the flames, but was counting on his speed and the inability of the wounded man to react very quickly. Even so, the man got off a shot, his rifle cracking as the muzzle flash lit up the barn for an instant.

Luke didn't have any idea where the bullet went. All he knew was that it didn't hit him. Using the rifle's flash as a guide, he reached out and the back of his hand hit the weapon's barrel. He grabbed it and wrenched it to the side as he rammed into the man. His other hand twisted in the man's shirtfront, and he swung him around. When the rifle came free, he slung it away.

"Take it easy!" Luke said. "I don't want to hurt you. I'll help you if you let me."

The man struggled weakly in his grip. "Why'd you do it?" he demanded. "Why'd you have to hurt her?"

"I didn't hurt her," Luke insisted. "I didn't hurt Martha." He figured that was the name of the man's wife.

The man stopped fighting suddenly and went limp in Luke's hands. It wasn't a trick. He had passed out . . . or died.

Luke got one arm around his shoulders

and the other behind his knees and picked him up, carrying him out of the barn. The man was slender and didn't weigh all that much.

Luke carried the grim burden several yards toward the house, until the light from the fire reached them. He knelt and lowered the man to the ground.

The blood that soaked the man's midsection was black in the flames' glare. When Luke saw how much of it there was and where it was located, he knew there was no chance he'd be able to do anything other than bury him. The rancher, if that's who he was, had been shot at least twice in the gut.

But he was still alive. Breath rasped harshly in his throat.

Luke whistled for his horse until the animal came trotting up to him. He didn't like the fire, but was well trained enough to answer Luke's summons.

Luke reached for one of his canteens, then changed his mind and delved into the saddlebags for a small silver flask. He unscrewed the cap as he knelt beside the wounded man.

He got a hand behind the man's head and lifted it, then trickled some whiskey into his mouth. Some of it spilled, but enough went down the man's throat to make him cough. That probably hurt like hell, Luke thought, but it brought him back from unconsciousness.

The man was in forties, with the whittled-down look of one who had led a hardscrabble life, as most small ranchers did. With firelight painting one side of his face a garish red, the man looked up at Luke and whispered, "Who . . . who are you?"

"I'm looking for the men who did this to you," Luke answered. "A white man and an Indian, isn't that right?"

"Y–yeah. The Injun was . . . an Apache, I think. He's the one who . . . shot me . . . Don't know why . . . I would've traded horses with 'em. . . ."

"Because that's the sort of men they are," Luke said, his voice hardening. "Worthless, no-good scum who aren't fit to breathe the same air as decent human beings."

"You must . . . know 'em . . . all right," the man forced out. "After they shot me . . . they went after my wife . . . poor Martha . . . Reckon they thought . . . I was dead. But I wasn't . . . I heard what they done to her . . . heard her scream just before one of 'em . . . cut her throat."

The whiskey seemed to have revived the man somewhat, but Luke knew that wouldn't last. "How long ago was this?"

"Dunno . . . hours . . . middle of the afternoon . . . sun was still up."

Luke frowned in puzzlement. From the place where he'd made camp, he'd seen the fire start. If the attack on the rancher and his wife had taken place that afternoon, why had Kelly and Dog Eater waited around so long to start the blaze and ride off? "What made them start the fire?"

The man's eyes were sliding closed again, but Luke's question made him open them.

"They didn't," he whispered. "I did. I passed out . . . lay there for I don't know how long . . . and when I come to and saw what they done to her . . . I took her in the house . . . laid her out in our bed . . . I knew I'd never be able to . . . bury her proper . . . couldn't have any varmints . . . gettin' to her . . ."

Luke turned his head and looked at the burning house, realizing now that it was the woman's funeral pyre. "All fled, all done," he muttered, part of a line from a half-remembered couplet.

The rancher had done what he could for his wife, and Luke was amazed at what he had managed as badly wounded as he was. If Luke had been more of a sentimental sort of a man, he might have said that was evidence of the power of love. . . .

Somehow, the rancher found the strength to clutch at Luke's sleeve. "You said you're . . . chasin' those fellas?"

"I am. I intend to bring them to justice."

"There's nothin' justice can do . . . that'll be bad enough to pay 'em back for what they done . . . They don't deserve justice. . . . What they're needin' . . . is revenge!"

The man's clawlike hand closed harder on Luke's arm. His body arched up from the ground as a spasm gripped him. His eyes grew wide, and his breath eased out of him in a final sigh. He was gone.

Gently, Luke lowered the man's head to the ground again. What had happened was two more marks against the ledger for Gunner Kelly and Dog Eater, he thought with a sigh of his own. Black marks . . . or maybe red for blood.

Luke wondered how many more marks there would be before he caught up to the murdering twosome.

Luke went into the barn, found a lantern, lit it, and looked around until he found an old blanket in the tack room. He used it to wrap the man's body and then carried the body into the barn and put it in the tack room, closing the door to keep predators out. In the morning he would dig a grave.

The only livestock in the barn was an old milk cow. Any horses the rancher had owned were gone, no doubt taken by Kelly and Dog Eater. A small flock of chickens was sleeping in a coop at the side of the barn, undisturbed by the violence and death that had descended on their home.

If Luke happened to pass a neighboring ranch, he would stop and let the people know what had happened. Until then, the cow and the chickens would have to fend for themselves. He would turn the cow loose in the morning so it could find some graze.

With those decisions made, he led his horse a quarter mile from the ranch and made camp again. He could still smell the burned-out house and didn't care for that. He had seen and smelled too many buildings that had suffered a similar fate during the siege of Richmond, when the big guns of Ulysses S. Grant and the Yankee army had pounded the city relentlessly for weeks on end. For a long time after that, he hadn't been able to get the bitter scent of ashes out of his nose.

He had learned to ignore the things that bothered him, so he was able to sleep. It was a light slumber, though. He didn't expect Kelly and Dog Eater to return to the scene of their latest crime, but anything was possible.

Because of that natural, instinctive alertness, Luke was able to come awake instantly when his horse let out a quiet whinny and shifted around a little. The animal had smelled or heard something, and Luke trusted the horse's senses. As soon as his eyes opened, he reached out and closed his hand around the butt of one of the Remingtons where his gun belt lay coiled on the ground beside him.

He drew the revolver with just the faintest whisper of steel on leather. His thumb looped over the hammer, ready to pull it back as he lay there listening intently.

He heard the faint thud of a hoof on the ground. The sound came from far enough away that he knew it wasn't his horse who had made it. Another horse was out there in the darkness.

A glance at the sky told Luke it was about an hour until dawn. He had been asleep for a while. He turned his head where he lay with it pillowed on his saddle. He could see the barn and what was left of the ranch house. The front door had burned, and through the opening that was left he saw a scattering of orange embers, the only remnants of the blaze that had consumed the inside of the dwelling.

Nobody was moving around over there.

The sound he'd heard had come from the other direction. Someone was moving up on his trail, and he recalled the feeling of being watched he'd had the day before. Whoever was following had caught up to him. They had probably used the flames to guide them, just as he had.

He heard another faint sound, the scuff of boot leather on dirt. The follower had left his horse and was advancing on foot. Luke knew that just as well as if he'd been watching the scene in broad daylight.

Breathing shallowly, he lay motionless and silent and let the unseen man come closer to him. The hombre moved pretty quietly overall, Luke had to give him credit for that, although not quietly enough to escape notice by a professional man hunter.

Finally, the man was close enough for Luke to see his dark shape creeping along. Starlight winked on the barrel of the rifle the man was carrying. If that rifle had swung toward him, Luke would have tipped up the Remington and fired from the ground. The man continued holding the rifle at a slant across his chest, though, instead of getting ready to use it.

The figure was only about five feet away,

lined up on a course that would take him within a step or two of the spot where Luke was lying, when Luke realized suddenly that the man didn't know he was there. The man had seen the burning ranch house and was approaching it stealthily to find out what had happened.

Luke was still fairly sure he knew the man's identity. He stayed where he was until the man stepped past him, then exploded into movement. As he pushed himself up, his right leg swung around and crashed into the back of the man's knees. The man let out a startled yelp as Luke swept his legs out from under him. He collapsed and dropped the rifle.

Luke landed on top of him and planted a knee in the small of the man's back to pin him to the ground, just in case he was wrong about his identity. He pressed the Remington's barrel against the back of the man's head and said, "Don't move or I'll blow your brains out."

"Don't kill me!" the man pleaded. "Please don't shoot!"

The familiar voice confirmed Luke's hunch. He didn't bother trying to keep the disgust out of his own voice as he said, "Hobie, what in the hell are you doing here?"

CHAPTER 8

The young hostler from Cyril Dunbar's livery stable in Rio Rojo gulped fearfully. "Mr. Jensen, is that you?"

"Who did you think?" Luke asked as he took the gun away from Hobie's head.

"I . . . I was afraid it might be one of those bank robbers."

Luke put his other hand on the ground to steady himself as he got to his feet. Hobie rolled over and sat up, taking deep breaths in an apparent combination of fear and relief.

Luke glared down at the young man. "If I'd been Gunner Kelly, you'd probably be dead right now. If I was Dog Eater, you'd *definitely* be dead. You haven't answered my other question. What are you doing out here so far from town?"

"I was . . ." Hobie swallowed hard. "I wasn't exactly following you. . . ."

"Except that you dogged my trail all day

yesterday after I left, didn't you?"

"That's sort of the way it worked out," Hobie admitted. "But what I was really doing was following Kelly and the Indian."

"Good Lord," Luke said, remembering one of the comments Hobie had made back at the livery stable. "You're after them, too, aren't you? You said you wanted to be a bounty hunter someday."

"It's all over town about the five thousand dollar reward Mrs. Vanderslice promised you if you caught them and recovered the loot from the bank robbery," Hobie said with a rising note of excitement creeping into his voice. "That's an awful lot of money!"

"Is it worth your life?" Luke demanded.

Hobie sounded confused as he asked, "What?"

"I said, is five grand worth your life? Because that's what it would have cost you if you'd actually found those two! They'd have killed you as easily as swatting a fly."

"I'm pretty tough," Hobie said defensively. "Tougher than I look."

That wouldn't take much to be true, Luke thought. He reached down with his left hand. Hobie grasped it, and Luke hauled the young man to his feet.

"Let me ask you a question. Did you know

I was there when you walked right past me, Hobie?"

"Well . . . I guess I didn't notice you —"

"Look over there." Luke lifted an arm and pointed. "My horse is picketed thirty feet away. Did you see him while you were creeping along like some phony Indian in a James Fenimore Cooper novel?"

"No," Hobie answered sheepishly. "A while back, I saw something burning up there, and I reckon I was concentrating too much on finding it. I had a hunch maybe Kelly and the Apache had something to do with it."

"That's one thing you were right about," Luke snapped. "The only thing, come to think of it." He paused and looked at the sky again. There wasn't much point in trying to go back to sleep, so he went on. "Go get your horse. I'll show you exactly what sort of men Kelly and Dog Eater are and why you shouldn't be trying to find them."

"Then I was right about them havin' something to do with that fire?"

"Just get your horse," Luke said.

While Hobie was doing that, Luke broke camp, gathering his gear and his bedroll and saddling his horse. By the time Hobie came back leading his mount, Luke was ready to go. They swung up into their saddles and headed for the ranch a quarter mile away.

The eastern sky was starting to turn gray by the time they got there. Hobie looked at the burned-out ranch house. "Did they do that?"

"Actually, no. But they were responsible for it."

Luke dismounted and handed his reins to Hobie. He went into the barn and brought out the body of the slain rancher. He placed the man on the ground and pulled back the blanket enough to reveal his face.

"Is that Mr. Anderson?" Hobie asked.

"You tell me. I'm not from around here."

"It's got to be him. Nelse Anderson. He owned this spread, him and his wife Martha." Hobie looked around. "Where is she? Did they —"

"She's in the house," Luke interrupted in a harsh voice. "They rode up and wanted to trade for some fresh horses. Anderson was agreeable, but they must have gotten a look at Mrs. Anderson. Comely woman, was she?"

"Yeah, she . . . she was real nice-looking. And she always treated everybody decent."

"Well, Kelly and Dog Eater gut-shot Anderson and left him for dead and then took turns attacking his wife until they got tired of it and cut her throat. Then they swapped horses and rode off, taking all the animals with them."

The sky was light enough for Luke to see how sick Hobie looked. The young hostler said, "I . . . I don't understand. If the bank robbers left, who set the house on fire?"

"Anderson did. He passed out for a while, then came to and found his wife's body. He knew he wasn't strong enough to bury her . . . might not live long enough to bury her . . . so he took her in the house and put her in their bed. Then he lit the fire. Sort of like a Viking funeral, except that adobe ranch house isn't a ship and we're a hell of a long way from the sea."

"How do you know all this?"

"He told me about it before he died. I don't think he would have had any reason to lie."

"This is awful," Hobie muttered. "Just awful. Why would anybody do such a thing?"

"I don't guess you ever ran into anybody like Gunner Kelly and Dog Eater before. Some people are just pure evil, kid. Those two are prime examples of that."

Hobie was silent for a long moment, as if he were having trouble comprehending the truth of what Luke had told him. Finally he said, "What are you going to do now?"

"I'm going to see to it that these two

people are laid to rest properly. It's not my responsibility, but someone ought to do it. And then I'm going after Kelly and Dog Eater. Somebody's got to do *that,* too."

"I'll help you."

"I certainly won't mind you giving me hand digging those graves —"

"I mean I'll help you go after Kelly and Dog Eater," Hobie said. "We can be partners."

Luke looked at the young man in disbelief. "Kid, have you listened to a word I said? You've got no business getting mixed up in this. Those two would chew you up and spit you out and not even slow down to pick their teeth."

"But there's two of them and one of you. They've got you outnumbered. I know I'm new at the bounty hunting game, but surely it'd help even the odds to have me along."

Luke took off his hat and scrubbed a weary hand over his face. "Hobie, are you familiar with the concept of negative numbers in mathematics?"

"Huh?"

"Never mind. Having you come with me wouldn't be like adding one to my side of the odds. I'd have to be looking out for you all the time, and I couldn't give all my attention to the job. That would actually subtract from my side and give Kelly and Dog Eater even more of an advantage over me. Do you understand?"

"Well . . . maybe," Hobie said grudgingly. "I've never been that good at ciphering."

"And one more thing. Bounty hunting isn't a game. It's a dirty, deadly, ugly business, and a lot of men get killed doing it. Men who are a lot tougher and more experienced than you are. Do you have a family?"

Hobie shook his head. "No, sir, not really. My folks are dead, and I don't have any brothers or sisters. I reckon Mr. Dunbar and his brother the marshal are sort of like my adopted uncles."

"How about a sweetheart?"

Even in the dim light of dawn, Luke could see the blush that spread over Hobie's face as the young man said, "I've sort of been courtin' Betsy Jane Hendricks."

"Then Betsy Jane would probably cry over your body, and I suspect the Dunbar brothers would mourn your loss, too. You don't want that on your conscience, Hobie."

"No, I wouldn't, but . . . the reward's five thousand dollars, Mr. Jensen!"

Luke took the shovel off his horse and tossed it to Hobie, who caught it awkwardly.

"Get down and start digging," Luke told

the young man. "We'll see if you still feel the same way when we get through."

The sun was a couple hand widths above the eastern horizon when they finished burying Nelse Anderson and his wife Martha. Luke and Hobie had taken turns digging until they had two graves ready on top of a small hill a short distance northeast of the house and the barn.

Hobie hadn't wanted to go into the house, but Luke had insisted. He wanted the young man to see everything Gunner Kelly and Dog Eater had left behind them. The ruins of the house were still too hot to walk on in places, so Luke and Hobie had to be careful, but they were able to recover the remains of Mrs. Anderson.

Then Hobie had stumbled behind a bush, fallen to his knees, and thrown up for a long time. His position was almost one of reverence, but the sounds coming from him were a long way from being prayers.

Sweat pasted Hobie's shirt to his torso by the time they were finished covering the graves. He leaned on the shovel, took off his hat, and sleeved moisture from his face. Turning his head to watch in disbelief as Luke started walking back toward the horses, he called out, "Wait a minute. Aren't you gonna say something over them?"

Luke paused and looked back. "They've both been dead for hours. If there's an afterlife, they're already where they're going to wind up. Nothing we say now can make any difference."

"If you believe that, why'd we go to the trouble of buryin' 'em? Why not just leave their bodies to be torn apart by coyotes and picked over by buzzards?"

"A simple matter of respect and dignity," Luke said. "And wherever they are, I think they'll rest easier knowing that didn't happen to what they left behind." He gestured toward the graves. "But if you want to say something, go right ahead. Don't let me stop you."

Luke heard Hobie mutter something behind him as he turned away again. A moment later the young man hurried to catch up to him, carrying the shovel. "What do we do now?"

"You go back to Rio Rojo," Luke said. "I pick up the trail and go after Kelly and Dog Eater."

"How can you catch them now? They're bound to be a long way ahead of you."

"I know which way they're headed. Even if I lose the trail, I'll find them sooner or later. After a while, they'll get careless.

Outlaws nearly always do. They won't go to as much trouble to hide where they've been. Besides, I know most of the trails and the places where men like that hole up. I've been tracking killers and thieves for years."

"Seems like they're heading a little south of due west. If they keep goin' far enough in that direction, it'll take 'em to the border."

Luke smiled. "Borders don't mean a whole lot to men like me. I'm not like a lawman with a set jurisdiction to worry about. I go wherever the trail leads me."

"But you can't collect the reward for them in Mexico, can you?"

"No, but I can put their heads in a sack and bring them back to prove I caught them."

Hobie stared at him and looked like he might be sick again. "You'd do something like that?"

"They'd already be dead," Luke pointed out. "They wouldn't care."

"What happened to dignity and respect?" Hobie muttered.

"Vermin like that don't deserve it. You want anything to eat?"

Hobie looked startled by the question. With a queasy expression on his face, he shook his head. "No, I . . . I don't think so."

"All right. I'll stop and fix a little breakfast for myself later. Right now I want to put a few miles behind me." Luke fixed the hostler with a stern stare and added, "Good-bye, Hobie."

"You're really sendin' me back to Rio Rojo?"

"That's where you belong. Keep doing a good job and Dunbar might make you a partner in the livery stable one of these days. Hell, you might wind up marrying Betsy Jane or whatever her name is and taking over the business. Go live your life, Hobie." Luke shook his head. "There's nothing waiting for you on the other trail but death."

Hobie looked like he wanted to argue, but after a moment he mounted up and turned his horse back toward the east. "Good luck, Mr. Jensen," he called as he lifted a hand in farewell.

Luke returned the wave, then stood there watching as Hobie rode away. He waited until the young man had gone several hundred yards before he went to his own horse and swung up into the saddle.

Picking up the trail of the outlaws wasn't very difficult. Kelly and Dog Eater were leading several horses now. Luke couldn't tell exactly how many. They would be able to switch back and forth so that they always had fresh mounts, though, and that would make his job that much more difficult.

The one advantage he had was sheer stubbornness. Once he was on a man's trail, he never gave it up. Days or weeks would go by, and Gunner Kelly and Dog Eater would become convinced that they had eluded any pursuers. They would believe that they were safe.

And then, sometime when they weren't expecting it, Luke would be there with his guns in his hands. Powder smoke and lead would fill the air, more than likely, because men like those two never came along peaceably.

No, Luke thought as he rode, somebody would die. Somebody always died.

So far it hadn't been him, and he was going to try to keep that streak going for a while longer.

CHAPTER 9

Two days later, Luke was forced to admit that he had lost the trail. There had been too many rocky stretches where the ground was too hard to take hoofprints.

But as he had told Hobie, he knew which way Kelly and Dog Eater were going, and he was confident that he could find them. For all its vastness, the frontier was a small place in many ways. Someone, somewhere, would have seen the two outlaws and would be willing to tell Luke how long ago they had been there and which direction they'd been going when they left.

The landscape was mostly flat and arid, broken up by ranges of small but rugged mountains running north and south. Luke had no trouble going around those mountains or finding passes through them, so they didn't slow him down much. Some of the valleys between the ranges were barren salt flats, while others had small streams running through them at least part of the year, resulting in enough vegetation to support small ranches. Those spreads had to have some sort of supply point, so Luke wasn't surprised when he spotted a few tendrils of chimney smoke rising in the pale blue sky. He followed them until he saw the scattered adobe buildings of a small settlement in the distance.

He didn't recall ever being in that exact spot before and didn't know the name of the place, if it even had one. But there would be at least one saloon or cantina, he thought, and he could ask there about the men he was pursuing. The same would be true at the general store. Kelly and Dog Eater might have stopped for supplies.

He could use a few things himself. No telling how long the chase might go on. There was bound to be a public well where he could fill up all four of his canteens. Anybody traveling in the dry country had to take on water wherever it was possible.

The town, if you could call it that, consisted of only a dozen buildings. The place seemed to be dozing in the afternoon sun. A few horses stood at the hitch rails, their heads down and their tails flicking lazily. A couple dogs were sprawled out sleeping. A gray and white cat sat on the seat of a parked wagon, giving itself a bath.

Luke didn't see any people moving around.

A faint prickle of unease stirred the skin on the back of his neck. He told himself he was worrying over nothing. It wasn't a ghost town, the horses and the wagon proved that, and it really wasn't that unusual for the street to be deserted at that time of day. It was siesta, after all.

He spotted a building with the word *Cantina* painted on it and was reminded of Rio Rojo and Magdalena. He didn't expect to be that fortunate again, but would settle for confirmation that Kelly and Dog Eater had come through there.

A couple horses were tied at the hitch rack in front of the building. As Luke rode up and dismounted, he took a good look at the hoofprints left by those animals, just on the off chance they were the two horses Kelly and Dog Eater had used to escape from Rio Rojo after the bank robbery. Nothing about the prints distinguished them. It was what Luke expected, but he was in the habit of being careful.

He went into the cantina and was immediately grateful for the relative coolness of its dim interior behind the thick adobe walls. It took a moment for his eyes to adjust after being in the bright sunshine outside.

Tables were scattered around the room. The bar was in the back. To the right was a big fireplace where an iron pot of something that smelled spicy and delicious simmered over a small fire. A couple vaqueros sat at one of the tables, playing cards without seeming all that interested in the game. Two more men stood at the bar passing a bottle of pulque back and forth. The short, fat bartender stood with his hands resting on the broad, thick planks laid across barrels that formed the bar.

Luke didn't see a woman anywhere in the place, let alone one as attractive as Magdalena.

He walked through the room to the bar. The card players didn't look up at him. The two men at the bar didn't pay any attention to him, either. One of them looked like a blacksmith, judging by muscular arms as thick as the trunks of young trees. The other could have been a stableman or even a clerk in the general store.

None of them carried a gun, Luke noted. In the case of the two townsmen that wasn't really a surprise, but he would have expected the vaqueros to be armed. You never knew when you might need to shoot a snake or something when you were out riding the range.

The bartender shifted over to face Luke across the planks and asked, "What can I get you, señor?"

"Beer will be fine," Luke told him.

The man seemed uneasy, and beads of greasy-looking sweat covered his face.

Luke went on. "Are you all right, amigo?"

"*Sí,* of course. What could be wrong?"

"I don't know. You tell me."

The bartender filled a mug from one of the barrels and set it on the planks in front of Luke. "Four bits. You should drink up and then ride on out of town, señor."

Immediately, Luke knew for sure that something was wrong. The cantina wasn't doing much business. Its proprietor wouldn't be anxious to chase away customers.

Luke took a sip of the beer. Not surprising, it was warm and not very good, but it cut the trail dust in his throat. He wasn't going to leave until he had asked a few questions, no matter how nervous the bartender was. He started by saying, "Does this place have a name?"

"The cantina, you mean, or the town?"

"The town."

"This is La Farva, señor. I'm sure you

115

have never heard of it."

That was true, Luke thought. The name meant nothing to him.

"It doesn't amount to much," the bartender hurried on. "No reason for anyone to linger here."

"I could use some supplies," Luke said. "I'm looking for a couple men, too."

The bartender shook his head without waiting for Luke to go on. "I have not seen them," he declared.

"That's odd," Luke said with a slight frown, "since I haven't even told you what they look like yet."

"You are the first stranger in La Farva in weeks, señor."

Luke didn't really believe that, but he supposed it could be true. Even if it was, it didn't explain the bartender's nervousness and the deliberate way the other men in the cantina were ignoring him.

"One of the two men I'm looking for is white and has red hair," he persisted. "The other is an Apache Indian."

The bartender shook his head stubbornly. "I told you, señor, I have not seen them."

Kelly and Dog Eater might be in town, Luke thought suddenly. They could have ridden in and taken over, terrorizing the citizens until everyone was afraid to cross them. That would explain things, even though it seemed like a big job for only two men to run roughshod over an entire settlement. Someone was bound to have stood up to them.

And then Kelly and Dog Eater would have killed whoever was brave enough — or foolish enough — to do that. More than likely, they would make an example of that poor soul so everyone else would be too scared to do anything except cooperate with them. It was certainly possible, Luke told himself.

"All right," he told the bartender. "I'm obliged to you for your help." He dropped a coin on the bar to pay for the unfinished beer.

"You are leaving La Farva, señor?"

"There's no reason for me to stay, is there?"

The bartender shook his head. "No reason, señor, no reason at all."

Luke turned away from the bar. He planned to ride out, wait until it was dark, and then return to La Farva under the cover of nightfall. He didn't think it would take him long to find out if the two bank robbers really were there.

He didn't make it out of the cantina. Several figures suddenly loomed in the doorway when he was halfway across the room. They were silhouetted against the light outside, so he couldn't tell much about them except that they wore broad-brimmed, steeple-crowned sombreros.

An air of menace came from them just as strongly as the smell of stewing chiles came from the pot in the fireplace.

Luke stopped where he was, since the doorway was blocked. He heard the bartender saying something under his breath and glanced over his shoulder. The man stood behind the bar crossing himself, which meant his mumbled words were probably a prayer.

That reaction didn't bode well, Luke thought. Maybe he had been wrong about Gunner Kelly and Dog Eater taking over La Farva. Somebody sure had the place spooked, though, and it appeared to be these men.

They came on into the cantina, their spurs clinking. The big, fancy rowels on those spurs told Luke they were Mexican. So did the short gray jackets and the tight gray trousers the men wore. Now that he could see them better, he recognized their garb as the uniform of the *Rurales,* the Mexican police force that patrolled the area along the border.

That didn't make any sense. As far as

Luke knew, he was still in New Mexico Territory. He was pretty sure he hadn't crossed the border.

The four newcomers definitely were Rurales, though. They carried rifles and had belted revolvers strapped around their hips. One of the men, a massive, swarthy individual with a thick black mustache, also wore crossed bandoliers of ammunition and had a machete stuck behind his gun belt.

The four of them walked straight toward Luke. The man who seemed to be the leader was short and slender, with such a bristling, animated personality that he was trembling a little, not from fear, but from eagerness. He was ready for trouble. He *wanted* trouble.

As the man came to a stop in front of Luke, he said in English, "Señor, it is not allowed for civilians to be armed in this town." He gestured toward the Remingtons. "You must hand over your guns."

"I was just leaving," Luke said. "It wasn't my intention to break the law, so I'll be moving on."

The man shook his head. "There are no exceptions to this rule."

Keeping his voice flat and hard, Luke said, "You can watch me ride out if you want. You'll see that I'm not staying in La Farva."

"There are no exceptions," the man said again, "and there must be consequences for those who break the law."

With an effort, Luke restrained the impatience and irritation he felt inside him. He'd had run-ins with the Rurales before. While some of the force's members were honest and wanted to bring a semblance of law and order to their country's isolated areas, overall, the Rurales were exceedingly corrupt, supplementing their meager wages with all manner of graft and extortion. Bribery was a way of life with them.

Momentarily putting aside the fact that they weren't in Mexico and the Rurales had no jurisdiction in La Farva, Luke knew the simplest thing might be to play along with them. "If there's a fine for this infraction, I'd be glad to pay it —"

The leader suddenly snapped his rifle around and centered the barrel on Luke's chest. His lips twisted in an arrogant sneer as he said, "You think you can come in here and do as you please, gringo? You think you can throw a little money around and everything will be all right?"

Luke fought the urge to reach for his guns. The Rurales had the drop on him. If he pulled the Remingtons, he would get lead in one or two of them, he was sure of that, but at the same time they would shoot him to pieces. He couldn't allow that to happen.

But he couldn't allow them to take his guns, either. He still had a job to do.

"Well?" the leader demanded imperiously. "Have you nothing to say for yourself?"

Clearly the man fancied himself a little tinpot dictator. He and his men must have crossed the border, ridden into La Farva, and turned it into their own kingdom, at least in their minds. If word got out about what was going on, the American authorities would move in and make short work of their reign, so they couldn't allow anyone to leave for fear of that happening.

Luke knew that if he surrendered, he would have to stay there as a prisoner, or more likely, he would be executed as a threat to the power held by these men.

"I've got something to say."

The rumbling voice came from the man Luke had taken for the local blacksmith. The man turned away from the bar and regarded the Rurales with a fierce scowl on his bearded face. "I say I'm sick and tired of you varmints lording it over us. You got no right to be here. This is our town, not yours!"

"Silence!" the leader of the Rurales shouted shrilly. "How dare you —"

"I'm an American. That's how come I dare!" the man bellowed back at him. "You can only step on us for so long, you little maggot!"

The Rurale jerked his rifle away from Luke to point it at the blacksmith. His face twisted with hate as he pulled the trigger.

But Luke was already moving, lunging forward to grab the rifle's barrel and wrench it upward even as the weapon roared. Luke shoved the rifle backward, smashing the butt into the leader's narrow chest.

As the man staggered back, he yelped, "Lopez!"

The big Rurale with the crossed bandoliers leaped forward. The machete seemed to spring into his hand and flash toward Luke's throat. The stroke would have lopped Luke's head right off his shoulders if it had landed.

The blacksmith tackled Lopez before that could happen. The Rurale was taller, but the two men weighed about the same. The impact drove the Rurale backward and caused the heavy blade to miss Luke by a couple feet.

The other two Rurales tried to bring their rifles to bear, but the struggling men were in the way. Luke palmed out both Remingtons from his cross-draw rig and had the guns ready when Lopez and the blacksmith staggered to the side as they wrestled desperately with each other.

Luke's left-hand gun barked. A howl of pain instantly followed the report as the slug tore through the shoulder of one of the Rurales. His rifle fell to the floor. The other man got a shot off, but the bullet went wild, causing the bartender to duck frantically as the bullet whined over his head and struck the wall. Luke's right-hand revolver roared. The shot shattered the Rurale's elbow. He screamed, dropped his rifle, and started running around in circles, momentarily driven mad by the pain.

That left the leader, who had gone pale and hunched over when Luke rammed him with the rifle butt, probably breaking one of the man's ribs. Cursing breathlessly in Spanish, the leader clawed at the flap of the holster at his waist, trying to free his revolver. Luke swung the Remington and smacked the barrel against the man's head, sending the gray sombrero flying.

The blacksmith had Lopez down on the floor, hands around his throat, beating his head against the ground. He glanced up at Luke and shouted, "Get out while you can, amigo!"

Luke didn't want to leave his unexpected

ally to face the wrath of the Rurales, but he needed to get out of La Farva and back on the trail of Kelly and Dog Eater. The thought that maybe the townspeople could disarm the invaders and lock them up, now that they were starting to fight back flashed through Luke's mind as he took a step toward the cantina's door.

Then he stopped short. More figures poured through the opening. He had hoped there were only four Rurales, but he saw that wasn't the case. At least half a dozen more charged into the building. All of them were armed, and when they saw Luke standing there with a gun in each hand, they opened fire.

CHAPTER 10

With all their compadres on the floor, the Rurales didn't care where their bullets went as they sprayed lead around the cantina. Luke would have been hit if the blacksmith hadn't reached out, grabbed his ankle, and jerked his legs out from under him even as the Rurales started shooting.

Luke hit the floor hard, but managed to hang on to his guns. Both Remingtons blasted in his hands as he rolled onto his belly. His slugs ripped into the cluster of Rurales and caused them to scatter. Everybody scrambled for cover, including Luke and the blacksmith.

They found themselves crouched behind an overturned table. Since both of them were pretty big men, the table wasn't really large enough to shield them, but with all the bullets flying around it wasn't safe to move.

"I'm obliged to you for the help," Luke

told his companion, raising his voice to be heard over the din of gunfire. "Reckon you've got yourself in a bad fix, though."

"We were already in a bad fix," the man replied in his gravelly voice. "Have been ever since those blasted deserters rode in and took over a couple days ago." He stuck out a hamlike hand. "I'm Thomas Sandoval, by the way."

"Luke Jensen." He put down his right-hand gun and shook with the man. "You're the local blacksmith, right?"

"That's right. You must be either a lawman or a bounty hunter."

Luke ducked his head lower as a slug whined close to the crown of his hat. "How do you know that?"

"I heard you asking about those two men. You sounded like you were on their trail, and you ain't their friend."

"You're right about that." Luke picked up the gun he had put down a moment earlier. "Was the bartender telling the truth about them not being here?"

"You're the first stranger unlucky enough to ride in since Captain Almanzar and his men showed up," Sandoval confirmed.

Unlucky was right. Kelly and Dog Eater hadn't even been there, and there was a good chance Luke was going to die in La

Farva, anyway.

Clouds of powder smoke clogged the air inside the cantina. The sharp, acrid reek stung Luke's nose and eyes. Outnumbered and outgunned, he knew the odds of him being able to fight his way out of there were pretty slim.

The chances of him surviving if he'd surrendered were even smaller, though. He hated to think that he might have to go down fighting and fail in his mission to bring Kelly and Dog Eater to justice, but he might not have any choice.

"Fill those hoglegs of yours," Sandoval said. "We're gettin' out of here."

"How do you figure that?" Luke asked as he followed the blacksmith's suggestion and thumbed fresh rounds into the revolvers until all the chambers were full.

"Just stay behind me and keep moving."

Before Luke could ask him what he meant by that, Sandoval had grasped the edges of the table. With a roar, he surged to his feet and charged toward the door. Bullets thudded into the table, but the boards were thick enough to stop them, although splinters flew wildly into the air.

Luke was right behind him, snapping shots right and left to make the Rurales duck. He heard Sandoval grunt and thought the blacksmith might have been hit, but Sandoval stayed on his feet and kept moving. A couple Rurales tried to get in his way, but he plowed right into them, using the table as a battering ram.

The collision knocked the Rurales off their feet and sent them flying like ninepins. Sandoval lost his balance, too, however, and went down. Instinct made Luke leap over his sprawled form and avoid the fallen table.

The door was right in front of him, and his horse was only a few feet away. He could be in the saddle in seconds, racing out of La Farva.

But Sandoval was struggling to get up, and as Luke glanced back he saw blood fly from the blacksmith's thigh as a bullet ripped a furrow in it. Sandoval fell again as that leg failed to support his weight.

He looked up at Luke and yelled, "Go! Get out of here!"

Luke knew that leaving Sandoval meant abandoning him to certain death at the hands of the Rurales. He jammed his right-hand gun back in its holster, kept the gun in his left fist roaring and spouting fire, and reached down to offer the blacksmith his other hand. "Come on!" he urged.

Sandoval reached up and clasped his wrist. Luke hauled him to his feet. They turned toward the hitch rack but hadn't even taken another step when a fiery lance burned across Luke's left arm. He stumbled, knowing that a slug had grazed him. The wound made his arm go numb.

A huge form flew through the cantina door in a diving tackle that smashed Luke to the ground. The big Rurale called Lopez was back in the fight. Fists like sledgehammers pounded into Luke as more Rurales bolted out of the cantina and surrounded Sandoval. Booted feet kicked and stomped, and rifle butts rose and fell in brutal blows.

Luke had dropped his left-hand gun when the bullet creased that arm. His other gun was in its holster, and he couldn't reach it with the bull-like Lopez on top of him, pummeling him relentlessly. He managed to throw a punch of his own that landed cleanly on Lopez's jaw, but he might as well have hit a slab of rock. Lopez ignored the blow and wrapped sausage-like fingers around Luke's throat. A red haze floated in front of Luke's eyes as Lopez began strangling him.

Faintly, as if from far away, Luke heard a high-pitched voice screaming in Spanish. He couldn't make out the words and didn't have time to ponder them because the red haze was quickly becoming a black tide. He couldn't hold it back. It swept over him and washed him away into nothingness.

The pain told Luke he was still alive. It started in his head and radiated all through his body. His throat was sore, and every rasping breath he took made it hurt worse.

He continued drawing air into his lungs anyway, grateful that he still could.

His brain was pretty foggy, but gradually his thoughts began to clear. Instinct had made him keep his eyes closed and lie motionless. He didn't know what was going on around him, and he didn't want to tip off his captors that he had regained consciousness until he had a better idea what the situation was.

He remembered the yelling that had been going on as he'd passed out. Now that he wasn't being choked halfway to death and could think a little straighter, he realized that somebody had been screaming orders not to kill him and the blacksmith. It must have been the little commander of the Rurales. Captain Almanzar was what Sandoval had called him, Luke recalled.

Almanzar hadn't stopped his men from killing them out of the goodness and mercy of his heart. No, Luke thought, the captain had had a lot more sinister reason for sparing them. No doubt he wanted them to die slowly and painfully, probably in full view of the townspeople so their deaths would serve as examples to the citizens of La Farva. Almanzar would want everyone to see what happened to anybody who dared to defy him.

To Luke that meant there was still a chance to turn the tables on the Rurales. As long as he was alive, he wasn't going to give up hope. He was pragmatic enough to realize, however, that the odds against him would be mighty high.

As he'd been thinking, he'd had time to take inventory of his body. He hurt like hell, but was pretty sure everything still worked. He was lying on something hard, either a dirt or stone floor, he guessed. He opened one eye to a narrow slit.

That little slice of vision was enough to show him a rock wall and a man's blood-stained trouser leg. Luke opened his eye a little more and saw Sandoval sitting with his back against that wall. The blacksmith's eyes were closed, but his massive chest rose and fell. He was resting, maybe even sleeping.

"Thomas," Luke said softly as he lifted his head and opened his other eye. He and Sandoval were inside a room with a small window in one wall and a heavy-looking door in the opposite wall. It wasn't a jail cell, although it might as well have been. Neither of them would be able to fit his shoulders through that tiny window.

It must have been a storage room of some sort, Luke thought.

At the moment, it was empty of everything except the two prisoners.

Sandoval hadn't stirred.

Luke said a little louder, "Thomas."

The blacksmith's eyes opened. He gave his great, shaggy head a little shake as he sat up straighter. "You're not dead. I didn't think you were, but I wasn't sure."

"I wasn't sure myself, for a minute there." With an effort, Luke pushed himself up until he was sitting against the wall opposite Sandoval. He groaned as the movement made the pain in his head worse. "Where are we?"

"Little room in the back of the store," the blacksmith replied. "Man named Lloyd Halligan owns it. *El Capitan* made him clean it out so the Rurales could use it to lock up anybody who didn't toe the line to suit them." Sandoval chuckled humorlessly. "We're the first occupants."

"They rode in a couple days ago, you said?" Luke didn't suppose it really mattered how long the Rurales had been there, but whenever he had a problem, he liked to learn as much about it as he could.

And staying alive in La Farva was definitely going to be a problem, he thought.

"Yeah," Sandoval said. "When they rode in, Almanzar started spouting a lot of big talk about how the governments of Mexico and the United States had made a deal and moved the border. He claimed the town was across the line now . . . in Mexico. That was bull and we all knew it. The border's a good fifteen miles south of here. There's no way the U.S. would give up that much territory. Even if they did, there would've been so much hoopla we would have heard about it."

"You're right about that," Luke said. "I was over in Rio Rojo just a few days ago, and there's a telegraph office there. They would have heard the news."

Sandoval scratched at his beard. "Yeah, it didn't take us long to figure out that Almanzar and his troop had deserted from the Rurales and crossed the border to turn outlaw. That wouldn't take much. Those Rurales are only a whisker less crooked than the bandidos they chase."

"Sometimes not even that much," Luke agreed. "I suppose they took over the town anyway, even though nobody believed their story."

"That's right. We're peaceful folks here. We weren't any match for a dozen well-armed border scum like that. They beat up a few men, threatened everybody else, and people fell in line. They didn't have any choice. Almanzar has patrols keeping an eye out to make sure nobody leaves."

"He's not as watchful about people riding in," Luke commented. "Nobody challenged me. I didn't even see anyone when I rode in, until I went into the cantina."

"I suspect his men have orders to lie low if anybody shows up. Let them come in, then close the trap behind them to make sure they don't leave. That's what happened to those two vaqueros who were in the cantina. They drifted in this morning. El Capitan's men disarmed them. They didn't put up any fight. They just want to keep their heads down and stay alive as long as they can."

"Can't blame them for that. This Captain Almanzar, he's the little banty rooster who was haranguing me in the cantina?"

"That's right."

Luke frowned. "What do you think his plans are in the long run?"

Sandoval shook his head. "I don't know.

I'd say he plans to loot the town, but La Farva doesn't exactly have a lot of money in it. Nobody around here has ever gotten rich. From the looks of it, the main thing Almanzar's interested in is strutting around like he's the cock of the walk."

"A man who would be king," Luke mused.

"Yeah, that's as good a way as any to put it. He'll stay here and enjoy it as long as he can keep his men in line. If they get too restless, though, he'll have to move on to greener pastures."

"And he'll wipe out everyone in town when he does," Luke predicted with a bleak look on his face.

Sandoval nodded gloomily. "I'm afraid you're right."

"I suppose he has plans for us sooner than that?"

"Oh, yeah. At sundown he's going to have us taken out and shot."

"Sundown?" Luke repeated. "Isn't it customary to have executions at dawn?"

"El Capitan's too impatient for that. Besides, he wants to make it clear to everyone right away that anybody who crosses him will come to a bad end. After we're dead, it wouldn't surprise me if he hacked our heads off and stuck 'em up on posts for everybody to see."

"An effective tactic for cowing the populace into submission. It goes all the way back to biblical times."

"You're an educated man," Sandoval observed.

"Self-educated, for the most part. Unfortunately, that doesn't do us much good in this situation." Luke gestured at the blacksmith's bloody leg. "How badly are you hit?"

"A couple deep grazes. This one in my leg, and another that took a chunk of meat out of my side. I lost some blood and they hurt like hell, but I reckon I'd be all right if not for the fact that they're going to shoot us to doll rags in another hour or so. How about your arm?"

Luke flexed his left arm and winced. The feeling had come back to it, so he could move it again. It was stiff and sore from the bullet crease, though. "Like you, I'd be fine under different circumstances. I'm curious. How much damage did we do to the Rurales?"

A wolfish grin spread across Sandoval's bearded face. "You killed a couple of them and wounded three or four others. And from the way Almanzar was moving around so carefully, I figure he's got a cracked rib. He acted like he was in pain every time he took a breath."

"Good," Luke said. "I hope he suffers the torments of the damned."

"If anybody ever deserved it, it's him," Sandoval agreed.

The two men were silent for a few minutes. Luke didn't know what Sandoval was thinking, but the wheels of his own brain were turning rapidly as he tried to figure out some move they could make. Finally, he asked, "Almanzar had a dozen men, you said?"

"A dozen counting him."

"Two of them are dead. That leaves ten. And I know at least a couple of the men I shot were hit bad enough that they wouldn't be any good in a fight. That brings the number down to eight, and some of them are injured."

"That's still four to one odds," Sandoval pointed out. "Plus they're armed and we're not. If you're thinking about trying to jump them when they take us out of here, I don't think we'd stand much of a chance."

"How many able-bodied men are there in town?"

The blacksmith rubbed his jaw and frowned in thought. "Eighteen or twenty, I reckon, counting those two vaqueros and everybody over the age of fifteen or sixteen."

"Probably not enough," Luke said. "Not

when they're unarmed and facing at least half a dozen rifles."

"They might be able to overpower Almanzar's men eventually," Sandoval said, "but some good men would get killed doing it."

"If they wait, Almanzar's liable to kill them off one by one, anyway."

The blacksmith's broad shoulders rose and fell in a shrug. "That's true, but when you're asking people to almost certainly die right now, as opposed to maybe dying later on . . ."

"I know. It's not a risk most of them would want to run." Luke's voice hardened as he went on. "I'll be damned if I'm going to stand in front of a wall and just let those deserters shoot me, though."

"Yeah, I feel the same way. What say we jump them as soon as we get a chance and make them fight to kill us?"

"That's what I —" Luke stopped in midsentence as he heard a key rattle in the lock. He forgot all about the aches and pains scattered throughout his body and came to his feet.

On the other side of the makeshift cell, Thomas Sandoval did the same as the door started to swing open.

CHAPTER 11

Luke was ready to throw himself forward as soon as the door was open wide enough. He knew their captors would be prepared for trouble, but even so he thought there was a chance he might be able to get his hands on a rifle before he was cut down. If he did, that could change everything . . .

"Mr. Jensen!" a voice whispered urgently through the opening. "Mr. Jensen, are you in there?"

Luke had heard people described as being thunderstruck. That was a pretty good way to describe how he felt at that moment. He was as surprised as he'd been in a long time. "Hobie?"

A slender figure in a battered old hat pushed the door open the rest of the way. Hobie had found a serape somewhere and draped it around himself, hiding the work shirt and the suspenders he wore. He had his Henry rifle in his hands.

Luke held out a hand to stop Sandoval from attacking the young man.

"We've gotta hurry," Hobie said. "I knocked out the fella standing guard in the store, but I don't know how long it'll be before he wakes up."

Sandoval asked, "You know this young fella, Jensen?"

"I do. And I have to admit, right now I'm mighty glad to see him."

A pleased grin flashed across Hobie's face. "See, I told you we ought to be partners. Come on."

The three of them hurried out of the back room and into the general store.

Sandoval limped on his wounded leg. He didn't want to hold up the others. "Don't let me slow you down. If I can't keep up, you just go on without me."

Luke didn't intend to do that. "Lean on me if you have to, Thomas. Nobody gets left behind."

A beefy, middle-aged man with white hair and a mustache stood behind the counter in the store. He looked scared, probably because of the Rurale who was stretched out senseless on the floor in the business's main aisle. The man stared at Hobie. "I don't know who you are, young fella, but you're gonna get us all killed!"

140

Luke said harshly, "The only chance you have is to fight back, mister. Keep letting those renegades have their way and all it'll get you sooner or later is a bullet."

"Tom, have you gone loco?" the storekeeper said to Sandoval. "We can't fight those Rurales!"

"Sorry, Lloyd, but if you won't fight, at least stay out of our way," Sandoval snapped. "Jensen and I need guns." He limped toward a case containing several rifles.

"You can't —" Lloyd stopped himself. With a sigh he went on. "Go ahead. Maybe you're right. Maybe this is the only chance we got." He stood up straighter, his back stiffening. "Hell, I'll take one myself. Nothin' to lose, is there?"

"Nothing but our lives," Luke said. "And those aren't worth a damned thing if we let animals like Almanzar and his men run roughshod over us."

Lloyd opened the gun case and handed Winchesters to Luke and Sandoval, then took one down for himself. "Got plenty of ammunition behind the counter. Come on."

He took a box of .44 shells off a shelf and opened it. The men gathered around the counter and fed ammunition through the rifles' loading gates until the weapons were full, then stuffed more shells into their pockets.

The Rurale started to stir and let out a little moan. Luke stepped over to him and kicked him in the head. It was a brutal thing to do, but he wasn't going to lose much sleep over anything that happened to the invaders. The man was still and silent again.

"It would probably be a good idea to tie and gag him and lock him in the back room while we have the chance," Luke said. They weren't going to kill the prisoner out of hand, and that seemed merciful enough to him. "How did you manage to get the drop on him, Hobie?"

"I stole this serape off a clothesline behind somebody's house," the young man explained. "When I came in here I had my head down so the guard couldn't see my face, and I kept my rifle hidden behind my leg until I was close enough to clout him with it." A note of pride in his voice, he added, "I told you I'm tougher than I look, Mr. Jensen."

"I'd have to say you're right about that," Luke admitted. "You're sneaky, too. You've been following me ever since I left the Anderson ranch, haven't you? You just did a better job of it, that's all."

"Well, I'll admit I thought I'd lost your

trail a few times. But I stuck with it."

Sandoval said, "I don't know what you hombres are talking about, but I'm glad you showed up when you did, young fella. We were in a pretty bad spot."

"We still are, but at least the odds are better now." Luke slapped a hand against the stock of the Winchester he held. "And this helps, too. Hobie, do you know where the rest of the Rurales are?"

"I saw some of them going into the cantina, but I don't know about the others."

Luke thought about it for a moment and said, "It doesn't really matter. They're going to be coming to us pretty soon."

"To fetch us for the firing squad," Sandoval said with a grin.

"That's right. All we have to do is sit back and wait."

Lloyd Halligan tied and gagged the unconscious Rurale as Luke had suggested, then went to the front of the store to keep watch.

Luke asked Hobie, "How did you know we needed help?"

"When I came in sight of the town, I thought I'd better stop and see if anything was going on before I just rode in. I've got a pair of field glasses in my saddlebags, so I used them to check the place out."

"It appears that once again I didn't give

you enough credit," Luke said. "Go on."

"Well, I saw some sort of ruckus in the street, and when I took a closer look through the glasses, I realized you were in the middle of it. I watched while they dragged you into the store here, along with this other fella."

"Thomas Sandoval," the blacksmith introduced himself.

"Hobie McCullough," the young man said as they shook hands.

Luke realized it was the first time he had heard Hobie's last name.

"Anyway, I recognized the men you'd been fighting with as Rurales, and that really threw me for a loop because I was pretty sure I was still in New Mexico Territory."

"They're deserters," Luke said. "Outlaws, now, instead of just corrupt lawmen."

"I didn't know what was going on," Hobie said, "but I knew I didn't want to just ride in bold as brass. That seemed like a good way to get in trouble. So I decided to sneak into town." Again, that note of pride entered his voice as he added, "I think I did a better job of it than last time."

"Evidently," Luke told him, smiling.

"I stayed out of sight and eavesdropped on some people talking at the livery stable. That helped me figure out you were in trouble and likely locked up here in the store's back room. Then I heard that you were gonna be executed at sundown. I couldn't let that happen."

"Nobody would have blamed you if you'd just ridden away," Luke said. "This wasn't your responsibility, and you were risking your life by going up against those Rurales."

Hobie shrugged. "Maybe. But it seemed like the thing to do."

"I really did underestimate you. But I won't again. I give you my word on that."

"Were they really gonna stand you up in front of a firing squad?"

"They certainly were." Luke's smile took on a grim cast. "We'll see how they like it when their would-be victims shoot back."

From the front of the store, Lloyd called, "Almanzar's on his way with three of his men. The other three are rousting folks out of the buildings and lining them up in the street at gunpoint."

"A play must have its audience, even if it's a captive one," Luke murmured. "Almanzar wants everyone to see what he thinks is about to happen."

"Once the lead starts to fly, those folks are going to be in danger," Sandoval said. "We need to hit the Rurales as hard and fast as we can, so the fight won't go on long."

"Surprise is our greatest ally." Luke looked at Hobie. "Are you sure you're ready for this?"

Hobie's face was pale under its tan, but he nodded. "I won't let you down, Mr. Jensen."

"After what you've already done today, I didn't think that you would. Let's go." As the three men walked toward the front of the store to join Lloyd Halligan, Luke quickly gave some instructions. "I'll go out first. The rest of you come fast behind me and spread out. Aim for Almanzar and the men with him first, then the ones guarding the townspeople. That'll give the citizens a few seconds to run for cover, anyway."

"Good luck," Sandoval said.

"Lord help us," Lloyd muttered.

Luke jerked the door open and stepped out onto the store's high porch that doubled as a loading dock. As he brought the Winchester to his shoulder in a smooth, swift, but unhurried movement, he saw Captain Almanzar stop in his tracks and stare at the building.

Shock made the Rurale officer's eyes widen. He shrieked something in Spanish and fumbled with the holstered pistol on his hip.

Luke fired.

He had drawn a bead on Almanzar's chest, but as he pressed the trigger and the sharp crack of the rifle filled the air, one of the Rurales lunged forward, trying to get a shot off. His shoulder struck Almanzar and knocked the smaller man aside. The .44 slug from Luke's rifle smashed into the man's body and twisted him around.

Luke bit back a curse. He'd hoped to kill Almanzar with his first shot. He worked the rifle's lever and fired again as more shots erupted from his three allies as they emerged from the store.

Luke's second shot punched into the belly of the man he had winged a moment earlier and dropped him to the ground. He tried to draw a bead on Almanzar, but the captain had retreated behind the other two men with him. He turned and ran.

Gunfire filled the street. A slug whipped past Luke's head as he fired again and saw a Rurale's head explode in a cloud of pink mist. He levered the Winchester and swung the barrel, tracking a man who'd bolted for cover. Luke pressed the trigger and felt the rifle kick against his shoulder. His bullet clipped the running man on the hip and spilled him off his feet.

Luke was about to finish off the fallen Rurale when one of La Farva's citizens, a middle-aged woman who was screaming at the top of her lungs, dashed in front of his target. With an effort, Luke held off on the trigger.

The Rurale used his rifle as a crutch and lunged awkwardly to his feet. He grabbed the woman from behind and dragged her in front of him as a shield. With his left arm around her throat, he lifted his rifle and fired it one-handed at the store. The bullet struck the porch to Luke's right, glanced off, and shattered the window behind him.

"Hunt some cover!" he called to the men with him. "Hobie, behind that rain barrel!"

Hobie leaped down the stairs at the end of the porch and crouched behind the rain barrel sitting there. Lloyd Halligan ducked back inside the store and started firing through the broken window. Sandoval leaped to the ground, but his wounded leg collapsed under him when he landed and dumped him. He rolled desperately to the side as slugs kicked up dust around him, coming up on hands and knees and scrambling behind the parked wagon Luke had noticed when he first rode into town.

Only a few hours had passed since then, Luke thought as he jumped off the porch and landed in the wagon's empty bed, although it seemed more like days. He dropped to one knee behind the seat and fired at the remaining Rurales, who kept blazing away as they retreated toward the building across the street.

Another man followed the example of the one who had grabbed the woman and snatched up a terrified boy to use as a hostage.

"Hold your fire!" Luke called to his friends. With the boy and the woman in danger, they had to stop shooting.

But then a man ran out of the nearby livery stable with a pitchfork in his hands. He lunged at the Rurale holding the kid and yelled, "Let that boy go!"

The citizens of La Farva had finally had enough. They were fighting back against the renegades who had invaded their town.

The Rurale turned at the shout, but didn't have a chance to defend himself. The liveryman plunged the sharp tines deep into his back. The Rurale screamed and twisted, trying unsuccessfully to arch away from the agonizing pain. His rifle roared. The shot hit the liveryman and knocked him backward.

The boy kicked loose, dropped to the ground, and streaked away. That left the wounded Rurale in the open, and a split second later he was blown to hell by four shots that were so close together they sounded like one huge blast. Luke, Hobie, Sandoval, and Lloyd Halligan had all drawn a bead him, and their deadly accurate rounds tore through him and dropped a quivering, bloody heap into the dirt.

The female hostage recovered from her hysteria and grabbed the barrel of her captor's rifle. Half mad with pain and anger, he clouted her on the side of the head with his free hand and knocked her away from him.

Realizing too late the mistake he had made, he turned and tried to run, but before he could take a step he was lifted off his feet by the slugs that smashed into him from the rifles held by Luke and Hobie.

One Rurale had made it to the building, but he backed out of the door even quicker than he went in, throwing his rifle aside and thrusting his hands into the air. An elderly townsman brandishing an ancient flintlock pistol followed him into the street, shouting, "You better keep your hands up, damn your hide! You didn't find this old pistol of mine 'cause I had it hid! It'll blow a hole in you just like it did your granddaddy at San Jacinto!"

"Keep him covered, old-timer!" Luke called from the wagon as he scanned the street, looking for more enemies. He counted quickly. Four gray-uniformed bodies sprawled in the street, plus the one who had surrendered to the old man. Luke didn't see any other threats.

Two of the Rurales were missing, though, and it was easy to tell who they were by the sizes of the one who had fallen. Captain Almanzar and the giant Lopez were nowhere in sight.

Luke stood up. They could hunt down the missing men later, he thought as he squinted against the clouds of powder smoke that still hung in the air. There were injured people to check on, wounds to patch up, and prisoners to secure along with the one they already had locked up.

La Farva was free again.

CHAPTER 12

Just as Luke suspected, Almanzar and Lopez had fled. A search of the town as night was falling failed to turn up any trace of the two Rurales.

The man who had wielded the pitchfork and skewered one of the Rurales was wounded, but according to the local barber, who doubled as the town's doctor, he was expected to live. The barber did a better job of patching up Thomas Sandoval's wounds, too, and also cleaned and bandaged the bullet graze on Luke's arm. Those were the only casualties among the town's defenders.

By that time, full darkness had settled over the town. Luke asked for volunteers to stand guard until morning. He didn't think it was likely Almanzar and Lopez would come back since they were badly outnumbered, but he didn't want to take a chance on the two renegades causing any more trouble.

La Farva didn't have a hotel, so Thomas

Sandoval invited Luke and Hobie to stay at his house overnight. They accepted the offer, putting their horses in a shed behind the blacksmith's shop and spreading their bedrolls in the little cottage next to the shop.

By the next morning, there had still been no sign of Almanzar and Lopez, so Luke thought it was safe to assume the two Rurales were gone for good. "They may have even gone back across the border," he said over the breakfast that Hobie had prepared. Their host's wounded leg had stiffened up overnight and made it difficult for him to get around.

Luke changed his mind. "But probably not. Since they're deserters, other Rurales may be looking for them. I doubt very seriously that they'll ever come back here."

"If they do, they'll find that we're a lot more ready for them next time," Sandoval said. "I think people realize now that you can't just let evil men come in and take over, no matter how scared you are. You have to fight back."

Luke sipped his coffee and nodded, but actually he was rather pessimistic about the blacksmith's prediction. The citizens understood that they had to stand up for themselves when they and their way of life were threatened, but over time they would forget.

They would become complacent again, and when the next evil arose — as it always did — they wouldn't be ready for it. They wouldn't realize how much danger they were in until too late, and then they could only pray that they had awakened in time.

Luke knew better than to think he could change human nature, though. He could only hope that the people of La Farva had learned their lesson. He had to move on. The minor wound on his arm wouldn't stop him from riding. He needed to get back on the trail of Gunner Kelly and Dog Eater.

He wasn't the only one thinking about that. Hobie said, "Are we going on after those outlaws today, Mr. Jensen?"

Luke finished his coffee and set the cup on the table. "Two things, Hobie. I think after all the help you gave me yesterday, you can call me Luke now."

Hobie looked a little uncomfortable at that idea, but he nodded. "Um, all right, Mr. Jensen . . . I mean, Luke. What was the other thing?"

"Are you sure you still want to ride with me?"

"Yes, sir," Hobie answered without hesitation. "Of course, I reckon I understand if you don't want me to. I did sort of horn in on this deal. You might not want to give up any of the bounty money."

"No, I'll split it fairly with you if we bring in Kelly and the Apache. The five thousand I'm owed for Monroe Epps is mine, though."

"Well, sure," Hobie said. "I wouldn't try to claim any of it."

"The reason I asked if you were certain you wanted to come along," Luke said, "is because you should be starting to understand that this is a hard, dangerous life for a man to follow. Most of the men you'll be tracking down won't hesitate to kill you if they get a chance. You have to be ready to kill them. You can't hesitate once your finger's on the trigger."

"I won't. I understand. I did all right yesterday, didn't I?"

"You did better than all right," Luke admitted. "But you also probably had quite a bit of luck on your side. Next time, things might not break so well for you."

"I'm willing to run that risk." Hobie paused, frowned, and went on. "Anyway, I may decide I don't want to keep on being a bounty hunter the rest of my life. I just want to do *something* to show the folks back in Rio Rojo that I'm more than just the orphan kid who mucks out the stalls at Mr. Dunbar's stable. Nobody's ever thought I was gonna amount to much, and I'd like to show 'em that they're wrong."

Hobie wanted glory as much as he did money, Luke mused. That was all too common. If young men never felt like that, there wouldn't be anybody to fight the world's wars.

He knew there had been some of that hunger for glory in his own decision to join the Confederate Army back in '61. Sure, he didn't think it was right for the Yankees to invade the Southern states the way they had, and he still didn't. But in the back of his mind, at least, had been the desire to hear the stirring music as he marched to battle under the flag of his homeland.

In the end, that hadn't gotten him any glory, only blood and mud and the closest brush with death he'd ever had. War, like bounty hunting, was an ugly, dangerous business.

He could explain that to Hobie McCullough until he was blue in the face, and it wouldn't do a damned bit of good. Men, especially young men, had to learn the hard lessons of life on their own.

So he nodded and said, "All right, Hobie, we'll ride together after those outlaws."

And God help us both, Luke added silently.

They rode out of La Farva with the shouted thanks and farewells of the townspeople ringing in their ears. They had stocked up on supplies, provided at no charge by a grateful Lloyd Halligan, and filled all six of their canteens at the public well.

Luke would have felt a little better about their mission if Kelly and Dog Eater had passed through there. It would have been nice to know that he and Hobie were still on the right trail, but all they could do was keep moving in the direction the fugitives had been traveling. He was confident they would pick up a lead to the outlaws' current whereabouts sooner or later.

Hobie talked a lot as they rode, and the incessant chatter reminded Luke of why he had never taken on a partner in his bounty hunting endeavors. Most of the past fifteen years he had spent alone, making few friends, and nearly all the female companionship he'd had was of the professional variety. Simpler that way. He enjoyed his own company, especially when he had a good book to read.

Months before, he had been reunited with his brother Smoke, who had told him he was welcome on the Sugarloaf ranch near Big Rock, Colorado, any time. Smoke wanted to introduce him to their adopted brother Matt and to the old mountain man called Preacher. For years, Smoke had considered them family, and now that he'd found his blood relative — Luke — again, he wanted him to be part of that circle.

So now *he* had a family, too, Luke mused, and Hobie was probably the closest thing he'd had to a friend in several years. Things were changing in his life, and Luke wasn't sure he liked that. The life he had led was rather bleak in many respects, true enough, but he was accustomed to it.

He didn't have the heart to tell Hobie to shut up, though, so he let him rattle on and didn't pay much attention to what was said.

If Hobie noticed, he didn't let it slow him down.

Several days after leaving La Farva, they came to another small settlement. It appeared normal, with people moving around on the street.

Luke reined to a halt in front of the Golden Buzzard Saloon. A carved wooden buzzard with a coat of gilt paint on it was mounted on top of its sign. Luke thought the figure was ugly, but at the same time it was certainly striking.

"Are we gonna get a drink?" Hobie asked.

"Among other things," Luke told him. "Let me do the talking."

They dismounted, tied their horses at the hitch rack, and went inside. The saloon was about half full. Unlike the cantina in La Farva, a couple women were working, both of them hard-faced veterans of the frontier who showed every year of their drab existence.

One of them perked up considerably at the sight of Luke and Hobie. She brushed a hand over her graying blond hair and smiled as she approached them. "Hello, boys. Can I get you a drink? You can sit down and I'll bring it right to your table."

Luke returned the smile. "Only if you'll agree to join us."

"Well, I'm really not supposed to" — she glanced at the bartender — "but I don't think Glenn will mind."

Luke was sure Glenn wouldn't mind, since it was the woman's job to sell drinks. She would try to keep them coming as long as she sat with her customers.

"My name is Doris, by the way," she added.

"I'm Luke and my young friend here is Hobie." Luke didn't see any point in giving her their last names.

"I'm very pleased to meet you. Just sit anywhere. I'll be back with a bottle and some glasses."

"Be sure to bring one for yourself," Luke told her.

"Oh, I don't know. I'm not used to drinking." Doris laughed. "You might try to take advantage of me."

"I swear on my honor as a gentleman that I wouldn't even think of it."

That brought another laugh from her.

She must have been considering the idea of a gentleman drinking in a place called the Golden Buzzard, Luke thought.

"She's kind of a nice-looking lady, isn't she?" Hobie said quietly as they sat down at one of the tables.

"Yes, and she's twice your age," Luke pointed out.

"That would make her just about right for you, then."

Luke chuckled in spite of himself at that gibe. Hobie's constant chatter out on the trail could be annoying, but Luke couldn't help but like the young man.

"Don't get any ideas about playing Cupid. I can handle that part of my life just fine, thank you."

"No, sir. I mean, yes, sir. I won't."

Doris came back with a bottle and two empty glasses. She had a third glass for herself that already contained a couple inches of amber liquid. Luke and Hobie stood up politely when she reached the table.

"My tastes run more toward brandy," she said. "I hope that's all right."

"Whatever you like," Luke told her, knowing full well that was weak tea in the glass, not brandy.

They sat down and Doris poured shots of whiskey for the two men.

Luke lifted his glass and said, "To making new friends."

"How sweet," Doris said. "I think maybe you really are a gentleman."

"I always endeavor to be."

Luke tossed back his drink. Hobie did likewise, then immediately got red in the face and started sputtering. He thumped a hand against the table a couple times.

"A little too strong for you?" Luke asked dryly.

"N-no," Hobie choked out in a hoarse whisper. "Smooth. J-just the way I like it."

Luke tried not to grin. He wasn't going to come right out and ask if that was the first drink Hobie had ever taken, but it wouldn't surprise him if that were the case.

"Speaking of friends," Luke went on, "a couple of ours may have ridden through here in the past few days. Wonder if you've seen 'em. A redheaded fella, sort of slender, traveling with an Indian."

Doris instantly stiffened at that description. "Those two are friends of yours?" The friendly tone she had displayed a moment earlier had vanished completely.

"Friends might be too strong a word," Luke said, instantly switching tacks when he saw her reaction. "More like acquaintances whose trail crossed ours, really."

"Well, those *acquaintances* of yours caused a lot of trouble when they were here," Doris said acidly. "That Indian, especially. He got in a fight over a woman and cut a man pretty badly. Almost killed him. And he smacked the woman around, too. Then when the marshal tried to step in, the redhead shot him!"

"Good Lord!" Luke exclaimed, trying to sound surprised even though what Doris had told them didn't shock him at all. "Did he kill the lawman?"

"No, but not for lack of trying. It was just luck that poor Marshal Bendix survived. As if that wasn't enough trouble they'd caused, those two robbed the general store! I hope they never come back here." Doris folded

162

her arms across her chest and frowned coldly at Luke and Hobie. "If they're friends of yours, I don't think you're welcome here, either."

Luke frowned. "I assure you, we spent less than one evening in their company, and going by what you've just told us, I'm thankful they didn't try to rob and murder us! Isn't that right, Hobie?"

"Yes, sir. They sound like really bad hombres."

Doris sniffed. "That's putting it mildly."

"Did you happen to notice which way they went when they rode out?" Luke asked.

"Why?" Doris shot back at him, instantly suspicious again. "Do you want to follow them?"

"Just the opposite. I thought we'd try to avoid them."

Her attitude eased a little. "Well, that would probably be the smart thing to do, all right. As a matter of fact, I did see them ride out. They were headed southwest."

"We'll go a different way, then. We sure don't want to run into them."

"Sorry I jumped to the wrong conclusion about you," Doris said. "I just don't want to have anything to do with anybody like those two."

"How long ago did you say they came

through here?"

"Three days, was it? No, four. Four days ago. That's right."

"Well, they're long gone by now," Luke said.

"And good riddance."

Luke poured another drink. "I'll drink to that."

CHAPTER 13

Luke came awake and stretched. He was aware of the warm figure stirring beside him in the bed. Doris's voice murmured sleepily, "Is it morning already, honey?"

"Indeed it is." Luke sat up and looked around Doris's room, which was located on the second floor of the Golden Buzzard. He hadn't paid much attention to the details the night before. The room was furnished simply with the bed, a dressing table, a ladder-back chair, and an old wardrobe that had been a nice piece of furniture at one time. Like everything else, it was showing its age.

Aren't we all, Luke thought as he swung his legs out of bed and stood up to stretch again, wearing only the bottom half of his long underwear.

Sunlight slanted through the gauzy yellow curtain over the room's lone window. He didn't normally sleep that late, but he'd had quite a bit to drink the night before, not to mention a good meal. And once they'd adjourned to her room, Doris had proven to be an energetic companion.

Luke wasn't stupid enough to believe that he could always tell when a woman was sincere, but he thought her enthusiasm had been genuine. As she had put it, "You're not the handsomest gent I've ever seen, but you really are a gentleman. I don't run into one of those in a month of Sundays!"

He had just pulled his trousers on and buttoned them when a tentative knock sounded on the door. He had a pretty good idea who was there, but drew one of his Remingtons from its holster, anyway as he went over to answer the knock. His thumb was looped over the hammer as he called, "Who is it?"

"Just me, Luke," Hobie replied. "I got the horses ready to go, like you told me last night."

Luke had to think for a second before he recalled telling Hobie to see to it that the horses were saddled and fed by sunup. He wanted to get an early start. Gunner Kelly and Dog Eater had quite a lead on them, and if he and Hobie were going to cut into that lead, they couldn't afford to waste any time.

Luke glanced out the window again and muttered a curse. Judging by the light, at least an hour had gone by since sunrise. There was no excuse for that, he told himself firmly. Hobie might wind up being a better bounty hunter than he was, sooner rather than later.

"Go order us some coffee and breakfast at the hash house," Luke said through the door. "I'll be right there."

"I already did," Hobie said. "The food will be ready in a few minutes."

Luke grunted. The boy was smart. Maybe a little too smart for his own good.

Luke pulled on the rest of his clothes, stomped into his boots, and buckled on the double gun rig. When he bent over the bed, he saw that Doris had gone back to sleep. Smiling faintly, he bent lower and brushed a kiss across her blond hair. She moved her head a little and smiled, but didn't open her eyes.

Luke left a double eagle on the dressing table. With the violent life he led, a moment of gentleness was well worth it. And he wanted Doris to have good memories of him, too.

Hobie was waiting in front of the saloon. They left the horses tied at the hitch rack, their saddlebags full of supplies, and went across the street to eat.

They didn't linger over breakfast and soon were mounted and riding out of the settlement. As they put the town behind them, Luke realized he hadn't even gone to the trouble of finding out the name. It didn't matter. It was just one more stop on the trail that led them after their quarry.

Hobie wasn't any less talkative, at least starting out, but Luke kept them moving at a fast pace that eventually grew tiring for man and horse alike. Hobie quieted down and reserved his strength for riding.

By the time two more days had passed, Hobie was taciturn most of the time and beginning to get a drawn, gaunt look about him. His eyes had dark circles under them, and patchy stubble covered his cheeks and jaw. It was probably the longest he had ever been out on the trail, away from civilization.

"This is the way you spend your days?" he asked once as they stopped to rest the horses.

"Most of them," Luke said.

"Don't you get lonely, 'way off out here in the middle of nowhere?"

Luke shrugged. "You get used to it. If you can't, you don't stay in this life for very long. But even when you're in a town, you're still alone for the most part. Most people don't have a very high opinion of bounty hunters. To them, we're just one step above the outlaws we hunt, and a pretty small step, at that. If that bothers you —"

"I know. You don't last long at the job."

"That's right."

A short time later, after they were riding again, Luke noticed a cloud of dust rising ahead of them. For a second, his pulse quickened with the thought that the dust might be coming from horses ridden by Kelly and Dog Eater, but then he realized that was pretty unlikely.

For one thing, the two fugitives would have had to stop for several days in order for Luke and Hobie to catch up to them so soon, and Luke didn't think they would do that.

For another, there was too much dust. Even with the extra horses they had taken from the ranch, Kelly and Dog Eater shouldn't have been kicking up a cloud like that.

Hobie saw it, too. "What's that?"

"I don't know. A big group of riders, maybe a wagon team. Look at the way the dust is moving. They're angling across our path from the northeast." Luke gestured to indicate what he was talking about. "It's

169

probably not Kelly and Dog Eater, if that's what you're thinking."

"I guess it's not really any of our business, then."

"You're right about that," Luke said.

Despite what he'd told Hobie, curiosity gnawed at him. The dust cloud was moving pretty fast, and if somebody was in a hurry, it usually meant trouble.

So did gunshots, and that's what Luke heard a moment later, floating through the hot air.

He reined in and motioned for Hobie to do likewise. The young man frowned as the shots continued. "Is that what I think it is?"

"Gunfire," Luke said. "Quite a bit of it, too. Somebody's fighting a battle up there, a mile or so ahead of us."

"Shouldn't we go see about it?" Hobie said eagerly. "Maybe Kelly and Dog Eater are mixed up in it."

"That's possible," Luke admitted. "Unlikely, but we can't rule it out." He lifted his reins. "Come on."

Their mounts were far from fresh, but Luke thought the horses had one good run left in them. Hobie matched his pace as they hurried toward the dust cloud, which didn't seem to be moving anymore. It was thinning as the breeze blew through it.

That fact, along with the continuing gunshots, told Luke it wasn't a running fight anymore. Pursuers and the pursued had come to a stop and were battling it out.

It was flat country for the most part, broken by ravines, shallow bluffs, and mesas. They came in sight of one of those tabletop formations, and Luke stopped to get his spyglass out of his saddlebags. Hobie followed suit, digging out his field glasses.

"Where did you get those glasses, anyway?" Luke asked as he tried to focus through the telescope.

"An old man back in Rio Rojo gave them to me as payment for some odd jobs I did for him. He fought in the War Between the States and said he used them then." Hobie paused. "Were you in the war, Luke?"

"I was. I suppose that makes me an old man, too."

"No, sir, I didn't say that. Which side were you on?"

Luke didn't like to talk about the war. Too many bad memories, culminating in the betrayal that had almost taken his life and set him on a lonely trail for a decade and a half afterward.

"I fought for the Confederacy," he said with a curt note in his voice, letting Hobie know he didn't want to discuss the subject at length.

"Oh. The fella who gave me these glasses, he was a Union officer."

"Plenty of good men on both sides. It was a shame so many of them had to die because of a bunch of damned politicians." Luke stiffened as the image came into focus through the spyglass. "Well, that doesn't look good."

"I don't — Oh, Lord. Is that a stage-coach?"

"It is," Luke said.

The coach was lying on its side near the base of the mesa. It appeared the team had broken loose when the wreck occurred, since the horses were no longer hitched to the coach and he didn't see them nearby. Puffs of powder smoke came from behind the coach as its defenders used it for cover.

Luke swung the spyglass, searching for the other side of the conflict. He found them a moment later, a dozen or more riders who had dismounted and stretched out on their bellies to snipe at the coach with rifle fire from a distance of about two hundred yards.

Hobie saw the men through his field glasses, too. "Do you reckon those hombres are outlaws?"

"More than likely. I can't think of any

other reason they would waylay that coach." Luke moved the spyglass back to the over-turned vehicle and frowned as he noticed something odd. Dust kept flying from the mesa as bullets struck the side of it behind the coach.

For some reason, the riflemen were aiming high. They were trying to keep the people behind the coach pinned down there, instead of picking them off.

Someone who had been riding in that coach was important to the attackers, Luke realized. They wanted to keep whoever it was alive. That put a slightly different slant on things.

And it made Luke more curious than ever.

"I don't think this is a simple holdup after all," he told Hobie. He explained what he had noticed and the conclusions he'd drawn from it. "They'll keep the driver, the guard, and the passengers pinned down until nightfall, and then they'll sneak in under cover of darkness and grab whoever they're after."

"We can't let 'em do that, can we?" Hobie asked.

"Again, it's not really any of our business."

"No, but they have to be planning something pretty bad, or they wouldn't have stopped the stagecoach and started all that shooting."

"It's possible the people with the coach don't have any rifles, either," Luke mused. "Just handguns and the guard's shotgun — which means they're wasting bullets. The riders are out of range."

"Not for us," Hobie said. "Not if we get closer."

Luke frowned at the young man. "You don't seem to grasp the concept of our job, Hobie. We go after wanted fugitives and bring them in, dead or alive, so we can collect the rewards for them. We don't ride around the countryside doing good deeds, like knights from some storybook."

"But those people are in trouble. Some of 'em are likely to get killed before this is over, if they haven't already."

Luke tried not to sigh. His own impulse was to pitch in and give those folks with the stagecoach a hand. If Hobie hadn't been there, he might have been able to resist that temptation. With the young man around to goad him into doing the right thing, there was no chance of turning and riding away.

"All right," Luke said as he put the spyglass away. He pointed to the north. "See that little knob over there? We'll circle around behind it. That'll give us some cover and also the high ground. From up there we ought to have a pretty good shot at those riflemen."

Hobie nodded eagerly and turned his horse toward the knob.

With the attackers concentrating their attention on the wrecked stagecoach, Luke figured it was unlikely they would be looking behind them. He and Hobie moved fast, galloping behind the rocky elevation and then reining to a halt when it was between them and the riflemen. Each tied his horse to a stunted mesquite and pulled his Winchester from the saddle boot.

The knob was about twenty feet high, its sides sloping gently enough that they were able to scramble to the top without any trouble. At the crest, Luke took his hat off and stretched out on his belly to peer at the landscape in front of them. Hobie did likewise, stretching out beside him.

The stagecoach's attackers were about fifty yards away, in easy range for a rifle.

Hobie swallowed hard and asked, "Do we shoot to kill?"

"Most of the time when you use a gun, you don't want to leave any doubt about the outcome."

"But we don't really know who those men are or what's going on here," Hobie argued. "Maybe they're a posse of lawmen. Outlaws could have stolen that stagecoach, and they're just trying to get it back."

That seemed like a pretty far-fetched idea to Luke, but he supposed they couldn't rule it out. Hobie was right that they didn't know the whole story.

Luke sighed. "Kid, you're going to be the death of me yet. But I guess you've earned that right since you saved my life." He nestled his cheek against the smooth wood of the Winchester's stock as he squinted over the barrel. "All right, let's see if we can spook them enough to make them run."

CHAPTER 14

Luke aimed for a spot about ten feet to the right of one of the attackers and squeezed the trigger. The rifle cracked and kicked against his shoulder, and dirt spurted into the air at the spot he had targeted.

The man jumped, obviously startled, made a motion like he was going to get up, and then pressed himself to the ground again as he looked around wildly for the source of the shot. Clearly, he didn't think it had come from the stagecoach.

Beside Luke, Hobie's rifle blasted. Another of the attackers flinched as the bullet hit close enough to spray grit in his face.

"Damn it," Hobie said. "I almost hit him. I was aiming to miss by more than that."

Luke had already levered his Winchester. He fired again and sent another man's hat flying through the air. "Yeah, I came a little closer than I intended there, too," he said dryly.

The attackers were stirred up and on the verge of panic. Several leaped frantically to their feet as Luke and Hobie continued to pepper the ground around them with slugs.

With no place to take cover, the riflemen broke off the assault and raced for their mounts being held by a man well back from the others.

"I just thought of something," Hobie said nervously as he paused in his firing. "What if they come after us now?"

"That's a risk you run when you stick your nose in somebody else's business," Luke said. "There's always the chance they'll try to cut it off."

As a matter of fact, some of the men were already throwing lead at the knob, having figured out where the shots were coming from. None of the bullets were coming close to Luke and Hobie yet, but that might not remain true for long.

It was time to send the attackers a message. Luke tracked his sights on one of the running men and squeezed off another round. The man tumbled off his feet as the bullet ripped through his thigh. His pained yell was clearly audible from where Luke and Hobie lay on top of the knob.

"I want them to know we missed those first shots on purpose," Luke said as he levered the Winchester and shifted his aim. His next shot hit a man in the shoulder and spun him around. He managed to stay on his feet and continued stumbling toward the horses.

One of the riflemen went back to help the first hombre Luke had shot. He got the wounded man up and helped him onto a horse. In a matter of seconds, all of the attackers were mounted. Instead of trying to circle around the knob and go after Luke and Hobie, they lit out to the south, causing a big cloud of dust to boil into the air again.

Hobie took off his hat and sleeved sweat from his forehead. He blew out a nervous breath and then laughed. "I thought we might have a real fight on our hands there."

"We were outnumbered, but we had the superior position," Luke explained. "And after I winged a couple, they knew they'd have to pay a pretty high price to roust us off the top of this hill."

Despite what he'd told Hobie, Luke kept a close eye on the gunmen until they had vanished in the distance. Then he stood up and said, "Let's go see what's so all-fired important about that stagecoach. Some of those folks could be hurt and need our help, too."

They got their horses and rode toward the overturned vehicle. Luke approached it warily. If the defenders had been paying attention, they would know that he and Hobie were responsible for running off those other men. People who had recently been fighting for their lives sometimes didn't really think straight, though, especially if they weren't used to such danger.

"Hold on," Luke told Hobie when they were still about fifty yards away. "Let's give them a minute to get it through their heads that we're friends."

He hadn't seen anyone moving around behind the coach, but knew somebody was still alive back there because they'd been shooting only a few minutes earlier. He took his hat off and waved it back and forth above his head. "Hello, the coach! Hold your fire! My partner and I are coming in! We mean you no harm!"

Luke put his hat on and nudged his horse forward at a slow walk. Hobie rode alongside him and asked quietly, "Are we really partners, Luke?"

"For now we are. Don't get used to it, though. I normally work alone, and once we've corralled Kelly and the Apache, I'm sure I will again."

"Sure. This is just a one-time deal."

Luke thought Hobie sounded a little disappointed. Maybe he had figured they would be trail partners from here on out. If that was the case, it was good that he learned the truth right away.

A man stepped out from behind the stagecoach. He wore a brown hat with a high, round crown. He took it off and returned Luke's wave. "Come on in!" he called.

Luke didn't miss the shotgun in the man's other hand. That and the long duster the man wore told Luke he was probably the driver or the guard.

As they came closer, the man lifted a hand in greeting. He was middle-aged, with a close-cropped, grayshot beard. "Howdy! Sure am glad to see you fellas."

Luke and Hobie reined in. Without dismounting, Luke leaned forward in the saddle. "It may be stating the obvious, but it looks like you've had some trouble here."

"We dang sure have. I'm Jim Pierce, jehu of this here stagecoach."

"Luke Jensen," Luke introduced himself. "My young friend is Hobie McCullough."

"I'm mighty pleased to meet you, Jensen. Reckon you saved us from those road agents. It *was* you takin' those potshots at 'em from the knob over yonder, wasn't it?"

"That's right." Luke disagreed with Pierce's contention that the attackers were outlaws, or at least that their primary intention was to rob the stage, but he didn't see any reason to go into that. "They jumped you a ways back, didn't they?"

"Yeah, and I done my dead-level best to outrun 'em, but that's hard to do with a team of horses pullin' a coach, especially one with four passengers in it. Still, we were stayin' ahead of the varmints until one of the leaders shied at something and made the whole team veer too sharp to the side. The coach went over, busted the singletree, and the harness snapped. We were stuck here."

"That's about the way I had it figured," Luke said. "Four passengers, you say? Any of them hurt?"

"I don't think so, but the fella who was ridin' guard has a busted leg. Maybe you can give me a hand fixin' him up."

"I'd be glad to try." Luke swung down from the saddle and handed his reins to Hobie. He told the young man, "Stay mounted and keep your eyes open. Those hombres can't double back at us without raising some dust. If you see anything suspicious, sing out."

"I sure will, Luke," Hobie promised.

"Looked like you were putting up the best fight you could," Luke said to Pierce as they walked around the coach.

"I been drivin' a stagecoach for near on to thirty years. Been held up before, but I don't like it. Any lowlife tries to stop my coach, he's gonna have a fight on his hands."

Another duster-clad man was propped up with his back against the roof of the coach, which was upright with the vehicle lying on its side. His legs were stretched out in front of him, but the right one had an odd bend in it. Luke could tell that it was broken between the thigh and the hip.

The man was awake, but his blocky face was pale and haggard from pain. He asked in a voice that also revealed the strain he was under, "Are they gone, Jim?"

"Yeah, and this is one of the fellas who chased 'em off," Pierce replied. "Jensen, this here is Ben Wallace."

Luke nodded to the shotgun guard. "Wish it was under better circumstances, Wallace."

"Yeah, me, too." Wallace's hat was off, revealing a thatch of sandy hair.

The four passengers — two men and two women — were also behind the stage. One of the women knelt beside Wallace. She had a wet handkerchief in her hand, and Luke supposed she had been wiping the injured man's face with it, trying to keep him comfortable.

She looked up at Luke. "Someone needs to set this man's leg."

The thick layer of dust that covered her clothes and face didn't keep her from being beautiful, Luke realized. Her vivid green eyes went perfectly with her fair skin and the bright red hair pulled into a bun on the back of her head. She wore a bottle green traveling outfit tight enough to reveal the lines of her slender but well-shaped body, and a matching hat with a little feather in it sat on that red hair. Luke figured she was around twenty years old.

The other woman was at least twenty years older, and from the way she huddled against one of the male passengers about the same age as he kept a comforting arm around her shoulders, the two of them probably were married, Luke thought. The second male passenger was in his thirties, reasonably well dressed in tight trousers, a frock coat, and a vest over a white shirt. He had a fancy stickpin in his cravat. His black hat was perfectly shaped. Luke took him to be a gambler.

He still had a pistol in his hand. He'd been one of the defenders firing from behind the coach, along with Pierce and possibly the other male passenger. He nodded a curt greeting to Luke.

"First things first," Luke said. "We need some splints for Ben's broken leg."

"We can bust some pieces out of the coach's door," Pierce suggested.

"That's a good idea," Luke agreed. He climbed onto the overturned stagecoach and used the butt of one of the Remingtons to knock several pieces of wood out of the door on the side that was up. With his knife, he shaped them into makeshift splints that would hold Wallace's broken leg in place once it was set.

Setting it would be a whole other story and might prove difficult, depending on how bad the break was. It wouldn't be the first broken bone Luke had tended to, however.

"Hobie, come around here and bring my horse," he called. There were some strips of rawhide in Luke's saddlebags that he could use to bind the splints into place.

Hobie rode around the coach and reined in sharply.

Luke wondered about the abruptness of the young man's action until he saw that Hobie was staring at the redhead kneeling next to Wallace. That wasn't a surprise. She was close to Hobie's age and definitely worth staring at, whether it was polite to do so or not.

The woman met Hobie's fascinated gaze for a second, then looked away. A flush spread over her face.

Hobie noticed and realized he was embarrassing her. He gave a little jerk of his head and turned to look at Luke. "What do you need me to do?"

"Keep watching to make sure those men don't come back," Luke said as he dug around in the saddlebags for the rawhide strips. When he found them, he took them and the splints over to Wallace and knelt on the injured man's other side.

"Do you happen to have a bottle of whiskey, Jim?" he asked Pierce.

The driver shook his head. "Naw, it's against stagecoach comp'ny regulations. I ain't sayin I never bent a rule in my life, but the district manager's mighty partic'lar about this one."

"I have some whiskey." The older male passenger took his arm from around his wife's shoulders and reached under his coat to take out a flask. As he handed it to Luke, he added, "Mr. Wallace can have as much of it as he needs."

Luke uncapped the flask and handed it to Wallace. "I'd advise drinking the whole

186

thing. It's going to hurt like blazes when I put that leg back the way it's supposed to be."

"I know that, mister. But it's got to be done, and I appreciate you doin' it." The guard tilted the flask up and took a long swallow. The whiskey gurgled inside the vessel.

"Have you ever done anything like this before, Mr. Jensen?" the redhead asked.

"As a matter of fact, I have, Miss . . . ?"

"Wheeler. Jessica Wheeler."

Luke nodded and touched a finger to his hat brim. "You'll need to move back, Miss Wheeler, so these gentlemen can hold Mr. Wallace down."

"I can stand the pain." Wallace's voice already seemed a little thicker. He took another slug from the flask.

"I know you think so, but we don't want to do any more damage than has already been done. Now, if you fellas will give me a hand . . ."

Jessica Wheeler stood up and moved back to join the older woman. The gambler took her place, telling Luke, "I'm Aaron Kemp."

"And my name is Stephen Langston," the older man put in.

Luke moved around to kneel beside the broken leg while the other three men arranged themselves around Wallace. Pierce and Kemp held the guard's shoulders while Langston took a firm grip on his left leg.

"Hang on just a minute," Wallace said. "Let me finish this first." He tipped his head back and emptied the flask with a final gurgle. Then he blew his breath out, closed his eyes, and leaned his head against the coach roof. "Go ahead."

Luke grasped the guard's right leg, one hand below the break and the other above it. It would be a process of trial and error, fitting the broken bone back together, and until he got it right, the jagged ends would grind together and cause excruciating pain for Wallace.

But delaying things wouldn't make them any better. With a sharp tug, Luke straightened the guard's leg.

Wallace's howl of agony rolled across the hot, flat land and echoed from the walls of the mesa.

CHAPTER 15

Between the liquor and the pain, Ben Wallace passed out before Luke finished setting the broken leg. That was a good thing, Luke thought.

He got the bone back the way it was supposed to be, as far as he could tell, and bound the four splints in place on the front, back, and both sides of Wallace's thigh. That would keep the bone from shifting around.

He stood up. "If I'd known he was going to pass out, I might have told him to save a little of that Who-hit-John. I could use a drink."

"I'll buy you as many as you want when we get to Harkerville," Pierce said. "That's the next stop on the route."

"How are we going to get there?" Langston asked. "The stagecoach is wrecked."

In a voice bordering on hysterical, his wife said, "We're stuck. We're all going to die out here."

"Don't worry, Mrs. Langston," Jessica said. "I'm sure we can figure something out."

Pierce nodded. "Yes, ma'am, we sure can. I've already checked the axles on the coach, and neither of 'em is broken. If the horses didn't run off too far, we can bring 'em back, tie them on to the side of the coach, and set it back up on its wheels. Got some work to do on the singletree, but I reckon I can fix it good enough to hold together until we get to the next stop. We'll be all right, don't you worry about that." He glanced at Luke and Hobie. "That is, if these two fellas can see their way clear to helpin' us out some more."

"Whatever you need," Hobie said without hesitation. "Just tell us what to do."

Luke didn't mind the young man pledging their assistance like that. He would have done the same thing, although maybe not so effusively.

He knew the reason for Hobie's eagerness to help. Hobie was still sneaking looks at Jessica Wheeler. He was just trying to be more discreet about it. There wasn't any doubt he was smitten with the young redhead.

Luke didn't wait for Pierce to give them orders. "The first thing we need to do is find that team."

"That's right," Pierce agreed. "While you're at it, I'll get my tools out so I'll be ready to work on the singletree."

Luke said to the gambler, "Kemp, you'll need to stand guard while we're looking for the team. If you see any dust clouds coming this way, fire three shots in the air."

"I'm afraid I don't have any ammunition left. I emptied my pistol at those outlaws."

"It's a thirty-two, right?"

"That's right."

"I don't have any rounds that caliber —" Luke began.

"That's all right. I still have bullets. If we need to signal you, Mr. Jensen, I can fire three shots." As if to prove it, Jessica reached into her handbag and pulled out a gun, handling it like she knew how to use it.

Luke recognized it as a .32 caliber Smith & Wesson. He realized she had probably been one of the defenders shooting at the ambushers.

"All right, Miss Wheeler. You keep an eye out for trouble, too."

"I intend to."

Luke swung up into the saddle. "Which way did those horses take off when they bolted?"

Pierce pointed to the west. "You shouldn't

have too much trouble findin' 'em. I'll bet they didn't go far."

As Luke and Hobie set off in search of the runaway team, the young man said, "Did you see Miss Wheeler take that gun out of her bag, Luke? I never figured she'd be the sort to carry a revolver!"

"It's not as if we're well acquainted with her," Luke pointed out. "We don't actually know what she's capable of."

"No, I guess not. But she seems like such a lady, I just can't imagine her shooting anybody." Hobie paused. "I think maybe she's the prettiest gal I've ever seen in my life."

Luke grunted. He wanted to find those horses and get back to the stagecoach. Hobie could rhapsodize about how beautiful Jessica was some other time.

The team had run about a mile, then stopped to graze on some of the sparse grass that grew in those parts. Luke and Hobie were able to catch them without much trouble. Hobie's experience working in the livery stable gave him a good touch with animals. He knew how to keep the horses from getting spooked and taking off again.

They rode back to the stagecoach leading the six horses. When they got there, Luke saw that Ben Wallace was still unconscious.

His breathing was deep and regular, though, so Luke figured he had slipped into a sleep brought on by the whiskey he had guzzled down.

Kemp and Langston moved the guard away from the stagecoach while Luke and Pierce used lassos to tie the brass rail around the coach's roof to the horses.

"Miss Wheeler, do you think you can lead those horses while the rest of us push on the coach?" Luke asked the redhead.

"Of course."

Luke handed her the reins, and she led the horses away from the stagecoach until the ropes were almost taut. Luke, Hobie, Pierce, Langston, and Kemp got on the other side of the coach and positioned themselves to lift and push on the vehicle.

"Take 'em on out!" Luke called to Jessica.

The ropes tightened and quivered under the strain. The five men heaved against the stagecoach. Luke felt the vehicle begin to shift position.

As the coach rose, Luke said, "Get under it!" He changed his grip, as did the others, and they all lifted. The stagecoach came up farther, its balance shifted, and it fell onto its wheels in an upright position again, rocking a little on the broad leather thorough-braces underneath as its weight settled.

Pierce hurried around the coach to check all the wheels for damage. "They're all right," he reported. "Now all we got to do is fix that singletree, mend the harness, and hitch up the team, and we'll be ready to roll again."

With Luke's help, Pierce vandalized both doors of the coach to fashion braces for the broken singletree, nailing it together so that it would hold long enough to reach Harkerville. That was the plan, anyway. They wouldn't know how well it was going to work until they tried.

It was late afternoon before all the work was finished. When Pierce declared that he had done all he could do, the men carefully lifted Ben Wallace and placed him on the floor inside the coach, so his splinted leg could remain straight.

Although mostly pale and tight-lipped, he woke up and grunted a few colorful curses because of the pain in his leg.

Pierce pointed out with Wallace on the floor of the coach, there wasn't room for all the passengers.

Hobie said, "You can ride with me if you want, Miss Wheeler. My horse can carry double just fine."

"That's all right, Mr. McCullough. I believe I'll ride on the seat with Mr. Pierce if he's agreeable to that."

The driver said, "You ride wherever you'll be the most comfortable, miss. I'm just sorry for all the trouble we've had this trip."

"It's not your fault," she assured him. "You did your best to get away from those awful men."

"Yeah, but I didn't make it, did I? The varmints could've killed us all."

Luke still wasn't convinced of that. He believed the men had been after one of the passengers. Langston, maybe, who had the look of a prosperous businessman. He doubted if any of the others had enough money to make kidnapping them worthwhile.

Jessica climbed to the seat with Pierce while Aaron Kemp agreed to ride on top of the coach.

"Don't get so rambunctious that I get bounced off," the gambler said with a smile.

"Don't worry," Pierce said. "With that busted singletree, I'll have to take it slow and easy to make sure the repair job don't come apart."

The coach set off for Harkerville with Luke and Hobie riding alongside. Hobie said quietly, "I sure am glad we decided to stop and help these folks."

Luke glanced at Jessica Wheeler and knew

why Hobie felt that way. He supposed he agreed, although given the difference in their ages, Jessica didn't hold the same fascination for him that she did for Hobie.

Luke just hoped the whole affair wouldn't delay their pursuit of Gunner Kelly and Dog Eater for too long.

It was well after dark before they reached the settlement. Luckily, Jim Pierce had been driving that run long enough that he had no trouble following the trail even after night fell.

The repaired singletree held together, but as Pierce brought the team to a stop in front of the local stagecoach station, he said, "I'm mighty glad we didn't have to go another five miles, or even two. I don't know if we'd have made it."

"We're here now," Luke said. "That's all that matters. Is there a doctor in this town?"

"Yep. His house is just down the street. He ought to have a stretcher we can use to carry Ben to his place."

The station manager had already come out of the building. "Jim, what the hell happened? You should have been here hours ago. I was just about ready to send somebody out to look for you."

"We ran into some trouble," Pierce explained as he climbed down from the seat. "Reckon it's pretty lucky we made it here at all."

Hobie dismounted hurriedly and stepped over to the coach. He looked up at the young woman on the seat. "I'll give you a hand, Miss Wheeler."

Jessica looked like she wanted to tell him she could manage just fine by herself, but then she nodded. "All right. Thank you, Mr. McCullough."

She stepped down onto one of the wheel spokes. Hobie put his hands on her waist to steady her as she climbed the rest of the way down to the street. When both feet were on the ground, she cleared her throat. Hobie let go of her and stepped back hurriedly. In the light that came through the station's front window, his face burned a bright red.

Getting old had its disadvantages, Luke thought as he tried not to grin, but so did being young.

A big barn stood next to the station. The manager sent one of the hostlers running down the street to the doctor's house. While they waited, Pierce explained about the attack and the running battle that had ended with the crash near the mesa.

"I reckon they were after the express box," the manager said. "I don't think there's much money in it, but those outlaws wouldn't have known that." He turned to the passengers and went on. "I'm mighty sorry about what happened, folks. We've got a hotel here in Harkerville, and while it's not the fanciest place in the world, the company will put you up there for the night. I'll have my men working all night to replace that singletree, and by tomorrow morning you'll be able to continue your journey. If there's anything else you need, you just let me know."

Pierce gestured toward Luke and Hobie. "Does that offer extend to these two fellas here? If it wasn't for them, there's a good chance we never would've made it out of that ambush alive."

The station manager didn't look happy about that, but said, "Of course. The company is grateful for your help, gentlemen."

Luke's mercenary side, ingrained in him by years as a bounty hunter, was tempted to suggest that if "the company" was really grateful, it could express that gratitude with a reward. But he supposed a night's lodging at the local hotel would have to do. It was certainly better than nothing.

The local sawbones and the hostler who had gone to get him showed up with a stretcher. The men loaded Ben Wallace onto it. The doctor examined Wallace's leg briefly by the light of a lantern and said, "It appears that whoever set this man's broken bone did a good job of it."

"That'd be Mr. Jensen here," Pierce said.

"If Wallace is able to walk normally again, he'll have you to thank for it, sir," the doctor told Luke. "Do you have medical training?"

Luke smiled faintly and shook his head. "No, Doctor, just more than my share of experience with trouble."

"It came in handy this time. Some of you men, get hold of that stretcher. Carefully, now . . ."

They carried Wallace down the street, leaving Luke and Hobie at the station with the passengers. The manager pointed out the hotel, a two-story frame structure, and told them to explain the situation to the clerk when they checked in.

"You fellas can leave your horses here in our barn tonight if you want," he added to Luke and Hobie.

"We'll do that," Luke agreed.

They led the animals into the barn, unsaddled and rubbed them down, and made sure the horses had plenty of grain and water before heading to the hotel.

Taking care of that chore meant the other

passengers had already checked in by the time Luke and Hobie got there. As they went in, Hobie muttered, "I was hopin' I'd know which room Miss Wheeler is in."

"I don't think the young lady will be in any mood for visitors tonight," Luke said. "It was a rough day."

"Oh, I know that," Hobie said quickly. "I just kind of wanted to keep an eye on her room, in case there's any more trouble."

"There shouldn't be any problems here in town," Luke told the young man.

They couldn't be absolutely sure of that, though, he mused as they went upstairs after checking in. Those bushwhackers had been after *somebody* on that stagecoach, and even though it seemed unlikely their quarry had been Jessica, Luke supposed it was possible.

He was in room twelve, Hobie in eleven. As usual, Luke had brought his rifle and saddlebags with him from the stage line's barn. He lit the lamp in the room, propped the Winchester in the corner, and draped the saddlebags over the back of the room's lone chair. As the station manager had said, the place wasn't fancy, but after several days on the trail, the bed looked pretty comfortable to Luke.

First, though, he wanted something to eat.

The hotel had no dining room, he had noticed, but there was a café across the street.

Hobie was coming out of the next room as Luke stepped into the hall. "I was going to get something to eat. . . ."

"Great minds think alike," Luke said. "Come on."

They went downstairs and walked across to the café, where the proprietor and his wife fed them tortillas, beans, and bowls of savory stew full of chunks of meat and chili peppers. They washed the meal down with several cups of coffee.

"Do you think Miss Wheeler got anything to eat?" Hobie asked as they were finishing up.

"I'm sure if she was hungry, she managed to find something," Luke said. Thinking of the gun she had taken out of her handbag, he added, "She strikes me as a capable young woman."

"And a mighty pretty one."

"That goes without saying."

"I wonder where she's bound for," Hobie said. "You think she's going to visit relatives?"

Luke shook his head. "I don't have any idea. And it's not really any of our business, is it?"

Hobie grinned. "We keep saying that, but somehow we get mixed up in one ruckus after another, anyway."

"Yes, I've noticed. And it's a disturbing trend, in my opinion."

They went back across the street to the hotel. As they entered the lobby, Hobie said, "Maybe I'll ask the clerk about Miss Wheeler —"

Luke put a hand on the young man's arm and steered him toward the stairs instead of the desk. "Go get some sleep, Romeo. We need to make an early start in the morning."

Hobie looked like he wanted to argue, but said, "Yeah, I guess you're right." They started up the stairs. "We still need to track down those two bank robbers —"

He stopped short as the sound of a woman's scream came from somewhere on the second floor.

CHAPTER 16

Hobie stood still only for a second, then exploded into motion again, lunging up the stairs as he shouted, "That's Miss Wheeler!"

Luke thought he was right, although it was difficult to tell one woman's scream from another. He charged after Hobie, drawing his right-hand Remington.

They reached the second-floor landing together, turning to their right as the screams continued. Two men were at the far end of the hallway, one of them struggling to drag Jessica down the rear staircase, the other bringing up the rear with a gun in his hand.

She was putting up quite a fight, Luke saw in the brief glimpse he caught before the man with the gun fired at him and Hobie.

Luke's instincts had already taken over. As the gun was coming up, he grabbed Hobie's shoulder and shoved the young man to the left, toward the wall. At the same time, Luke darted right.

The bullet sizzled through the air between them.

A fraction of a second later, Luke's Remington blasted. He couldn't afford to get fancy and try for a disabling shot that might miss and hit Jessica instead. He aimed for the gunman's body.

The slug smashed into the man's chest and drove him backward, crashing into the two people wrestling at the top of the stairs. A shout of alarm came from the second gunman as he and Jessica toppled out of sight.

"No!" Hobie yelled. He sprinted along the hall toward the rear stairs, fear for Jessica's safety making him move so fast Luke couldn't keep up with him.

Hobie disappeared down the stairs. Jessica had stopped screaming, which was a good sign — or a bad one.

Luke reached the far landing, stepped past the body of the man he had just shot, and looked down to see Hobie at the bottom of the stairs, locked in desperate combat with the second gunman. Jessica lay sprawled at their feet, apparently unconscious.

Hobie's opponent had lost his hat, but he'd held on to his revolver. He had it in his hand, fighting to bring it to bear on Hobie.

The young man had both hands wrapped around the would-be kidnapper's wrist, holding the gun muzzle away from him. He ducked his head as the man threw a punch with his other hand. The blow glanced off his skull. He brought his head up and used it as a weapon, butting the gunman in the face.

Blood spurted as the man's nose flattened under the impact. He yelled in pain and hauled Hobie around, smashing the young man into the wall. The impact knocked loose his grip on the kidnapper's gun hand and the man jerked back, flinging the gun up.

Luke had the Remington already leveled. Having only a small target, and aiming down at an angle made the shot trickier. He had only a split second to save Hobie's life. At point-blank range, the gunman couldn't miss.

Luke fired.

The gunman's head snapped back as the slug caught him in the forehead and bored on into his brain. A dying reflex made him jerk the trigger, but his gun had already swung out of line, and the bullet struck one of the stair risers. The gunman's legs folded up, dumping him on the floor next to Jessica.

Luke's shot was deafeningly loud in the close confines of the narrow stairwell. His ears rang, but he still heard Hobie desperately calling Jessica's name as he dropped to his knees beside her and gathered her up into his arms.

Luke wanted to find out whether Jessica was still alive, too, but first he checked on the gunman at the top of the stairs. As he'd expected, the man was dead. He had seen the tag on the tobacco pouch in the man's shirt pocket jump when the bullet struck, which meant there was a good chance he had gotten him in the heart.

With that confirmed, Luke went down the stairs quickly, taking them two at a time. When he reached Hobie, he asked, "How is she?"

"She's still breathing. I was afraid she'd broken her neck falling down the stairs. But she won't wakeup!"

"She probably hit her head on the way down." Luke holstered his gun and knelt beside the two of them. He reached out and gently explored Jessica's head. Her red hair was loose, falling around her shoulders and down her back. That, along with the nightdress she wore, told Luke she had been getting ready for bed when the two men burst in and dragged her out of her room.

"Yes, I thought so. There's a goose egg here where she hit her head. She should be all right, Hobie. We'll know more when she wakes up."

"When's that going to be?" the young man asked miserably.

"That's hard to say in a case like this. Can you carry her back upstairs to her room?"

"Sure." Hobie's arms were already around her. He shifted them a little and stood up, grunting with effort as he came to his feet. Even a slender young woman like Jessica was quite a bit of dead weight when she couldn't help out any.

"I can give you a hand —"

"No, I've got her," Hobie insisted.

He was on the first step, when a man's loud, harsh voice said, "Hold it! Nobody move there!"

Luke started to reach for a gun, but the ominous double click of a Greener being cocked stopped him. Stalking along the first floor corridor toward them was a tall man with a drooping white mustache and a double-barreled shotgun. The newcomer also had a badge pinned to the lapel of the sober black coat he wore.

"Take it easy, Marshal," Luke said. "You don't need that scattergun. The shooting's all over, and we have an injured girl here."

"I'll be the judge of when the shootin's over," the lawman snapped. He kept the twin barrels leveled at Luke and Hobie as he came up to them. "You two are strangers, and I don't cotton to it when folks I don't know start shootin' up my town."

"What about this man?" Luke asked with a nod toward the corpse at their feet. "Is he a stranger, too?"

The lawman squinted at the body for a second, then said, "As a matter of fact, yeah, he is. That don't make it any better."

With worry pulling his voice tight, Hobie said, "Miss Wheeler needs a doctor. She took a bad spill down these stairs."

"Carry her into the lobby, then. I'll send for the doc."

"I can't do that." Hobie lowered his voice to a whisper. *"She's in her nightclothes!"*

"Reckon I can see that. Do what I told you." The marshal jerked the shotgun's barrels toward the front of the hotel to emphasize the command.

"Better do what he says," Luke advised Hobie. He didn't know how steady the old-timer's trigger finger was. It was always better not to take chances with a shotgun.

Hobie sighed and carried Jessica toward the lobby as the marshal moved aside. The lawman motioned for Luke to go ahead, too. At least he hadn't demanded that Luke and Hobie give up their guns, and Luke was grateful for that. The two dead kidnappers might have partners somewhere close by.

Luke's thoughts were racing. While it was possible the two men had tried to abduct Jessica simply because she was a very attractive young woman, he didn't think that was what was going on. It was more likely the attempt was related to the attack on the stagecoach earlier in the day. Luke was fairly well convinced that Jessica had been the target of that, as well.

When they reached the lobby, the marshal told Hobie to put Jessica down on a divan that had a potted plant at each end. Hobie lowered her carefully to the cushions. She was pale and still unconscious.

The hotel clerk and a number of townspeople were gathered in the lobby. Luke knew the citizens had been drawn by the shooting.

The marshal told the crowd, "Somebody run fetch Doc Bismarck. And bring Cassius Mulvaney back here, too!" He glanced over at Luke. "Mulvaney's the local undertaker."

"He'll have work to do, all right," Luke agreed. "There's another dead man up on the second floor."

The marshal glared at him. "Are you

responsible for both of 'em, mister?"

"I killed them, yes, but in self-defense and in defense of my young friend here," Luke replied. "Do you know Jim Pierce and Ben Wallace, the driver and guard on the stagecoach run?"

"What if I do?" the marshal asked with a suspicious frown.

"They'll vouch for us."

A new voice said from the main stairs, "So will I, Marshal."

Luke looked up and saw Stephen Langston descending toward them, wearing a long nightshirt with a coat over it.

"And who might you be?" the marshal asked.

"Stephen Langston, owner of Langston's Emporium and Freight Company, over in Moss City, Arizona."

Luke thought his guess that Langston was a successful businessman looked like it was correct.

"These men saved the stagecoach from outlaws earlier today," Langston went on. "They saved all the passengers from certain death, including my wife Edna and me. If they're involved in some sort of trouble here tonight, I assure you they're in the right."

The marshal squinted at Luke. "Supposin'

you just tell me what in blazes happened here?"

Luke did so, starting with the attack on the stagecoach and continuing to their rescue of Jessica from the two men. "Miss Wheeler started screaming while Hobie and I were going up the stairs. You can ask the clerk about that. He's bound to have heard her, too."

The marshal looked over at the man. "How about it, Ambrose?"

The clerk nodded without hesitation. "It's like Mr. Jensen said, Marshal. The trouble started before he and his friend ever reached the second floor."

The marshal told Luke, "It's startin' to look like I got no choice but to believe you." He didn't look particularly happy about that, however. "What I want to know now is what all this ruckus is about. If these two varmints tonight are part of the same bunch that jumped the stage, what's so all-fired special about this gal that makes them want to grab her so bad?"

"I'm afraid we're going to have to wait for Miss Wheeler to wake up and answer that," Luke said.

"Hasn't somebody got a blanket or something so we can cover her up?" Hobie asked. "She shouldn't be lying here in her nightclothes with all these people around gawking at her."

Ambrose went through a door behind the registration counter and came back with a blanket. Hobie took it and spread it carefully over Jessica, nodding in satisfaction when he stepped back. "That's better."

The doctor came into the lobby a few minutes later. He frowned when he saw Luke and Hobie. "Does trouble just follow you two around?"

"It's starting to seem like it," Luke said.

"Never mind that," Hobie said with a note of impatience in his voice. He gestured toward the divan where Jessica's blanket-covered form lay. "There's your patient. She fell down a flight of stairs."

"Any broken bones?" Dr. Bismarck asked as he bent over Jessica and lifted one of her eyelids.

"I don't think so, but she's been unconscious ever since she fell."

"How long ago was that?"

"Five minutes, maybe," Hobie replied with a shrug.

Bismarck checked Jessica's other eye, then said, "Not an uncommon amount of time to be out cold after a good knock on the head. She needs to wake up soon, though." He quickly ran his hands over her limbs.

212

"Like you said, no breaks. She's lucky in that respect. Her eyes look all right. Let's try some smelling salts."

He took a small bottle from his black medical bag, uncorked it, and held it under Jessica's nose. At first, she didn't react, but after a second she flinched away from it and her eyelids began to flutter. A moment later, she opened her eyes all the way and gasped.

"There you go," the doctor said as he put the cork back in the bottle. "Works every time."

"What . . . where am I?" Jessica asked as she tried to sit up.

Bismarck's hand on her shoulder held her down.

"You're in the hotel lobby, Miss Wheeler," Luke told her. "Don't worry, you're safe now."

"Those men . . . two men . . . they burst into my room and grabbed me when I about to go to bed —" Jessica stopped short and looked down at herself, then at the crowd of people around her. "Oh, my God. This . . . this is so embarrassing."

"You don't need to be embarrassed," Hobie said. "This isn't your fault."

"How . . . how did I get away from them?"

Langston waved a hand at Luke and Hobie. "These two desert knights saved you,

Miss Wheeler, just like they saved all of us earlier when those outlaws attacked us."

Jessica looked at them. "I can't thank you enough."

"No thanks necessary," Hobie said. "And you almost got hurt bad while we were trying to help you, so if you had, I reckon that would've been our fault."

"Nonsense," Luke said. "It would have been the fault of those two men who tried to kidnap Miss Wheeler."

"That's right," Jessica agreed. "Please don't blame yourself for anything, Mr. Mc-Cullough."

"Hobie."

She smiled and nodded and said, "Hobie," which put a big grin on the young man's face. Jessica went on, "Do you think I could go back up to my room?"

Luke looked at the doctor, who said, "I don't see why not. Does your head hurt, my dear?"

"Yes, it does."

"I'm not surprised, after feeling that lump on your head. It may hurt for a day or two, but I think you're going to be all right. If the pain suddenly gets worse, you'll need to let me know."

"But . . . I won't be here. The stage is leaving again in the morning."

Bismarck frowned. "I'm not sure it would be a good idea for you to travel so soon."

"But I have to!" Again, Jessica started to sit up, clutching the blanket around her.

"All right, all right," the doctor said. "You'll be better off if you just stay calm and quiet. I'll check on you again in the morning before the stagecoach leaves, and we'll see how you're doing then. For tonight, you need rest."

Jessica nodded, then winced. The movement made her head hurt worse. "Thank you, Doctor."

"Is there anyone who can sit up with you?" Bismarck asked. "It might be a good idea if you weren't alone."

Hobie opened his mouth to say something, but the stern look Luke gave him made him stop before any words came out.

Stephen Langston said, "My wife can sit up with Miss Wheeler. I'm sure Edna won't mind." He smiled slightly. "She gets a little spooked when people are shooting at us, but normally she's very level-headed."

"That'll be fine," Bismarck said. "Now, let's help the young lady up."

Hobie was quick to help. He and the doctor got Jessica on her feet again. With the blanket wrapped around her and the two men supporting her, she went slowly up the stairs. Luke followed, along with Langston. The crowd in the lobby began to break up.

Langston went to fetch his wife. Luke, Hobie, and the doctor accompanied Jessica to her room. Luke examined the lock where the door had been kicked in. It would need to be repaired before it could be fastened properly again.

While Bismarck was getting Jessica settled in bed, Luke took Hobie aside and showed him the damaged door. "We'll need to take turns standing guard tonight."

"You think something else is going to happen?"

"It's not likely, but we can't rule it out."

"I can stay up all night," Hobie said without hesitation. "I'll get a chair and sit out in the hall. If anybody tries to get in, they'll have to go past me."

"We can take turns," Luke said. "Whoever is on guard will be more alert that way."

"Well, all right. But I'll do whatever I have to, to keep her safe."

The doctor told Jessica he would be back to see her in the morning, then left the room. Hobie shifted his feet awkwardly and held his hat in front of him as he said, "If you need anything, Miss Wheeler —"

"What you really need to do, Miss Wheeler, before Mrs. Langston gets here, is to tell us just why those hardcases keep trying to kidnap you," Luke interrupted.

CHAPTER 17

Jessica stared up at him from the pillows. "I . . . I don't know what you mean. Those men broke in here tonight, but I don't know what they wanted."

Luke thought he saw fear in her eyes. "They wanted you," he said flatly, "and they were part of the same bunch that jumped the stagecoach earlier today."

"Wait a minute," Hobie said. "How do you know that? Did you recognize them?"

"I didn't get a good enough look at any of them to recognize them," Luke admitted. "But it's the only thing that makes sense. I saw the way those men were shooting at the stagecoach. They were being careful to keep you pinned down and not kill anybody. I think they planned to sneak up once it got dark and take all of you prisoner."

Jessica insisted, "They must have been after one of the other passengers, not me. There's no reason anybody would want to kidnap me."

"Then why did those two men try to carry you off tonight?" Luke shook his head. "I can't believe it's just a coincidence."

"I'm sorry. I just don't know."

Luke was sure she was lying. The fear in her eyes was obvious. He didn't like trying to browbeat her, but he was convinced the men who were after her would make another try. He and Hobie would be able to protect her better if they knew what was going on.

Hobie didn't seem to understand that, though. He said angrily, "Luke, the doctor told us that Jessica needs to rest. I think we should leave her alone."

Luke frowned, but nodded slowly. "You think about it, Miss Wheeler. We can help you, but we need to know the whole story. Maybe you'll feel more like talking about it in the morning." He shrugged. "In the meantime, one of us will be right outside the door all night to make sure that nothing else happens."

"You mean in case anyone else tries to . . . to kidnap me?"

"That's right." *And to keep you from sneaking off and trying to give us the slip,* Luke added to himself. He didn't know if she would do that, but when a person got scared enough it was hard to predict what they might do.

Edna Langston came in wearing a thick robe over her nightdress. She shooed Luke and Hobie out of the room, saying, "Let this poor girl get some sleep. She needs it."

"Yes, ma'am. Hobie and I will be standing guard in the hall all night."

She looked relieved to hear that as she pushed the door closed, even though the lock wouldn't fasten.

Hobie frowned at Luke and said quietly, "You shouldn't have jumped all over Jessica like that."

"She's lying to us," Luke said. "She's right in the middle of all this trouble. Do you think we ought to just ride off and leave her to deal with it herself?"

"Hell, no. But —"

"So we need to be ready for it to happen again, and to do that we need to know what's behind the whole thing."

"I guess that makes sense," Hobie admitted grudgingly. "I just don't want to upset her. She's been through a lot already."

Luke couldn't argue with that. His instincts told him that there was a good chance Jessica Wheeler's problems would get worse before they got better.

Hobie insisted on taking the first shift on

guard duty.

Luke relieved him after several hours. He sat in a straight-back chair outside the door of Jessica's room, with only the glow from a wall-mounted lamp turned low lighting the corridor. He didn't doze off. He had stood watch too many times in his life, going all the way back to the war, to allow himself to go to sleep on duty.

But he was tired the next morning and had to stifle a yawn as he knocked on the door of Hobie's room a little before dawn.

Hobie looked sleepy, too, when he came to the door in a pair of long underwear. "Any problems?"

"No, everything was quiet. I thought you might want to go across the street to the café and get some breakfast and coffee for Miss Wheeler."

That idea perked Hobie up and he nodded. "I'll do that. Should I bring some for us, too?"

"That's an excellent suggestion." Luke handed three silver dollars to the young man. "That ought to cover the bill."

Hobie didn't waste any time. He dressed quickly and fetched the food and a pot of coffee. He held the big tray from the café while Luke rapped on Jessica's door.

Edna Langston opened the door. She had

a wary look on her face, but relaxed when she saw Luke and Hobie.

"How's Miss Wheeler?" Luke asked.

"She was a bit restless, but she slept. She's awake now, waiting for the doctor to come by."

"We brought some breakfast," Hobie explained.

"I see that." Mrs. Langston turned and asked, "Do you think you could eat, dear?"

"Actually, I'm famished," Jessica replied.

Mrs. Langston stepped back and ushered the two men into the room. Jessica was sitting up in bed with pillows propped behind her, wearing a dressing gown. She was still a little pale, but Luke thought she looked considerably less shaken.

"I'll leave the three of you to enjoy your breakfast," Mrs. Langston said. "I'm sure, being older, that you'll be a proper chaperone, Mr. Jensen."

Luke wanted to point out that he wasn't exactly ancient, but he thought it would be smarter to just nod and say, "Of course, Mrs. Langston. Thank you for your help."

"I was glad to do what I could." The older woman patted Jessica on the shoulder. "You take care of yourself, dear, and if we don't see you again, I wish you all the best."

"You'll see me again," Jessica said. "I'm

going to be on that stagecoach when it leaves."

Luke wasn't so sure about that, but he didn't see any point in arguing with her about it before the doctor had even been there.

They ate the breakfast of flapjacks, fried eggs, and thick slices of ham, washed down with cups of hot coffee. That made Luke feel considerably more human after the long night and not enough sleep. He was sipping the last of his coffee when Jessica said, "I've been thinking about what you asked me last night, Mr. Jensen."

"You mean about trusting us enough to tell us why those men are after you?" he asked, ignoring the warning frown that Hobie gave him.

"That's right." She directed a cool, level look at Luke as she went on. "And you were right. They were trying to get their hands on me. Those men who attacked the stage, I mean, not just the ones last night. They work for a man named Milton Dietrich."

That name meant absolutely nothing to Luke. He glanced over at Hobie. The young man shook his head to indicate that he didn't recognize it, either.

Jessica said, "I'm not surprised that neither of you have ever heard of him. He's a wealthy, powerful man, with interests in railroads and shipping and Lord knows what else, but he likes to conduct his business behind the scenes, I suppose you'd say. He lives in Boston. That's where I'm from, as well. My father . . . well, he used to do business with Dietrich before he died."

"I wasn't aware that your father had passed on," Luke said. "I'm sorry."

"There was no way you could know about my father or any of the rest of it. But my mother died when I was a little girl. After my father was gone, I didn't have any relatives in Boston. I have an older brother who lives in California, though. He's actually my only relative that I know of."

"That's unusual. Most people have large families."

"I know," Jessica said. "I would have loved to have a large family. If I did, Dietrich might not have decided that he could just announce out of the blue that he and I were to be married."

"Married!" Hobie exclaimed. "How old is this fella, anyway?"

Jessica smiled, but there was no warmth in the expression, only disdain. "At least twice my age. But it's not uncommon for men of his years to marry much younger women, especially successful men."

"Maybe not," Luke said, "but I can understand why you weren't all that enthusiastic about the match, especially if it was all Dietrich's idea."

"It was, I assure you. Like I said, my father had done business with Dietrich. He built ships for Dietrich's line. So Dietrich had been to our house. I've known him for years. Evidently he's had his eye on me for . . . quite some time."

"Why, that randy old goat!" Hobie said. Instantly, he looked embarrassed. "I'm sorry, Miss Wheeler —"

"You can call me Jessica," she told him. "As much as you've both done for me already, even though we haven't known each other for twenty-four hours yet, you've earned the right."

"So Dietrich decides the two of you are going to get married," Luke said, "and you don't agree. That prompted you to leave Boston and head for California to live with that brother you mentioned."

"That's right, but how did you know?"

"It's not very hard to figure out," Luke said with a shrug. "Then, when Dietrich realized what you'd done, he sent those men to find you and bring you back to him."

Jessica nodded solemnly. "Yes, that's exactly what he did. He's so arrogant he thinks he can do whatever he pleases, and if anyone defies him, he'll just crush them and take what he wants."

"In this case . . . you."

"Yes." Jessica's voice was little more than a whisper.

"Well, by God, we have to put a stop to this," Hobie declared. "Why didn't you go to the law? It's illegal to make people do something they don't want to do."

"Dietrich doesn't just have hired gunmen working for him," Jessica said. "He has a small army of lawyers, too, along with plenty of judges and other officials who are in his pocket. He'd just make it sound like he was trying to help the daughter of an old friend and business associate and didn't have any ulterior motives. He . . . he'd paint me as unstable and claim that my grief over my father's death had driven me mad." She looked back and forth between Luke and Hobie. "I honestly don't think he would hesitate to have me placed in an asylum or something until I agreed to go along with what he wants."

"We've got to figure out some way to stop him," Hobie said.

Jessica reached over and put a hand on his arm as he sat in a chair beside the bed. "I can't allow you to get mixed up in my troubles any more than you already have. Those men are killers."

"Well, they don't know who they're dealin' with," Hobie blustered. "Why, Luke here is a famous bounty hunter!"

Jessica's eyes widened a little as she looked at Luke. "Is that true?"

"Never mind about that. What makes you think that Dietrich would leave you alone if you reached your brother in California?"

"He wouldn't have nearly as much influence clear on the other side of the continent. He can't tell judges and lawmen out there what to do. And my brother has been pretty successful himself. Nowhere near the level of Milton Dietrich, of course, but Jacob has a fine ranch and plenty of friends. I think I'd be safe there."

"More than likely you would be," Luke agreed. "But first you've got to get there."

Jessica's chin jutted out defiantly as she said, "I won't let that horrible man stop me. I'll find a way to get there. I will."

"Darn right you will," Hobie said. "We'll —"

A knock on the door made him pause before he could promise anything. In the long run, though, that wouldn't help, Luke thought. He knew what was going through Hobie's mind just as well as if it were printed on the young man's face.

In the meantime, Luke drew his right-hand Remington as he stepped over to the door. "Dr. Bismarck?" he called through the panel.

"That's right," the medico answered.

Luke opened the door and looked out into the corridor. The tall, spare doctor was alone. Luke holstered the revolver.

"My patients don't usually meet me with a gun," Bismarck said.

"I'm not your patient," Luke pointed out. "Miss Wheeler is." He stepped aside to let the doctor come into the room.

"If you two gentlemen would give us some privacy . . ." Bismarck said.

"We'll be right outside the door," Hobie told Jessica.

When they were out in the hall and the door was closed, Luke crossed his arms, leaned against the wall, and said to Hobie, "You were about to tell her we'd take her to California, weren't you?"

"Well, somebody needs to. With a bunch of hired killers after her, you don't think she can make it there alone, do you?"

"Actually, I'm rather surprised that she's made it this far. Boston is a long way off."

"So if we don't help her, who will?"

"I don't know. But if we don't track down

228

Gunner Kelly and Dog Eater and get the bank's money back, who will?"

"That's just money," Hobie said.

"A necessary evil in this world we live in."

"But it's not important compared to a young woman's life, is it?"

"That depends who you're asking, I suppose."

"I'm asking you, Luke."

"Let's wait and see what the doctor says," Luke suggested.

Hobie looked like he wasn't satisfied by that answer, but he didn't argue any more. They stood there waiting in a somewhat tense silence until the door opened and Dr. Bismarck stepped out into the hallway.

"Miss Wheeler appears to be in remarkably good condition for someone who took a header down a flight of stairs twelve hours ago. She has some bruises and sore muscles, and I'd feel better about that knock on the head if she was agreeable to spending the next few days resting in bed. But she's determined to resume her journey, and medically, I can't really forbid it."

"So she can travel on the stagecoach?" Hobie asked.

"That's what I just said, isn't it? I think she should be examined again by a competent physician at the next available opportunity, though."

Luke said, "There'll be doctors in the other towns along the coach's route. Did you tell her she could travel?"

"I did. I suspect she's already packing and getting dressed. She wanted me to tell you to be sure and not let the stagecoach leave without her."

"Thanks, Doctor." Luke glanced at Hobie and added, "I guess we'll take it from here."

A pleased grin spread across the young man's face.

A few minutes later, Luke and Hobie walked up to the stagecoach station carrying their rifles and saddlebags. They had checked out of the hotel. The stagecoach sat in front of the barn, where a couple hostlers were finishing up the job of hitching a fresh team of horses to it. The new singletree was in place.

Jim Pierce walked around the coach inspecting everything, the way a careful jehu did before setting off on a run. He raised a hand in greeting to Luke and Hobie. "I was hopin' I'd see you fellas again before we left this mornin'."

"You'll see more of us than that," Luke said. "With Ben Wallace laid up, who's going to be your shotgun guard?"

Pierce scratched at his beard and admitted, "We don't have one. There's a relief guard waitin' at Moss City, just across the border in Arizona, but until we get there I reckon I'll be driver and guard both."

"Not necessarily. I've got a guard for you."

"Who might that be?" Pierce asked.

Luke turned and leveled a finger at a startled Hobie McCullough.

CHAPTER 18

Hobie was a little surprised, but once he realized what Luke had in mind, he was enthusiastic about the idea.

The station manager wasn't so sure, though. He frowned and said, "I don't know how the company would feel about me hiring you for the job, young man."

"You don't have to hire me. Luke and I are headed in that direction anyway. I'll just tie my horse on at the back of the stage and ride with Mr. Pierce. You don't have to pay me anything."

Hobie's argument convinced the station manager.

Pierce was pleased with the development, too. "I ain't expectin' any more trouble, but you never know. It'll be good to have you boys ridin' with us for the next leg of the trip."

Luke and Hobie had promised Jessica they wouldn't reveal her secret. She hadn't done anything wrong, of course, but still didn't want people to know she was being pursued by an older man who had been lusting after her for years.

Knowing what he did, Luke felt a little bad about not warning Pierce of the very good chance there would be more trouble. The stagecoach would continue on its way regardless, so Luke figured he and Hobie were doing what they could to help it get through to Moss City.

Hobie wanted to go all the way to California with Jessica. If that was his decision, Luke would wish both of them the best. As for him, he had a couple outlaws to catch.

Jessica and the Langstons walked down to the station from the hotel a short time later. Luke and Hobie had saddled their horses, and Hobie's mount was tied at the back of the coach.

"Where's that gambler, Kemp?" Stephen Langston asked.

"Reckon he's stayin' here in Harkerville," Pierce replied. "His ticket was only good for this far, and I ain't seen him since we got in last night. He probably spent the night in some saloon, playin' cards, and he'll sleep away the day."

"That means there's room for you to ride in the coach if you want to," Langston said to Luke, who shook his head.

"I'll be scouting our route," he explained. Besides, the last thing he wanted to do was spend hours sitting on a hard bench seat in a stagecoach that rocked as much as a ship in rough seas. The dust was always bad inside a coach, too, blowing in despite the canvas covers over the windows. He would be a lot happier out in the fresh air.

The passengers climbed into the coach and settled down for the journey.

Hobie was right there to give Jessica a hand getting in. "If you need anything, I'll be up top. You just give a holler."

Luke swung into the saddle as Hobie joined Jim Pierce on the driver's seat and picked up the shotgun that was lying on the floorboard at his feet.

The white-mustachioed marshal came along the street and regarded Luke with a disapproving frown. "Can't say as I'm sorry to see you go, bounty hunter," he snapped. "I can do without a bunch of gunmen in my town."

"Don't worry, Marshal. I won't be in any hurry to come back here." Luke grinned and lifted a hand in a mocking wave of farewell as he heeled his horse into motion.

They soon left Harkerville behind as the coach rolled on toward the border between

New Mexico Territory and Arizona. Luke hadn't had a chance to ask around the settlement about Kelly and Dog Eater, but he was confident they were headed in the right direction.

Anyway, the outlaws probably would have avoided the town unless they needed supplies or planned to rob the bank. They would have been more likely to stop at one of the way stations along the stagecoach line to water their horses or buy a meal.

Luke ranged ahead of the coach by as much as a half mile at times, and he dropped back a similar distance now and then to check their back trail. He didn't see any signs of trouble, but knew better than to think those hardcases hired by Milton Dietrich would give up. It was only a matter of time until they struck again.

The coach stopped at an isolated way station at midday to change horses and let the passengers stretch their legs, as well as have a meal of beans and stew. While they were there, Luke asked the man in charge of the station, "Have you seen two men come through here in the past week or so, leading several extra horses?"

The man, who was wiry and wizened with age and had a brush of gray hair that stuck straight up from his head, tilted his head and frowned. "Are you talkin' about a white man and a Injun, mister?"

Luke felt his pulse quicken slightly. "That's right. The Indian is an Apache."

The man spat. "I seen 'em, all right. Let 'em water their horses. But somethin' about 'em wasn't right, and it wasn't just that the one fella was a 'Pache. Those red devils make everybody in this part of the country uneasy. But I tell you, that white man spooked me just as much or more than the Injun. I stood in the door with my rifle in my hands the whole time they was here. I was mighty relieved when they rode off."

"How long ago was this?"

"Three days, I think," the man replied with a squint-eyed frown. "The days sort of run together out here, but yeah, I'm pretty sure it was three days ago."

Luke and Hobie had cut into their lead, somehow. Kelly and Dog Eater must have been just ambling along, Luke thought, supremely confident that no one was on their trail.

He was about to thank the man for the information and move on, but something else occurred to him. "I don't suppose you heard them say anything while they were here about where they were going, did you?"

The way station manager squinted some

236

more, then finally said, "Come to think of it, I did hear the white hombre say somethin' that sort of puzzled me, but it wasn't about where they were headed. He mentioned somebody called Don del Oro."

"Gift of gold," Luke translated. "I wonder what that was all about."

"Or maybe it was somebody's name," the man suggested again. "All I know is, I wouldn't want to have those two lookin' for me. That Don fella better have eyes in the back of his head if those two are after him. They was pure poison."

Luke couldn't argue with that.

The passengers climbed into the stagecoach and it rolled on. Luke knew from talking to Jim Pierce that it would stop for the night at another way station, then move on in the morning, crossing the Arizona border and arriving at Moss City around the middle of the day.

As he rode alongside the coach, Luke asked the jehu, "Have you ever heard of somebody or something called Don del Oro?"

Pierce thought about the question for a long moment, then shook his head. "Can't say as I have. A lot of the fellas who own big ranches down in Mexico are called dons. Maybe it's one of them."

Luke supposed that was possible. For some reason the phrase didn't really sound to him like a man's title and name, though.

"What's that about, Luke?" Hobie asked.

"I was talking to the fella back at the way station. Kelly and Dog Eater were there three days ago. They said something about Don del Oro while they were watering their horses."

"Those are the bank-robbin' varmints you're after?" Pierce had talked to Luke and Hobie enough to know that they were tracking the two men who'd robbed the bank in Rio Rojo.

"That's right," Luke said. "I was hoping to pick up a clue to their destination. I don't know if Don del Oro is it, but I'll have to keep it in mind."

Hobie didn't say anything else. He was torn between wanting to continue on the quest that had brought him that far and his desire to help Jessica Wheeler safely reach her brother's ranch in California.

Luke suspected Hobie's infatuation with Jessica would win that battle. That was fine. He had set out after Kelly and Dog Eater alone, and was perfectly willing to continue going after them alone. It was the way he had spent most of his time during the past decade and a half, after all.

The afternoon passed without any trouble. The sun wasn't far above the western horizon when the next way station appeared up ahead. The adobe building was a dark, squat shape in the sea of reddish gold light washing over the landscape.

Luke rode ahead of the stagecoach and reached the station a few hundred yards ahead of it. As he reined in, two men came out of the building. One of them called, "That the stage from Harkerville comin' up behind you?"

"That's right."

"Who are you, mister?" the other man asked with a note of suspicion in his voice.

"Outrider. Actually I'm just traveling along with the stage as far as Moss City, so I thought I might as well do a little scouting."

"Run into any trouble?" the first man asked.

"Not so far." Luke looked around the station. There was no barn, but behind the building he saw a big corral where the fresh teams were kept.

Something struck him as odd about several of the horses, though. Their sides were flecked with drying sweat, as if they had been put in the corral recently after a hard run.

Before he could ponder that thought, the stagecoach rattled up and Pierce hauled back on the lines to bring the team to a stop, calling, "Whoa!" The cloud of dust kicked up by the team's hooves and the wheels swirled around the vehicle for a few seconds before the breeze began to carry it away.

"Howdy, fellas," Pierce said to the two men who had come out of the building. "Where's ol' Banty Sinclair?"

"He, ah, took sick," one of the men replied. "The company sent us out to take his place."

Pierce frowned. "That's odd. I would've figured those two boys of his could handle everything."

That brief exchange on top of the drying sweat he had noticed on several of the horses in the corral suddenly came together in Luke's mind to form a picture, and he didn't like what he was seeing.

His right hand reached for a gun as his left pulled his horse's reins and sent the animal lunging between the stagecoach and the station. "Jim, get that coach out of here!" he shouted.

The shutters on the station's windows flew open, and gun flame lanced from inside the building.

Luke returned the fire and kept his horse dancing and wheeling so he would be a harder target to hit. From the driver's seat, Hobie's shotgun boomed as Pierce bellowed at the team and lashed them with the reins. The coach lurched into motion again.

The two men who had come out of the station jerked guns from under their shirts and triggered the weapons at Luke. He felt the hot breath of one slug as it whipped past his head. The Remington in his hand blasted as he downed one of the men with a bullet through the body. He sent the horse pounding straight at the other one.

The man didn't have time to get off another shot. He screamed as the horse's shoulder rammed into him and knocked him down. The animal's steel-shod hooves slashed at him.

Luke twisted in the saddle and sent two more slugs sizzling through an open window into the station. That emptied the Remington. He rammed the revolver back in its holster and kicked the horse into a gallop after the stagecoach. More dust boiled up from the rapidly turning wheels.

Luke looked back and saw two men run out of the station holding rifles. They fired after him and the coach, but the fading light made accurate shooting difficult. Luke leaned forward to make himself a smaller target, just in case the riflemen got lucky enough to come close.

He thought back to the horses he had noticed in the corral. He was pretty sure only four of them had been flecked with sweat, meaning only four bushwhackers had been lurking at the station, waiting for the stagecoach to arrive. Luke had shot one of them and trampled another under his horse's hooves. The two throwing lead after the stagecoach were the only ones left.

He didn't think those two were likely to give chase, now that they had lost the element of surprise. Their trap had failed.

Luke raced to catch up to the stagecoach. As far as he could tell, Hobie and Pierce were all right. The jehu didn't seem to be hurt as he kept the team moving at top speed. The horses couldn't keep that up for much longer, though.

Luke drew even with the coach.

From his position facing the rear and kneeling on the seat so he could fire back over the roof, Hobie called to him, "I don't see them comin' after us!"

"I don't think they will," Luke said. "But keep an eye on our back trail anyway, Hobie!"

Hobie waved a hand to signal that he

understood.

Luke motioned for Pierce to slow down and shouted out, "Better stop and let those horses blow, Jim!"

Pierce nodded and hauled back harder on the reins. The team slowed to a walk and then stopped.

One of the coach doors opened, and Stephen Langston popped out of the vehicle with a pistol in his hand. "What happened back there?" he demanded. "My God, are we going to be plagued with outlaws for the entire journey?"

Luke knew the men at the way station weren't outlaws. They were more of Milton Dietrich's hired hardcases. He wasn't going to reveal Jessica's secret, though. It wasn't his place to do so.

He didn't have to.

Jessica looked out the coach window and said, "This is all my fault, Mr. Langston. All the trouble that's been following us is because of me."

Langston frowned. Inside the coach, his wife said, "I don't hardly see how that's possible, dear."

Jessica stepped out of the stagecoach to explain. "Those men who attacked us both times — the ones who tried to kidnap me back in Harkerville — all work for a man named Milton Dietrich. He . . . he's got his mind made up that he's going to marry me, even if he has to force me into it."

Edna Langston, poised on the step to exit the coach, gasped, while her husband said, "Good Lord! That's outrageous!"

"I know, but it's true," Jessica said. "The two of you have been so nice to me, I just couldn't keep the truth from you any longer. I feel terrible that I didn't tell you earlier. You've been in danger — again! — because of me."

Langston shook his head. "It's not your fault, Miss Wheeler. You're a victim of this man's evil intentions." He looked at Luke. "Did you and Mr. McCullough know about this, Mr. Jensen?"

"Miss Wheeler explained the whole thing to us this morning," Luke admitted.

"Don't look at me," Pierce put in. "This is the first I'm hearin' about it." He paused, then asked, "How'd you know they was layin' for us back there at the way station, Luke?"

"The first clue was the sweat drying on some horses I saw in the corral at the station. There were four of them, and they looked like they'd been unsaddled and put in there pretty recently. I knew they couldn't be part of a stagecoach team, because this run is the only one going through right now. Then when you asked about the fella who runs the station —"

"Banty Sinclair." Pierce's voice was grim with anger. "An old friend of mine. He got stuck with the nickname Banty because he's so small. Got two big strappin' sons who help him at the station, though."

"When you mentioned them I knew something was wrong, and the most likely thing was that Dietrich's men had taken over the station and set up an ambush for us. I'm sorry. I think there's a good chance your friend and his sons are dead. Dietrich's gunmen may have shot them when they rode in."

"Could be they're just tied up."

"That's possible," Luke said. "I can go back and check. It'll be dark soon, so if any of Dietrich's bunch is still there, they won't be able to see me coming. I think it's more likely they lit a shuck out of there, though, when they weren't able to grab Miss Wheeler."

"I feel like those men's blood is on my hands," Jessica murmured. Guilt wracked her voice.

Luke shook his head. "No. Mr. Langston is right. None of this is your fault. Lay the blame where it belongs." Luke's voice grew harsh. "Right at the feet of Milton Dietrich."

CHAPTER 19

The question was what to do next.

They couldn't be sure Dietrich's surviving men had abandoned the way station. And there was the possibility that more hired hardcases had shown up following the shoot-out. It might not be safe for the coach to turn around and go back to the station.

But they didn't have the option of continuing on. The horses in the team were played out. It was Jim Pierce's opinion the animals couldn't make it the rest of the way to Moss City. "I reckon I could follow the trail in the dark if I had to, but them hosses would be dead before we got there, even takin' it slow and easy."

"Do you know of any place not far from here where we could hole up for the night?" Luke asked. "Some place that can be defended?"

Pierce rubbed his bearded jaw and frowned in thought for a moment before answering. "Maybe. I seem to recollect a little box canyon not far from here. The mouth of it is narrow enough that a few men with rifles could hold it."

"Can you find it in the dark?"

"I think so. But I got to warn you, like I said, it's a box canyon. We can keep those varmints from gettin' in, but if they want to, they can keep us from gettin' out."

"If you have a better idea, I'm wide open to hearing it," Luke said.

Pierce chuckled humorlessly. "That's just it, I don't."

Luke turned to the three passengers. "What do you folks think? You've got a stake in this, too."

"If Mr. Pierce thinks we can put up a fight in that canyon, then that's where we should go," Langston answered without hesitation. "I may be a businessman now, but when I came to Arizona it was about as untamed a place as you've ever seen. I've smelled my share of powder smoke."

"Stephen, you're a little old to be talking so fierce," his wife remarked.

Langston snorted and shook his head. "I'm not *that* old," he declared. "The only one I'm worried about is you, my dear. I wish I hadn't taken you with me on that business trip to Albuquerque."

"I'll be fine," she told him, but her voice held an undercurrent of nervousness.

Hobie turned to Jessica. "What about you, Miss Wheeler? What do you think we should do?"

"The smartest thing for all of you to do would be to leave me right here by the side of the road and drive on," Jessica said bluntly. "Some of Dietrich's men are bound to come along and find me sooner or later. That way you'd all be safe, because they wouldn't have a reason to go after you anymore."

"I wouldn't be so sure about that," Luke said. "We've killed four of them and wounded several more. With men like that, it hurts their pride when somebody gets the better of them. Not only that, it hurts their reputation. If they don't settle the score with Hobie and me, they might not be as likely to get the job the next time somebody needs some gun work done."

"You're saying they're going to have a grudge against you no matter what?"

"That's right."

"Well, then, I suppose we should find a place where we can fight if we have to," Jessica said.

"I feel the same way," Hobie added. "If you can get us to that canyon, Mr. Pierce, we'll spend the night there."

The jehu nodded. "We're all agreed, then. Climb back in, folks, and we'll get goin'."

A minute later, with Hobie on the seat beside him and the passengers back inside the coach, Pierce started the team moving. They traveled at a slow pace. The horses were so tired, night had fallen, and it was more difficult to see where they were going.

Luke rode alongside the coach. There was no point in him scouting ahead, since he didn't know how to find the canyon Pierce had mentioned.

Half an hour later, the jehu brought the team to a halt and pointed to a cliff visible in the moonlight, about a quarter mile away. A black slash in the upthrust rock face marked the location of the canyon.

"Place ain't got a name, far as I know," he said. "It runs back up into that cliff for about half a mile."

"It looks a bit ominous," Luke said. "I'd better reconnoiter first."

"I'll come with you," Hobie volunteered.

Luke shook his head. "No, you stay here with the coach, just in case there's any trouble while I'm gone. I shouldn't be long."

"Please be careful, Mr. Jensen," Jessica said from the coach window.

"The chances of any of Dietrich's men

being in there is pretty small," Luke said. "I'm more worried about a cougar or some wild animal like that."

Hobie said, "If you run into trouble, fire three shots into the air. I'll be ready to jump on my horse and come a-runnin'."

Luke didn't say anything, but thought if he ran into any really bad trouble, he might not have time to waste firing shots in the air.

He trotted his horse toward the canyon mouth. As he neared it, he pulled the Winchester from its sheath and laid it across the saddle in front of him. Dressed all in black like he was, he would blend into the darkness, making him harder to hit if anybody tried to take a shot at him. It was one reason he had always chosen such somber garb.

Luke always paid attention to his mount's reactions, especially in unknown situations. If the horse had caught the scent of a big cat, a bear, or anything like that, he would have been spooked. He would have reacted to other horses in the canyon, too. But it didn't appear there was any danger. His horse walked into the canyon without hesitation.

Luke rode slowly. The canyon floor was rocky in places and sandy in others. The thudding hoofbeats echoed back from the sheer walls on both sides. Anyone who had a problem with small, enclosed spaces wouldn't like this, Luke mused. The canyon was only about fifty yards wide, and its walls rose at least two hundred feet.

Those walls came together and closed off the far end of the canyon after about half a mile, as Jim Pierce had said. The cliff they formed loomed ahead of Luke, black as sin in the faint light that filtered into the canyon. As far as he had been able to tell, the place was completely deserted except for maybe a few lizards and rats.

He turned his horse and rode back out. When he emerged from the canyon he found the five people with the stagecoach waiting anxiously for him.

"Everything looks all right," he reported. "Take the coach on in, Jim."

Pierce heaved a sigh of relief and picked up the reins. He flapped them against the backs of the team and got the horses moving.

"Hobie, there are some piles of rocks in there," Luke said to the young man as he rode beside the vehicle. "I think you can build a fire among one of them so that it can't be seen from outside the canyon. That's important. We don't want to announce where we are."

"That makes sense," Hobie said. "But why can't you build the fire, Luke?"

"Because as I said earlier, I'm going back to that way station. I want to check on the man who was supposed to be running it and his sons."

Pierce said, "I planned on borrowin' a horse and doin' that myself."

"I think it would be best if you stayed here," Luke said. "If you have to make a run for it, you handle that team better than any of the rest of us could."

"Banty and his boys could be hurt and needin' help."

"I know. That's why I'm going. I should be back before morning." Luke added dryly, "I'll sing out before I come in. Don't shoot me."

"I won't get trigger-happy," Hobie promised. He didn't offer to go along, and Luke knew why. Hobie wanted to stay there so he could protect Jessica.

That seemed like a good idea to Luke, too. He turned his horse and said over his shoulder, "I'll be back." Then he rode out of the canyon and headed toward the way station.

Luke had kept a close eye on their route

while Pierce led them to the canyon, so he would be able to backtrack and find the way station. He steered by the stars, stopping fairly often to listen for the sound of hoof-beats floating on the night air. Any group of riders likely represented trouble for him and his companions, so he wanted to steer clear of them.

He didn't hear anything except the occasional call of a night bird. There was a good reason outlaws had come to be known as owlhoots. They rode dark, isolated trails where the only sound was likely to be the lonely hooting of an owl. Saying that a man rode the hoot owl trail was the same as branding him as being on the wrong side of the law. Over time, that had gotten switched around so that such men sometimes were called owlhoots.

Luke had tracked down more than his share of them. He would have been willing to bet that some of the men working for Dietrich had bounties posted on their heads. For once, though, he wasn't interested in those rewards. At the moment, sheer survival was more important.

That and getting Jessica Wheeler safely to where she was going.

Eventually the way station came in sight. Luke saw it as a deeper patch of darkness in the night. No lights were burning anywhere around it. As he rode up, he didn't see any bodies lying in front of the building. Dietrich's gunnies must have pulled out and taken the two dead men with them.

Either that, or they were holed up inside the station, waiting to bushwhack anybody who showed up.

Luke dismounted and took his rifle with him as he cautiously circled the station. It continued to look deserted. After a while, he approached the open door at an angle.

Pausing just outside the door, he held the rifle ready and sniffed the air. He smelled a faint tang of gun smoke coming from inside the station, left over from the earlier ambush.

He lowered the rifle, leaned it against the wall, and drew both Remingtons, instead. With the revolvers in his hands, he went through the door fast, crouching low as he entered the building. He was ready to return the fire if any muzzle flames spurted at him from the darkness.

The room remained silent. Slowly, he straightened and took another deep breath. A mixture of smells filled the air — the gun smoke he had noticed a moment earlier, human sweat, horses, and something even more ominous. Luke recognized the coppery scent of blood.

He holstered his left-hand gun and reached into his shirt pocket for a match. He fished one out and snapped it to life with his thumbnail. His eyes narrowed against the glare as the match flared up.

The light revealed exactly what he had been afraid he would see. Three bodies were piled against the far wall of the station's main room. They lay limp and unmoving. Luke had seen enough dead men to know what he was looking at.

To be sure, he moved closer and worked the toe of his boot under the shoulder of the nearest man, who lay facedown. Luke rolled him onto his back.

Wide, sightless eyes that didn't flinch from the match's glare stared up at him. They were in the weathered face of a balding, middle-aged man whose cheeks were covered with silvery beard stubble. He had been of fairly small stature in life. Luke knew he was looking at the body of Banty Sinclair.

The other two men were just as dead. They were young, in their twenties, and despite their much greater size bore a distinct family resemblance to Sinclair. Luke would have guessed that they were the man's sons even if Pierce hadn't mentioned that fact.

All three had been shot numerous times at close range.

Luke had a pretty good idea what had happened. Dietrich's men had ridden up, Sinclair and his sons had gone out to see what they wanted, and the killers had opened fire with no warning. It had been an act of wanton, cold-blooded murder.

Of course, any man who would sign on to kidnap a young woman and force her to marry a ruthless man more than twice her age wouldn't be the sort to think twice about murder.

Luke went outside to look around. Half a dozen horses were still in the corral. In the normal course of events, they would have been hitched to the stagecoach when it stopped there, and the worn-out team would be allowed to rest until the next stagecoach came along. The four saddle mounts he had seen earlier were gone.

Luke didn't like leaving the bodies unattended, but it would take him all night to dig three graves and he wanted to get back to the canyon where he had left Hobie, Jessica, and the others. He would tell the stationmaster at Moss City what had happened and he could send someone out to tend to the horses and bring back the bodies of

Banty Sinclair and his sons.

Luke went back into the station, hunted up some blankets, and used them to wrap the bodies. When he left, he made sure the door and the shutters were closed to keep scavengers out. For now, that was all he could do for the dead men.

He rode away, wishing that when he and Hobie had first encountered Dietrich's men attacking the stagecoach, they had taken advantage of the opportunity to kill a few. At the time, though, they hadn't known what was going on.

Luke certainly wouldn't hesitate to send more of them to hell in the future. They had it coming.

The moon was just about to set by the time he neared the canyon again. He could see the black slash in the cliff face that marked its location. In another minute or two he would be close enough to call out to Hobie.

Suddenly, a burst of gunfire ripped out, muzzle flame blooming in the darkness of the canyon's mouth.

CHAPTER 20

Luke's first impulse was to gallop straight ahead, right into the thick of the fracas. His natural caution made him suppress that urge.

He hurriedly drew rein and tried to figure out what was going on. Maybe Hobie, Pierce, and Langston had heard him coming and gotten nervous, despite being warned not to get trigger-happy.

The shots weren't being directed at him, though, Luke realized a moment later as more guns opened up from outside the canyon. Men were shooting *toward* the dark slash in the cliff. It was pretty easy to come up with an explanation for why they were doing that.

Dietrich's men had found the hiding place and were attacking again, attempting to root out the defenders.

If they didn't know he was out there, away from the canyon, it could make a difference.

Luke sat still on his horse, hiding in the darkness.

"Hold your fire!" a man bellowed. "By God, hold your fire!"

Something about the voice struck Luke as odd. After a moment, he realized the words had a broad, flat intonation to them, marking the speaker as being from Boston.

Luke would not have known that if he hadn't run into several sea captains from that Massachusetts city during his visits to San Francisco. He had spent an entire evening sitting across from such a man in a marathon poker game in one of the Barbary Coast saloons.

That thought flashed through his mind as he recalled Jessica saying that she was from Boston, as was Milton Dietrich. He wondered if Dietrich had come all the way out to New Mexico Territory in pursuit of the woman he intended to marry.

Whoever had yelled the order to stop shooting got results. The attackers' guns fell silent first, and then the shots from the canyon's defenders trailed off. An uneasy hush descended on the landscape as the echoes rolled away.

Luke stayed where he was, listening.

After a few moments, the man with the Boston accent shouted, "Jessica! Jessica, darling, can you hear me?"

Several long seconds ticked past, and Luke began to wonder if she was going to answer.

Then she said, "Go away, Mr. Dietrich. I'm not going to marry you. I'll never marry you, no matter what you do."

That confirmed Luke's hunch about the man's identity. Dietrich hadn't been content to send his hired killers after Jessica. He had come west himself to ramrod the effort to find her.

"Jessica, thank God you're alive!" Dietrich said. "I was deathly afraid that something had happened to you."

"It's no thanks to you that it hasn't! I've nearly been killed by your men several times."

"You have my abject apologies. My men were . . . overzealous . . . in their efforts to find you." He paused. "But that's all over now that we have a chance to talk to each other again. I'm sure we can work out our problems —"

"The problem is that I'm not going to marry you!" Jessica broke in. "And that you're insane!"

If that accusation bothered Dietrich, his calm, carefully controlled voice didn't show any sign of it. "My dear, I just want to help you —"

"I know what you want!" Jessica cried raggedly. "My poor father was barely in his grave when you came slobbering after me like a dog after a bone! You're a horrible, horrible man!"

"That's not true," Dietrich protested. "Your father was an old friend of mine. Before he passed away I promised him that I'd see to it you were taken care of. He was worried about what might happen to you after he was gone."

A new voice broke into the conversation as Hobie yelled, "Reckon he had good reason to be worried, you old lecher, if he knew what kind of lowdown snake you are!"

Dietrich didn't say anything for a moment. When he spoke again, his lips pursed with disapproval. "Is that ill-mannered young frontiersman your new suitor, Jessica?" he demanded. "Can he give you all the things I can? I've offered you a fine, comfortable life with me back home in Boston. What sort of life can you have out here in this drab, godforsaken wilderness?"

"I'll be free!" Jessica cried. A sob wracked her voice. "I'll be free . . ."

More shots roared from the canyon.

Luke figured that was Hobie losing his

temper and blazing away at Dietrich and the hired gunmen. Pierce and Langston joined in. Luke saw multiple muzzle flashes winking like fireflies in the dark mouth of the canyon.

"Hold your fire!" Dietrich shouted again to his men. He didn't want to risk a stray shot hitting Jessica. "Everyone stay down! They'll run out of ammunition eventually."

That was true. Hobie had quite a few rounds for his rifle and pistol, but they wouldn't last forever. Langston probably didn't have more than a dozen or so extra cartridges for his pistol. Luke didn't know how much extra ammunition Pierce had for his revolver and shotgun, but not enough to hold off the attackers indefinitely.

Luke didn't know whether there was any water to be had in that canyon, either. A small water barrel stood in the boot on the back of the coach, and Hobie had a couple canteens on his saddle, but once the sun came up the heat would come with it, and that water wouldn't be enough to last more than a day.

The long-term prospects for defending the canyon didn't look good, Luke thought. A siege would end badly for the defenders.

But they had one advantage. Luke was behind Dietrich's men, and evidently they didn't know he was back there.

He swung down from the saddle and reached for his rifle, then stopped with his hand resting on the smooth wood of the stock. He didn't know how many men Dietrich had or where they all were. If he opened fire on them, he would take them by surprise and no doubt would account for a few of them.

But doing so would reveal his presence, and the element of surprise would last only a few seconds. Once it was gone, he would be outnumbered and outgunned.

The challenge called for a stealthier response, he realized.

He left the rifle in the saddle boot and let the horse's reins dangle. Well trained, the animal wouldn't stray very far, ground-hitched like that.

Reaching into one of his saddlebags, he took out a chunk of charcoal wrapped in a piece of soft leather. He always kept some of the black, sooty stuff with him for night-time work. He wiped it on his hands and face, covering his skin with dark streaks that would help him blend in with the night. Years of man hunting had taught him plenty of such tricks.

He wrapped up the charcoal and slipped it back in the saddlebag. Leaving his revolvers in their holsters, he moved warily on foot toward the area where he had seen the flash of rifles from Dietrich's men.

As he crept closer, Luke remembered a story Smoke had told him about the old mountain man Preacher.

As a young fur trapper in the Rockies, some fifty years earlier, Preacher had had a long-running feud with the Blackfoot Indians. Several times he had been pursued by large war parties. In order to demoralize his enemies, Preacher would wait until nightfall, slip into the Blackfoot camp, cut the throats of several warriors as they slept, and slip back out again without anyone knowing he had been there until the bodies were discovered in the morning. The gruesome practice had led the Indians to give Preacher the nickname "Ghost Killer."

Luke was about to attempt something similar, although he wasn't interested in demoralizing Dietrich's men. He just wanted to kill as many of them as he could in order to whittle down the odds against him and his companions.

While the shooting was still going on, he had tried to pin down the location of as many gunmen as he could. He had memorized those spots, another habit his years of experience had taught him, so he headed for the nearest one. When he judged that he was getting pretty close, he dropped to hands and knees and crawled forward.

A low cough sounded no more than ten feet in front of him. Luke froze. His keen eyes scanned the darkness ahead of him. After a moment, he made out an irregular shape that had to be the hired killer. The man was stretched out behind a small hummock of earth that served as cover for him during the assault on the canyon.

It didn't offer any protection from the deadly danger coming up behind him, though. He seemed completely unaware of that as Luke closed in on him, inch by inch, in utter silence.

The blade of Luke's knife made only the faintest whisper of steel on leather as the bounty hunter drew it from its sheath. As far as he could tell, none of the other gunmen were close by. Luke gripped the knife tightly, came up in a crouch, and dived forward.

He landed with his knee in the small of the man's back, pinning him to the ground. His left hand went around the man's head and clamped over his mouth, stifling any outcry as the blade in his other hand flashed forward. The eight inches of cold steel drove into the hired killer's back, rasping through the ribs and penetrating his heart. Luke hung on tight as the man's body bucked in its death spasm.

After seeing how mercilessly Dietrich's hardcases had gunned down Banty Sinclair and his sons back at the way station, Luke wasn't going to lose any sleep about killing any of them. He waited until he was sure the hombre was dead, then withdrew his knife and wiped it on the back of the corpse's shirt.

That was wasted effort, he told himself grimly. The blade was just going to get more blood on it before the night was over.

The scent of tobacco smoke drifted to his nose, coming from somewhere to his right. Luke started crawling again, following the smell. A couple minutes later, he spotted the tiny orange glow of a quirly's tip as the smoker drew in on it.

The distance to the canyon mouth was too great for any of the defenders to see that glow and aim at it. It served as a beacon for Luke, though, as he closed in on the man kneeling in a little hollow.

In the dark, Luke couldn't tell if the formation was a natural one or if the gunman had scooped it out of the dirt. Either way, it was going to serve as the location of the man's last stand; he just didn't know it yet.

Luke attacked, his left arm looping around the enemy's neck, forcing his head up and back, and drawing his throat taut. Pressure on the man's jaw kept him from crying out as Luke brought the knife across his throat in a deep slash that cut almost all the way to the spine. Blood gushed out onto the sand, a black fountain in the starlight.

The dying man's struggles lasted only a couple seconds before he went limp. Luke lowered the body to the ground.

He didn't bother cleaning the knife.

He stretched out on the ground again as he heard two men talking in soft tones not far off. He tried to remember how many men had been in the group of hired killers when he and Hobie first ran into them. About a dozen, he thought. Maybe fourteen.

At least six were dead. That left Dietrich with eight gun wolves, at most . . . unless Dietrich had had more men in reserve that Luke didn't know about.

He couldn't worry too much about that possibility. No matter how many men Dietrich had, the more of them Luke killed, the better.

He crawled away from the spot where he heard the two men talking. He might have been able to dispose of both of them, but not without making enough racket to alert the rest of the bunch. He continued his stealthy stalking until he found another man kneeling behind a slab of rock.

That one died quietly, too, with his blood gurgling out of the gaping wound in his throat that Luke's knife opened up. The sandy soil was drinking deeply.

Dietrich had been quiet for a while. He tried again, calling to Jessica. "My dear, think about the people who are with you. If you've befriended them at all, you don't want anything to happen to them, do you? Surely you understand that if this keeps up, someone could get badly hurt."

"Like the people you've already killed?" Jessica shouted back at him.

"My orders were that no one should be harmed! But bad things happen sometimes. You should understand that."

"I do. The day I first laid eyes on you was a very bad thing. I just didn't know it yet."

Dietrich's control was slipping. He yelled, "You damned little tease! You always enjoyed making me want you! You may have thought I didn't know what you were doing, but I did! And now you have to pay the piper!"

By that time, Luke was close enough to

tell Dietrich's voice was coming from a cluster of boulders about fifty yards to his right. If he could get into those rocks and capture Dietrich, it might end the fight. Without Dietrich to pay them, the hired killers might be less likely to continue risking their lives.

With that thought in his head, Luke began working his way carefully toward the boulders.

It was doubtful that Dietrich would be alone. The man from Boston would have at least one of the gun wolves with him. Luke wouldn't be able to take them without raising a ruckus.

But if he got his hands on Dietrich, that wouldn't matter. With the man who had hired them taken as a hostage, the gun wolves would have to let those in the stagecoach go.

Luke slipped across the ground, keeping to the shadows cast by scrubby mesquite bushes and using shallow gullies to conceal himself. He had covered about half the distance to the boulders where Dietrich had made his headquarters when hurried footsteps suddenly sounded, practically on top of him.

One of Dietrich's men must have decided to change position, Luke realized, but the varmint had done it at the worst possible time. Before Luke could get out of the way, one of the man's feet struck his thigh, and with a startled grunt the hardcase lost his balance and fell sprawling to the ground, landing half on top of the bounty hunter.

Luke still had the knife in his hand. He twisted out from under the man and his free hand shot upward. His fingers hit the man's face and slid over his mouth, clamping down with a grip of iron. At the same time, Luke struck with the knife and felt it rip into his opponent's midsection.

The razor-sharp blade went into the man's belly like a hot knife into butter. Luke ripped it to the side and felt a hot flood spill over his hand. The wound was a mortal one, but Luke wasn't going to wait for the man to die. He pulled the knife free and plunged it into the hardcase's chest, again and again.

The man went limp.

As Luke rolled him to the side, a grimace of distaste tugged at his mouth. He had done plenty of grim, ugly work in the past, but had never grown completely hardened to the killing, even when the men who died richly deserved their fate.

But when you got right down to it, he told himself, the man was one less he'd have to kill later.

One less man who might kill *him.*
Luke started after Dietrich again.

CHAPTER 21

Luke hadn't seen any horses so far, and the reason for that became apparent as he closed in on the boulders where Dietrich was holed up. He heard several whinnies and the stamping of hooves as the mounts shifted around among the big slabs and chunks of rock. The gunmen had brought their horses into cover to keep them safe from any stray slugs.

At least one of the hired killers . . . and maybe one or two others . . . would be posted with Dietrich to tend to the horses. The businessman could have as few as five or six men left overall, Luke realized. He might be able to get the drop on half of them at once. He wasn't going to count on being that fortunate, however. In a deadly struggle, it was always smart to expect the worst.

A man who did that was seldom taken by surprise. Disappointed, maybe, but not surprised.

Luke paused at the outer edge of the boulders and listened intently. In addition to the small sounds coming from the horses, he heard voices muttering.

Then Dietrich's eastern-accented tones said clearly, "Build a fire, Pardee. There's no reason for us to sit here shivering all night. Put some coffee on to boil, too."

"I'm not sure that's a good idea, boss," another man said. "Even if they can't see the flames from where they are in that canyon, they'll see the glow and know we're here. It'll give 'em something to aim at."

"These rocks provide excellent shelter. You said so yourself."

"Yeah, but when a slug goes to bouncin' around, you never know for sure where it's gonna go."

"Build the fire, anyway," Dietrich ordered. "I'm already chilled to the bone, and it'll be even colder by morning."

He was right about that. Even in summer, the temperature dropped quite a bit at night in the high, dry country.

Luke stayed where he was, motionless in deep shadow next to one of the boulders, while he listened to the hired gun build the fire as Dietrich had ordered. He heard the man moving around, heard the rasp of a match, and a moment later caught the faint crackle of flames and smelled wood smoke. After a few more minutes went by, the scent of coffee brewing was added to the mix.

The gunman was right that Hobie and the others in the canyon would be able to see the reflected glow from the fire, but that didn't mean much. They didn't have an endless amount of ammunition, so firing in the general direction of the rocks in the hope that a ricochet might find one of the enemy was too risky. It would just exhaust their supply of bullets that much quicker.

Luke had already sheathed his knife. He drew one of the Remingtons and began slipping around the boulders, staying in the shadows and working his way closer to the fire.

He could hear Dietrich and the other man talking in low tones, discussing what they would do in the morning. A feint toward the canyon would draw the fire of the defenders and determine whether they still had any ammunition. If not, the men could ride in and take Jessica. If the defenders continued to put up a fight, Dietrich's men would withdraw and continue the siege.

Luke came to a huge slab of rock that rose at a slant. It was steep, but not so steep that he couldn't climb it, he thought. He holstered the gun and started the ascent, leaning far forward to rest both hands against the rock.

The surface was rough enough to provide handholds and footholds. As he began to climb, he hoped the noises coming from the restless horses would cover up any small sounds he made.

When Luke reached the crest of the rock about fifteen feet off the ground, he took off his hat, went to his belly, and edged forward so he could look over the far edge. The rock dropped off sheer. Dietrich's hired gun had built the fire against its base.

By the flickering light of the flames, Luke saw three men standing near the fire. He had heard only two voices, so he knew one of the gun wolves had to be the taciturn sort.

He didn't have any trouble figuring out which one was Milton Dietrich. The man from Boston wore a gray suit and a homburg hat. He was a little below medium height and of average build. His hair was steely gray and his face had a slightly pinched look about it, as if he were used to disapproving of just about everything. He was about as ordinary-looking a gent as Luke had ever seen.

And yet his evil was far from ordinary.

Dietrich was responsible for the deaths of at least three innocent people, as well as for terrorizing a young woman and endangering a number of other folks.

Luke knew that from where he was, he could put a bullet through the man's brain, and he was sorely tempted to do just that. The only thing stopping him was knowing that if Dietrich was dead, the men he had hired might go on a killing spree. They wouldn't have anything to lose. As long as Dietrich was alive, even if he was a prisoner, there would still be a chance the gunmen might get the money he owed them.

One of the men filled a tin cup with coffee and handed it to Dietrich. The easterner swallowed a sip of the brew and grimaced, but he took another sip. Whether it tasted good or not, coffee would have a bracing effect on the cool night.

"Pardee, we need to talk about what's going to happen once we have Miss Wheeler in our custody," Dietrich said, making it sound like they were lawmen of some sort, rather than the worst kind of trigger-happy scum. "I don't want anyone coming after us or trying to set the law on us."

"That's what I figured, boss," replied the man who had handed Dietrich the cup. He was a stocky hombre with a ragged black mustache. He wore a black hat and a cow-hide vest. "Don't worry, we'll take care of cleanin' up."

"I'll promise her that if she surrenders, the others won't be harmed, but I think we both know what needs to happen in the long run."

Pardee chuckled. "We don't want to leave any witnesses behind, that's for sure. They know we killed those fellas back at the way station."

"It's very important that nothing happens until Miss Wheeler and I are gone," Dietrich went on. "I still have hopes of winning her affections, so she needs to believe that I kept my word and her new friends weren't hurt."

"We'll handle it," Pardee assured him. "You can tell her we'll just hold 'em prisoner here until y'all are gone and then let 'em go."

"But as soon as we're well out of earshot —"

"No need to spell it out, boss. We'll bury the bodies all the way up in that canyon where nobody's likely to find the graves for a long time. Maybe never."

Luke's anger grew as he listened to them callously plotting the slaughter of Hobie, Jim Pierce, and the Langstons. From his vantage point he could see the horses and knew there wasn't anyone with them. He figured the third man by the fire was responsible for them.

Luke had to take care of two men — three if he counted Dietrich — but he didn't figure the older man represented much of a threat. He drew both guns, knowing he would have to shoot swift and sure to bring down both hardcases. Once that was done, he could drop down and take Dietrich prisoner.

Before he could make his move, a harsh voice suddenly yelled from behind him, "Look out, boys! One of 'em's up there on that rock!"

The shout was followed immediately by the roar of a gun.

Instinct sent Luke twisting around. A bullet spanged off the slab beside him, sending dust and rock chips flying into the air. Being spotted was a stroke of bad luck and the one thing he couldn't plan for.

The gunman behind him let fly with another shot, but the slug whistled past Luke's ear.

Luke aimed at the muzzle flash and triggered twice. A howl of pain split the night, telling him that at least one of the shots had scored.

He would be a good target as long as he was up there on top of the boulder, so he got down the quickest way he knew how. He rolled over, came up in a crouch, and leaped off the rock, aiming at the camp below.

Pardee and the other hardcase had their guns out, but they didn't know exactly where Luke was and certainly didn't expect him to come diving out of the night sky at them. As professional gunmen, though, their reactions were quick, and each man got a shot off as Luke plummeted toward them. Neither bullet came close to him.

Chance aimed Luke's dive at the second man. He landed feet-first, his boot heels smashing into the man's chest and driving him to the ground. Bones snapped and splintered under the impact.

Luke's momentum carried him forward in a roll as he hit the ground. He came up on one knee, twisting toward Pardee as the man fired again. The slug whipped over Luke's left shoulder and past his ear.

Both Remingtons spewed flame as he fired. The pair of .36 caliber slugs pounded into Pardee's chest and drove him backward in a jittering dance. His gun sagged toward the ground and boomed again as a spasm made his finger jerk the trigger. He lost his balance and fell into the fire, landing on his back and causing an explosion of sparks in the air around him. He screamed as his clothes and hair started to burn, but he was too weakened by his wounds to escape the flames.

Luke bounded to his feet and lunged toward Milton Dietrich, who stood there with the cup of coffee still in his hand, looking stunned and dumbfounded by the sudden violent turn of events. Too late, he dropped the cup and tried to turn and run, but Luke's left-hand gun came crashing down on his head, denting the fancy hat and sending Dietrich stumbling to his knees.

Luke holstered that Remington, reached down, grabbed the collar of Dietrich's coat, and hauled the man to his feet again. He pressed the barrel of the other revolver against Dietrich's back. "It wouldn't take a hell of a lot to convince me to blow your guts out, Dietrich. So you better listen and listen good."

"Don't kill me!" Dietrich babbled. "Please don't kill me!"

That was typical, Luke thought. Like most men drunk on their own power and arrogance and accustomed to riding roughshod over anyone who opposed them, once his own life was threatened Dietrich turned into a pathetic, mewling coward. Luke turned him toward the fire, where Pardee still whimpered and thrashed around weakly. The stomach-turning smell of burning flesh filled the air.

As Pardee's moans faded away, Luke said to Dietrich, "I ought to throw you in the fire with him. It's just what you deserve."

"No, no, I'll pay you. I swear to God I'll give you anything you want —"

"Shut up!" Luke heard footsteps pounding quickly toward them and knew the rest of the gunnies were coming to see what all the shooting and yelling was about. "Tell your men to back off. Now!"

"Stop!" Dietrich shouted. "Stop where you are! Don't come any closer!"

"Boss?" one of the gunman called tentatively. "What's going on over there?"

"Don't come any closer," Dietrich said again. "This . . . this madman will kill me!"

"Damn right I will!" Luke said, lifting his voice so the other men could hear him and know that he wasn't bluffing.

He prodded the gun barrel harder into Dietrich's back. "You know how a revolver like this works, Mr. Dietrich?" Luke's voice dripped with scorn as he asked the question. "I've already tripped the trigger. My thumb on the hammer is all that's keeping it from firing. It would behoove you to keep that from happening."

"You . . . you sound like an educated man. Surely we can come to some sort of agreement, work out an arrangement —"

"I like money as much as the next fella, Dietrich, but I wouldn't touch any of yours. It's too dirty even for me." Luke hauled him toward the edge of the cluster of boulders. "Now, you and I are going to walk over to that canyon, and if your men get any bright ideas about shooting me, this gun will go off when I let go of the hammer and you'll die, too. So what do you think you should tell them?"

"Hold your fire!" Dietrich practically screamed. "Whatever you do, for God's sake don't shoot!"

Although Dietrich had given that order, the skin on the back of Luke's neck crawled as he stepped out of the cover of the boulders and forced Dietrich ahead of him. Even with just starlight to aim by, those gunmen were probably good enough shots to ventilate him. He hoped they would follow the orders of the man paying them and hold their fire.

No shots sounded as Luke strode out into the open. He whistled for his horse, knowing the animal would respond. Sure enough, the horse trotted up out of the darkness a moment later and gave Luke a friendly nudge on the shoulder with his nose.

Luke kept a tight grip on Dietrich's collar as the man stumbled along in front of him. The horse walked along easily behind them. The open ground between them and the canyon mouth seemed a hundred miles wide, rather than a few hundred yards.

As he pushed Dietrich along, Luke wondered what Hobie and the others were thinking about all the shooting a few minutes earlier. They had to be curious, especially once they realized the bullets weren't coming toward them. It must have sounded like a battle had broken out among Dietrich's men. He wondered if they had spotted him and Dietrich walking toward the canyon mouth.

When he was about fifty yards away, Luke stopped and called, "Hobie! Hey, Hobie, can you hear me?"

"Luke?" the young man's voice came back instantly. "That's you?"

"Yeah, so hold your fire! I've got Dietrich with me."

"My God!" That was Jessica. "You've taken him prisoner?"

"I have a gun in his back," Luke replied. "He's ordered his men not to shoot. We're coming in."

"You're never going to get away with this," Dietrich said in a low, furious voice. His immense pride asserted itself as he seemed to have gotten over being scared. "I'll see to it that you're hunted down and killed." His voice shook a little from the depths of his rage as he added, "I don't care how long it takes, you're a dead man."

Luke said, "Talk like that makes me think I ought to go ahead and let this hammer drop." He chuckled. "Is that what you want, Dietrich?"

"If you're as intelligent as you seem, that's exactly what you'll do. Do you really want a man like me as your enemy?"

"They say you can judge a man by the sort of enemies he makes," Luke drawled. "If that's true, I'm pretty well satisfied to be on the opposite side from you, mister."

Dietrich didn't say anything else as they covered the rest of the distance to the canyon. As they stepped into the thick shadows at its mouth, Hobie said, "Over here, Luke."

Luke followed the voice to some rocks along the canyon wall. The stagecoach was parked behind them, and the embers of a small fire glowed beyond the coach. By the faint light they cast, Luke saw the vague shapes of Hobie, Jessica, Pierce, and the Langstons as the defenders gathered around them.

"I was hoping I'd never have to see you again," Jessica said to Dietrich.

"You'll regret this," he snapped. "All of you will. I'm not accustomed to such treatment."

"You're not used to bein' on the receivin' end of it," Hobie said. "You sure can dish out the misery, though."

Pierce asked, "What did you find back at the way station, Luke?"

Luke's tone was gentle as he said, "I'm sorry, Jim. We were right about what happened there. Your friend and his boys are dead."

Pierce muttered a heartfelt curse. Then he lifted his shotgun and said, "This hombre here is the one responsible for what happened, even if he never pulled a trigger. Step away from him."

"No!" Dietrich gasped. "You can't just kill me in cold blood."

"That's what your men did to poor ol' Banty and his boys," Pierce said. "Hell, a double load of buckshot is better'n you deserve. It'll kill you quick, and what you've really got comin' is a slow, painful death."

Dietrich's head jerked around toward

Luke. "You . . . you can't allow this lunatic to —"

"I'd mind my tongue if I was you," Luke said. "Jim, I hate to say it, but right now Dietrich is worth more to us alive."

"Reckon I know that," the jehu growled as he slowly lowered the scattergun. "But if I had my druthers, his insides'd be scattered all over this canyon by now."

"Maybe you'll get your chance later," Luke said. "I guess it all depends on whether Dietrich's men want to let us out of here in the morning."

CHAPTER 22

It was only a few hours until dawn. No one had slept much, but Luke figured it would be safe enough for them to take turns grabbing a few winks while Dietrich was their prisoner.

"He only has three or four of those hardcases left," Luke told the others while he was tying Dietrich's hands behind his back. "The odds are as close to even as they've ever been since this trouble started."

"Are you willing to bet your life on that?" Dietrich asked coolly. "For all you know, I have more men working for me than you've seen so far."

Luke knew that was true, but he wasn't going to admit that to Dietrich. Instead, he sat the man down on the ground with his back against one of the stagecoach wheels and said, "I'll take my chances."

Hobie said, "So will I. You're beat, mister. You just don't know it yet."

Dietrich glared up at him. He seemed to have a special hatred for the young man. He had seen the protective way Hobie stayed so close to Jessica. Even in bad light, anybody with half an eye could tell how Hobie felt about her.

Luke thought those feelings were beginning to be returned, judging by the way Jessica stood close to Hobie, smiled at him, and rested a hand on his arm from time to time while they were talking.

Taking advantage of the opportunity to get a little rest, he wiped the charcoal streaks off his face, then sat down with his back against a rock, stretched his legs out in front of him, and tipped his black hat down over his eyes, even though he didn't really need the brim's shade at the moment.

In a matter of minutes he had fallen into a light doze, a manhunter's sleep that would allow him to come awake instantly and completely at the first sign of trouble.

Nothing disturbed him, though, until the smell of coffee roused him. When he opened his eyes he saw that the eastern sky was gray with the approach of daylight.

Luke stood up and stretched. He looked around and saw that Dietrich had gone to sleep, too. The man's head hung forward over his chest as he snored. A few yards away, Jim Pierce sat guarding him with the shotgun ready.

"Any problems?" Luke asked.

Pierce shook his head. "Nah, those buzzards out yonder have been quiet. To tell you the truth, I ain't sure they're even still out there."

"I'd bet a hat they are," Luke said. "They're not going to give up on the job just yet. It wouldn't surprise me if Dietrich promised them a bonus when he got what he wanted, and they'll still try to collect that if they can."

"You're probably right. Hombres like that are mighty stubborn when it comes to their money."

Luke looked around some more and asked, "Where is everyone else?"

"Mr. and Mrs. Langston are inside the coach. Far as I'm concerned, the ground's just about as comfortable as them seats, but I reckon folks like them are used to havin' a roof of some sort over their head when they sleep. Miss Wheeler's over there behind them rocks. Hobie made her a bedroll there so's she'd have some privacy. As for the young fella hisself, he's taken a *pasear* out to the canyon mouth to have a look around."

"I hope he's being careful not to show himself," Luke said as he picked up his rifle.

"I wouldn't put it past those men to try sniping at him."

"Neither would I. If you want to go get him, I got Arbuckle's boilin'. Stuff's a real eye-opener, the way I make it."

"I'll fetch him," Luke said with a smile.

He walked the fifty yards or so to the canyon mouth, staying close to the wall so he wouldn't present much of a target in the pre-dawn gloom. When he had nearly reached the opening, he called softly, "Hobie?"

"Right here," the young man replied from a thick patch of shadow behind a jutting rock.

"Everything quiet out there?"

"Too dang quiet, if you ask me. I think those varmints are up to something."

"They might try to sneak up on us, all right," Luke agreed. "But I think they're more likely to wait until we're out of here to make their move."

"We're leaving the canyon?"

"We can't stay here indefinitely. We don't have enough food, water, and ammunition for a long siege. We're less than half a day's journey from Moss City, so I think we ought to make a run for it."

"Taking Dietrich with us as a hostage," Hobie said.

Luke nodded. "That's right."

"They'll try to stop us," Hobie warned. "If there's any law in Moss City, they can't afford to let us get there or they'll have murder charges hinging' over their heads. They'd probably rather see Dietrich dead than let that happen."

"On the other hand," Luke said, "they probably don't have the advantage in numbers anymore. There's a chance they'll decide to cut their losses and light a shuck."

"If they do, that'll be just fine with me," Hobie declared fervently.

The two men went back to camp. Stephen and Edna Langston were standing beside the fire, and Jessica came out from behind the rocks a few minutes later, carrying the bedroll Hobie had put together for her.

"Were you able to get any sleep?" he asked her.

Jessica smiled. "Some. The bedroll was actually pretty comfortable, Hobie."

"Aw, you don't have to say that. I know it wasn't."

"No, really, I mean it," she insisted.

"Maybe you can spend tonight in an actual bed. I sure wouldn't mind if I did, too." Hobie started to get red in the face. "I mean . . . not the same bed. A different bed. In a different building. I never meant —"

"That's all right, Hobie," she told him with a smile. "You don't have to explain."

"That's good. My tongue seems to get all tangled up mighty easy these days."

And everyone knew the reason for that, Luke thought with a smile as he bent to pick up the coffeepot.

The bleeding edge of the sun had just peeked over the eastern horizon by the time everyone had eaten and the team was hitched to the stagecoach again. The horses still weren't exactly fresh, according to Pierce, but they had rested enough overnight that they could make the rest of the trip to Moss City.

"We better hope we don't have to run 'em too hard, though," the jehu said. "I don't know how much they got in 'em at top speed. A mile or so, at most."

"Maybe it won't come to that." Luke swung up into his saddle. "I'll scout ahead a ways. Everyone's guns are fully loaded?"

A chorus of assent came from the travelers.

Hobie added with a worried frown, "We're running a mite low on cartridges, though, Luke."

"I figured as much. If there's trouble, make every shot count."

From the top of the coach, where he sat

293

with his wrists bound in front of him and his ankles tied together, Milton Dietrich said, "It's not too late to make a deal, Jensen. Leave Jessica and me here so my men can pick us up, and the rest of you can leave. You won't be harmed and no one will try to stop you. I give you my word on that."

"Your word doesn't mean a damned thing to me, Dietrich," Luke said. "Putting you up there in plain sight, where a stray bullet is just as likely to hit you as any of us, is just about the only value you've got right now."

Dietrich glared at him, but didn't say anything else. The man's gray hair was askew, and his face had grown haggard. Fear still lurked in his eyes, but hatred and arrogance had the upper hand at the moment.

Pierce whipped up the team and got them moving. Luke rode ahead of the coach. His eyes scanned the landscape outside the canyon.

He didn't see anything out of the ordinary, but that didn't mean much. The terrain might look pretty flat from a distance, but close up that wasn't exactly the case. There were plenty of places where a group of horsemen could hide, ranging from arroyos to small mesas.

Luke waved Pierce ahead, and the stagecoach rolled into the open. Pierce kept the horses moving at a brisk pace, although not at an actual run.

Luke slid his Winchester from its sheath and rode with the rifle across the saddle in front of him. His eyes never stopped moving as he swept his gaze over the landscape, searching for any sign of impending trouble.

Nothing. He spotted some buzzards wheeling around in the pale blue sky in the distance, but that was all.

Pierce had left the trail between Harkerville and Moss City to reach the canyon the night before. He drove back to the stagecoach's usual route and swung the vehicle to the west, toward the Arizona border.

Hobie turned to look at Dietrich. "Looks like your hired killers don't think highly enough of you to come to your rescue after all."

Dietrich sneered at him. "You want Jessica for yourself, but I can promise you, you'll never have her. Never."

"Go to hell," Hobie grumbled.

"You'll be there before me," Dietrich said.

Luke heard that exchange and didn't care for the confidence he heard in Dietrich's voice. The man was mighty sure of himself, considering the situation he was in, and that confidence seemed to grow with every turn of the stagecoach's wheels.

Luke wasn't sure what Dietrich expected to happen. It seemed to him that if the surviving gunnies were going to try anything, it would have been an ambush at the mouth of the canyon or at least somewhere close to there.

That uneasy feeling stuck with Luke, even after Pierce announced that they were getting close to the Arizona border. "We'll be outta New Mexico Territory soon. He pointed. "See those hills up ahead? They're across the line in Arizona. Of course, it don't really matter all that much. One flat, dry, dusty stretch of ground is pretty much like any other flat, dry, dusty stretch of ground, I reckon."

He was right about that. A stone marker beside the trail indicated the spot where they entered Arizona, but to Luke the surrounding countryside all looked the same, at least right along the boundary.

A short time later, though, they entered the low, rocky hills Pierce had pointed out. The trail followed a fairly deep cut between two of those hills.

Luke's instincts kicked in. The location was perfect for an ambush. He was about to ask Pierce if there was another way around the hills when Hobie called out an alarm.

"Luke! Behind us!"

Luke twisted in the saddle and looked back the way they had come. Seven or eight riders had appeared seemingly from nowhere, although Luke knew they must have been hidden in a gully. The horsemen thundered after them.

Pierce looked back and saw the pursuers, too. He ripped out a curse and slashed at the horses with his whip. They surged ahead in a gallop.

And that was the wrong thing to do, Luke realized. He shouted, "Jim, no!" but it was too late. The stagecoach careened into the cut between the hills at high speed, tossing the passengers around inside.

Puffs of powder smoke appeared on the slopes on both sides as hidden riflemen opened fire on the racing coach. Luke's worry about Dietrich having more men had just come true.

It was too late to turn back or go around. Luke knew all they could do was fight their way through. He flung the rifle to his shoulder and started raking the near hillside with lead, hoping to distract the bushwhackers at the very least.

Hobie twisted back and forth on the seat next to Pierce and fired his rifle at both slopes, squeezing off rounds as fast as he could work the Winchester's lever. Pistol shots cracked from inside the coach as Jessica and Langston put up a fight, too. Pierce had his hands full just keeping the team under control. Puffs of dust kicked up from the trail as bullets struck around the flashing hooves of the team.

If one of those horses went down, the others probably would, too, and then the coach would pile up. When Luke saw the way the gunmen were shooting at the team, he knew they didn't really care about saving Dietrich's life anymore. They just wanted to stop the coach from getting to Moss City.

Dietrich yelled in alarm as he was thrown back and forth on top of the stage. He twisted to his side and grabbed the brass rail around the edge of the roof to keep from being thrown off.

From the corner of his eye, Luke saw Dietrich raise his legs and lash out with them. He slammed his feet into Hobie's back.

The unexpected blow sent Hobie flying forward off the seat and his rifle crashing to the ground. The young man seemed to hang in mid-air above the team, a split second away from falling under the slashing steel-shod hooves of the galloping horses.

CHAPTER 23

There was nothing Luke could do to save his young partner. It was all up to Hobie's own instincts and quick reactions.

With both hands free, Hobie made a desperate grab for the harness on the horses on either side of him. His right hand caught and held, but his legs dropped toward the ground.

One foot hit the singletree. He scrambled for purchase on it and lunged, wrapping his left hand around the same harness. Holding on with two hands, he managed to get his other foot on the singletree. His position was still perilous, but better than it had been a few seconds earlier.

Up on the top of the stagecoach, Dietrich pushed himself to his knees and faced forward. He raised his arms, spread them as much as he could with his wrists tied, and brought them down around Jim Pierce's neck. Dietrich yanked back, choking the jehu.

The attack made Pierce drop the reins. They coiled around loosely on the floorboard like crazed snakes, allowing the team to run wild.

Luke couldn't risk a shot at Dietrich while the man was locked in such a close struggle with Pierce. He still had the rest of the gunmen to deal with, too. Seeing one man rise from his hiding place behind some brush on the slope, Luke snapped a shot at him and was rewarded by the sight of the would-be killer doubling over and then tumbling down the hillside.

Luke levered the Winchester and swung the rifle to the side as he triggered another shot, but couldn't tell if he hit anything.

Hobie carefully worked his way along the singletree back toward the coach as Pierce and Dietrich continued their battle. Pierce's whiskery face was turning bright red as Dietrich's brutal hold on his throat cut off his air. Pierce jammed an elbow into Dietrich's body, but the man's grip didn't loosen.

Luke realized he had underestimated how much of a threat Milton Dietrich really was. The man was fighting with the crazed strength of a lunatic.

Hobie reached up and grabbed the floorboard. He hooked a foot over it and hauled himself up as the coach careened along the trail. If it had hit a big bump just then, he would have been flung loose and fallen under the team, the fate he had narrowly avoided a moment earlier.

He managed to reach the floorboard and surged up to throw a punch over Pierce's shoulder that caught Dietrich in the face. Dietrich's head rocked back. Hobie caught hold of the businessman's arms and fought to wrench them free from Pierce's throat.

Somehow, they were past the bushwhackers. They had run that deadly gauntlet without anyone getting killed. The gunmen on horseback were still coming up quickly from behind, however. Luke twisted in the saddle to throw another shot at them, but the Winchester's hammer just clicked when it fell.

Empty.

He jammed the rifle back in its scabbard and hauled his mount around. He took the reins in his teeth and filled both hands with the Remingtons. Using his heels, he sent the horse charging straight at the group of gunmen.

It was a damned fool play, and he knew it. But he also knew that doing the unexpected was sometimes a man's most effective weapon, and charging into the face of such odds was certainly unexpected.

He bent low and cut loose with the revolvers, trading shots from hand to hand as he guided the horse with his knees. He had another small advantage in that he had plenty of targets to choose from, while his enemies had to concentrate their fire on him. The horse veered back and forth at slight angles in response to Luke's urging. Bullets sang past him, but failed to find the mark.

He saw two of the gunmen rock back as his slugs smashed into them, and another man threw up his arms and pitched out of the saddle in a limp sprawl that signified death.

That broke the nerve of two of the other gunmen. They whirled their horses to flee, ignoring the shouted curses of their companions. With that, the odds against Luke suddenly dropped to two to one.

He almost felt like he had them outnumbered.

The distance between Luke and his enemies had dwindled to almost nothing. He aimed for the gap between their horses and flashed through it, firing to both sides as he did so. They twisted in their saddles and tried to bring their guns to bear on him. The air around Luke's head buzzed like a hornet's nest as bullets fanned past his ears.

Still untouched, he leaned back and clamped his teeth down hard on the reins, slowing his horse. He dropped the reins and turned his head in time to see both gunmen topple off their mounts. He didn't know if he had hit them or if each had accidentally shot the other, but it didn't matter. He was still alive.

And the stagecoach was still a runaway. Luke holstered the left-hand Remington, grabbed his horse's reins, and wheeled the animal so he could race after the coach.

Up ahead, Hobie had succeeded in pulling Dietrich's arms away from Pierce. The jehu slumped on the seat, gasping for breath.

Dietrich clubbed his bound hands together and swung them at Hobie's head. Hobie ducked under the sweeping blow and hooked a punch into Dietrich's ribs. In the frenzy of hate that gripped him, Dietrich didn't even seem to notice the blow. He lunged at Hobie, rammed into him, and knocked the young man off the seat onto the floorboard. Dietrich fell on top of him, landing with his knees in Hobie's stomach. His fingers locked like iron bands around Hobie's throat.

From Luke's position galloping up behind

the coach, he couldn't see the two of them anymore, only Jim Pierce's hunched form as the jehu tried to draw life-giving air through his bruised throat.

Hobie lifted a knee into Dietrich's groin. Even in his berserk state, Dietrich couldn't ignore that. His hands slipped a little on Hobie's throat as he curled his body around the pain.

Hobie got a flailing hand on Dietrich's face and clawed for the man's eyes. Dietrich flung his head back to get away. He let go of Hobie's throat and dived for the Colt still on the young man's hip. The thong over the hammer had held it in the holster despite Hobie's near-fall under the galloping team.

Dietrich got his hand on the gun and ripped it free. At the same time, Pierce, barely recovered, made a grab at Dietrich's shoulder. Dietrich twisted and swung the gun at Pierce's head. The barrel raked the jehu's jaw and made him fall back against the seat, momentarily stunned again.

Using both hands, Dietrich pointed the gun at Hobie and pulled back the hammer. "I told you you'd never have her!" he yelled triumphantly.

Almost even with the stagecoach again, Luke heard Dietrich's shout, and knew he had to act. The Remington in his right hand came up and blasted a shot. The .36 caliber slug struck Dietrich in the back of the head, bored through his brain, and exploded out between his eyes. Already dead, the man with the ruined face flopped forward, somersaulting over the horses and dropping among them.

The hooves did their gruesome work, followed by the wheels of the stagecoach. They chopped Milton Dietrich's body into something that barely resembled a human being.

Luke urged his horse alongside the team and leaned over to grab the harness. He hauled back on it, yelling, "Whoa! Whoa, damn it!"

Gradually the horses slowed, and after another hundred yards or so, the coach lurched to a halt. Before he did anything else, Luke yanked out the Winchester and reloaded as he scanned the trail behind them.

He saw several sprawled bodies and riderless horses, but nobody was coming after them. The rest of Dietrich's men appeared to have given up.

If they had seen what was left of their employer, they knew they wouldn't collect any more blood money from him. No one ever would. They must have decided to take their chances with the law coming after them for the killings at the way station. Men like that often had murder charges hanging over their heads to start with.

With the coach no longer moving, Hobie dropped to the ground and jerked the door open. "Jessica!" he cried. "Jess, are you all right?"

She practically threw herself out of the coach and into his arms. "Hobie! Oh, Hobie, I thought you must be dead!"

"It was pretty dang close," he told her as he held her tightly. "But I was lucky, and then Luke saved my life."

Luke rode over to the coach so he could look in one of the windows. Stephen and Edna Langston were huddled together on the rear seat, but appeared to be unhurt.

"Are you folks all right?" Luke asked.

Langston nodded. "We weren't hit. But I don't see how, with all that lead flying around!"

"Hitting a moving target is a lot more difficult than some people make it out to be," Luke said with a faint smile. "And sometimes there's a great deal of luck involved, too. I'd say that luck was on our side today."

"Ain't no denyin' that," Pierce rasped from the driver's seat. "Dietrich damn near choked me to death, that no-good varmint."

"He paid the price for that and all his other sins," Luke said as he looked back at the ragged, bloody remains of Milton Dietrich. Sometimes all the money and power in the world didn't matter a damned bit, he thought.

Hobie was still holding Jessica. He saw where Luke was looking and asked, "Do we have to take what's left of him on to Moss City with us?"

"What, and cheat the buzzards out of a good meal?" Luke asked.

They all agreed. If anyone back in Boston wondered what had become of Milton Dietrich, it was best to let them wonder. After the scavengers were done with what was left of Dietrich, no one would ever be sure who he was or what had happened to him.

Dietrich's disappearance somewhere in the West would just be . . . a mystery.

When the stagecoach reached Moss City later that day, Jim Pierce reported to the local stationmaster that Banty Sinclair and Sinclair's two sons were dead, apparently murdered by unknown outlaws who had raided the way station and then tried to waylay the stagecoach. That was true enough, in its own way. No one knew who had pulled the triggers when the three men

307

were gunned down.

Luke hoped the killers had met their own ends during the battles at the canyon or in the hills.

Pierce blamed his hoarse voice on an illness, and the stationmaster told him to see the doctor. Another driver and shotgun guard would be taking the coach on the next leg of its journey to California, starting bright and early the next morning.

Luke got a hotel room and cleaned up, glad for the chance to do so without anybody shooting at him. He had lost track of Hobie, but assumed the young man was with Jessica or somewhere close by her, wherever she was.

The hotel had a decent dining room, and that evening Luke was carving his way through a thick steak when Hobie came in, glanced around the room, and spotted him. The young man had cleaned up and changed clothes, too. He took his hat off and walked across the room toward Luke.

When he reached the table, Luke gestured toward one of the empty chairs. "Why don't you join me?"

"Sorry, Luke, but I, uh, can't. I'm supposed to meet Jessica in a little while and have supper with her. She's staying at the Sunset House."

That was the other hotel in Moss City, a little nicer than the one where Luke had taken a room. He patted his lips with a napkin. "All right, but you look like you have something to tell me. You can sit down long enough to do that, anyway."

"Yeah, I suppose so." Hobie pulled out the chair and sank into it. "Jess and I have been talking about her plans now that Dietrich's dead."

"Jess," Luke repeated, smiling. "From the sound of that, the two of you have gotten pretty friendly in a hurry."

"Yeah, bein' in the middle of a hell of a lot of trouble together will do that, I reckon."

"Is she going back to Boston?"

Hobie shook his head. "No, she's decided she wants to go on to California, anyway. Her brother's still the only family she has left."

"That makes sense," Luke said with a nod. "I think it's a good decision."

Hobie took a deep breath. "And I'm going with her." He rushed the words out as if he were afraid he couldn't say them if he didn't.

Luke just sat there, still smiling slightly.

"Well?" Hobie demanded. "Aren't you going to try to talk me out of it?"

"Why would I do that?"

"Well . . . well, you and me are partners! We set out to bring in Gunner Kelly and Dog Eater!"

"If you remember correctly," Luke said, "we didn't exactly set out to accomplish that goal together. You followed me from Rio Rojo."

"Yeah, and it's a darned good thing I did, too, or those Rurales would've put you up in front of a firing squad in La Farva!"

"Possibly," Luke admitted. "Our time together has had its benefits, I won't deny that. But I'm used to working alone, Hobie. I've been doing that for years and years."

"You're sayin' you don't want me partnering up with you anymore." Hobie sounded a little hurt.

"I'm saying that you're in love with a fine young woman who evidently returns that feeling, and you'd be a damned fool to turn your back on that. Think about it, Hobie. Fate brought you and Jessica Wheeler together, and something . . . some force . . . kept both of you alive until you came out on the other side of all the trouble. I don't believe you should fly in the face of what's obviously meant to be."

"You really think so?" Hobie asked with a frown.

Luke nodded. "I really think so."

Hobie heaved a sigh. "Well . . . I reckon you've got a point. It does seem like me and Jess were meant to be together."

"There you go. Fate."

"But you're going on after Kelly and Dog Eater?"

"They have my five thousand dollars," Luke said, his voice hardening. "I intend to get it back."

"You think you can find them?"

"I can find them. However long it takes, however far I have to ride."

CHAPTER 24

Crossing from Arizona into Mexico was like crossing the border between Arizona and New Mexico Territory. If there hadn't been a marker beside the trail, burned into a weathered slab of wood, Luke wouldn't have been able to tell that he had passed from one country into the other.

The brushy, semiarid terrain was the same almost as far as the eye could see. Several small ranges of hills broke it up in the distance.

Luke was about a hundred miles southwest of Moss City, where he had said goodbye to Hobie and Jessica several days earlier. Jessica had hugged him and told him to be sure and stop at her brother's ranch to see them if he ever got to that part of California. Luke had promised that he would, but didn't really expect to keep that promise. He had ridden alone for too long to break the habit.

He had used his time in Moss City to find out whatever he could about the mysterious Don del Oro, mentioning the name in every saloon and cantina in town. For a while, it seemed like he was going to be frustrated in his efforts, but one night he had bought a beer for an old desert rat with a scruffy beard and a battered hat with a turned-up brim and had been rewarded.

As he rode farther into Mexico, Luke remembered the conversation.

"Oh, yeah, sure, the Don del Oro mine," the old-timer said after licking beer foam off his mustache and sighing in appreciation. "Gift of gold, they called it, and maybe it was for a while, but the vein played out a long time ago. Place has been abandoned for twenty years or more. Reckon that's why most folks have never heard of it."

"Is it here in Arizona?" Luke asked.

The desert rat took another long swallow from his mug and then shook his head. "Nope, down across the line in ol' Meh-hee-co. In the Sierra Diablitos."

"The Little Devils," Luke muttered.

"Yep. Good name for 'em, too. Them mountains might not be too tall, but they're rugged as all get-out. Back in them days, too, they was full o' Yaquis and bandidos. It was worth a man's life to be caught out alone. Or so I've heard, you understand. I never laid eyes on the place myself, but I knowed several fellas who worked there. I think they was just as glad when the vein petered out. They didn't have to risk their lives workin' there no more."

"What about now? Are the Yaquis and bandits still in those parts?"

"I could use a mite more lubrication," the old-timer whined. "My throat's gettin' dry."

Luke signaled for the bartender to send over another beer.

When it arrived, the prospector sucked down a healthy slug of suds and then wiped the back of his hand across his mouth. "The way I hear it, them Yaquis has pulled out and gone farther south into the mountains. The Rurales made it pretty hot for 'em for a while. Most of them Mex lawmen are crookeder 'n a snake with the rheumatiz, but they're decent Injun fighters when they put their minds to it."

Thinking of the Rurales pulled Luke from his memories. After meeting up with Captain Almanzar and his men at La Farva, he had his own opinion of the Rurales, and it wasn't a favorable one. He hadn't brought that up in his conversation with the old prospector, though.

He shifted in his saddle and continued his

ride, mulling over what he had learned about Don del Oro.

"As for the bandidos, though," the old-timer went on, "I couldn't say. That's mighty lonely country down yonder, just made for owlhoots."

"So you think that mine is still deserted?" Luke asked.

"No reason for it not to be," the desert rat replied. "Unless somebody come along and found some more gold in it, and I think I'd have heard about that if it happened. I keep my ear pretty close to the ground, you know. No tellin' when or where you might hear news of a strike."

The old man licked his lips. The thirst for gold that lurked inside him was even stronger than his thirst for beer or whiskey. It was the sort of powerful drive that sent some men out into the desert or the mountains again and again until they either struck it rich or found a final desolate resting place for their bones.

"You said you'd never been to the Don del Oro," Luke prompted.

"Yeah, but I know where to find it, if that's what you're after, son." The old man's rheumy eyes narrowed. "You wouldn't be holdin' out on me, would you? You ain't heard rumors that there's been a strike there?"

"I give you my word that I haven't," Luke

said. "Some men I know mentioned the place. I thought I might look for them there."

"If they're at the Don del Oro, they must not like comp'ny. That's about the lonesomest place an hombre could find."

"That sounds just like what they would look for," Luke said.

The old-timer hadn't been able to give Luke exact directions to the abandoned mine, but he'd told him enough to get to the Diablitos. They loomed ahead of him, a rugged line of gray peaks.

As usual, the mountains were farther away than they appeared. By the time Luke made camp that night, he didn't seem any closer to them than he had been when he first sighted them. He knew from experience that he had to just keep going until he reached his destination.

He was aware that in Mexico he had less legal standing than he did in the States. Because of that, he made sure his fire was small, using it only to boil coffee, and he doused the flames with sand, putting it out before night had fallen completely. His supper consisted of jerky and some hard biscuits he had bought in a tiny settlement not far north of the border.

After circling his lasso around his bedroll

to keep snakes out, he crawled into his blankets and slept. His horse was picketed nearby and would let him know if anybody or anything came around. The animal was a better sentry than a lot of humans Luke knew.

In the morning, Luke pushed on toward the Little Devils. By midday, the mountains were starting to look somewhat closer. He lost sight of them, however, when he entered an area of ridges and gullies that formed a forbidding badlands. There was no telling how far the breaks stretched to either side, so he had no choice except to cross them.

Luke had been following a serpentine path through the rugged terrain for about an hour when he spotted a little plume of dirt and pebbles sliding down a steep slope ahead of him and to the left. That served as a warning that something had just moved up there above him. He reined in, jerked his head back to look up the slope, and reached across his body with his right hand for the Remington.

A shot rang out, its echo bouncing around crazily from the multitude of rock walls all around him. Dust flew as the bullet chipped stone to his right. A voice called out in Spanish, ordering him not to move.

The same man's voice continued in English, "Take your hand away from your gun, señor. I would hate to have to tell my men to shoot you."

Luke wasn't convinced the fella would hate it all that much. He lifted his hand away from the Remington's walnut grips and raised it shoulder high while he held the reins in his other hand. His eyes scanned the slopes. At first, he didn't see anything, but then he picked out several rifle barrels protruding menacingly from behind rocks.

"You have the advantage of me, my friends," he called. "I'm not looking for trouble, though."

"You are an American," the unseen speaker said. He made it sound like an accusation.

"That's true," Luke admitted.

"What are you doing in my country?"

"Looking for two more Americans." As an Apache, Dog Eater might not take kindly to being called an American, but since he'd been traveling with Gunner Kelly, Luke thought it was all right to lump the two of them together.

"Stay where you are," the man told him.

"All right," Luke agreed. He heard more rocks rattling as somebody shifted around.

Suddenly, a gray, steeple-crowned sombrero came into view above one of the boulders that littered the slope to his left. Luke recognized it instantly. The sombrero was the sort of headgear worn by the Rurales.

This could be bad, he thought grimly. If he had run into a Rurale patrol, there was every possibility they would try to kill him and steal his horse and all his other belongings.

The man who came out from behind the boulder and slid down to the trail wore the gray trousers and short jacket of the Rurales. He was young and clean-shaven. Lines etched around his eyes and mouth showed that he wasn't quite as innocent as he first appeared. "I am Lieutenant Diego Sanchez," he announced.

"Luke Jensen. I'm pleased to make your acquaintance, Lieutenant. At least . . . I hope I am."

"You are alone?"

"I suspect that you've been watching me for a while and you know I am."

Sanchez shrugged. "At least you did not lie. You are more than a day's ride from the border, Señor Jensen. What brings you to Mexico?"

"I'm looking for someone."

"Friends of yours?"

"Acquaintances." Luke had traded shots

with Kelly and Dog Eater. That was enough reason to say they were acquainted, he supposed.

"What makes you think they are here?"

"I was told they were bound for the Diablitos." That was stretching the truth, but it made sense. The outlaws had mentioned the name of an abandoned mine in the Little Devils, and a place like that would make a good hideout.

"Have you seen any other Rurales?"

The sharply-voiced question took Luke by surprise. He was about to say that the only other Rurales he had seen had been across the border in New Mexico Territory, at the settlement called La Farva, but some instinct made him stop.

He shook his head. "You and your men are the only ones I've run into since I crossed the border."

That statement was true, when you came right down to it.

"You are fortunate," Sanchez said. "The men we seek are criminals. They deserted their post and have become *renegados.* They would have killed you without a second thought and taken everything you own."

Luke thought it probably wouldn't be a good idea to mention that the same idea had crossed his mind about the lieutenant and his men. He said, "So you're looking for some of your own, eh?"

Sanchez turned his head and spat eloquently on the ground. "Not my own," he said with a note of outrage in his voice. "They are traitors! They have turned their backs on their duty. Their captain, a man named Almanzar, is nothing more than scum."

Having had the dubious pleasure of meeting the man, Luke couldn't disagree. While Lieutenant Sanchez, on the other hand, seemed to be that rarest of creatures: an honest Rurale. He appeared to be genuinely offended by Almanzar's lawlessness.

"I appreciate the warning, Lieutenant. I'll certainly keep my eyes peeled for those men and do my best to avoid them."

"You should turn around and return to the United States, Señor Jensen. The Diablitos are not safe for anyone, especially a gringo."

"It's important that I find those men," Luke said. "They have something that belongs to me."

Five grand, to be precise, but he wasn't going to mention *that* to Sanchez, either. Whether the lieutenant was honest or not, there was no point in tempting him.

"I could order you to return to your country," Sanchez said sternly. "I could take you into custody."

"You have a job of your own to do," Luke pointed out. "You don't need to be burdened with a prisoner. And even if I turned around and started north, you wouldn't know whether I kept going or doubled back."

Sanchez's dark eyes narrowed. "I could just have you shot."

"For no good reason? I don't think you'd do that, Lieutenant." Luke knew he was gambling his life on the judgment he had made about Sanchez's character.

After a few seconds, Sanchez sighed and said, "No, I would not. Consider yourself warned, Señor Jensen, and if you ride on, it will be at your own risk."

"It usually is," Luke said dryly.

"If I ever find out that you lied to me about the men I seek, I will find you and make you regret it."

That seemed like a pretty empty threat to Luke, but he nodded solemnly. "I understand."

Sanchez stood aside and motioned for Luke to go ahead.

As Luke nudged his horse into motion and rode past the lieutenant, he was acutely aware that an unknown number of men were still staring at him over the barrels of their rifles. All he could do was hope they would follow their officer's orders and allow him to pass.

No shots rang out as he followed the trail on through the badlands and emerged from them half an hour later to enter a wide stretch of flats that ran all the way to the base of the mountains. Not until then did he heave a sigh of relief.

As he rode on toward the Little Devils, he thought about the encounter with the Rurale patrol. They were a long way from La Farva, over in New Mexico Territory, which was the last place Almanzar and the giant Lopez had been seen.

At least, as far as Luke knew that was the last place the two surviving renegade Rurales had been. Maybe Almanzar and Lopez had crossed back over the border and headed for the Diablitos, thinking they would find sanctuary there. They could have been spotted somewhere along the way and reported to Lieutenant Sanchez. That made sense, Luke decided.

Of course, he might not ever have a full explanation, and if he didn't that was just fine with him. As long as they didn't interfere with his mission, the Rurales — good or bad — were no concern of his. He just wanted to find Kelly and Dog Eater.

He made a cold camp that night and pushed on toward the mountains the next morning. If nothing happened to delay him, he would reach them today, he mused as he rode toward the peaks. Then there would be the matter of locating the Don del Oro mine, which was supposed to be located at the head of a valley near the northern edge of the mountains, under a sawtooth peak that could be seen for miles.

Luke had spotted that sawtooth a couple days earlier and had been steering toward it ever since.

As he approached the mountains, he came across a pair of ancient ruts worn deeply into the ground. Reining in, he studied them and realized they were wagon ruts, etched into the earth by the iron-tired wheels of heavily loaded wagons passing along that route by the score. Loaded down with gold from the Don del Oro mine, Luke thought. It was the best indication yet that he was on the right trail.

If the man who had heard Kelly and Dog Eater mention the name hadn't made a mistake about what they said . . . *If* they had actually been talking about the abandoned mine . . . *If* they were still there . . .

He would have answers to those questions soon, Luke told himself. All he had to do was keep moving.

He reached the foothills by midday and pressed on into the mountains. Close up, the peaks were more impressive than they had appeared from a distance. Even though they were considerably shorter than the Rockies, they still loomed massively over a man to make him feel small and insignificant.

With the sawtooth mountain as his guide, he found a valley that penetrated into the Little Devils range. Once some ancient river had run through there and carved out the valley, he thought, although the ground was rocky and dry now.

According to the old desert rat — and it was just hearsay, since he hadn't been there but had heard about it from others — the mine was located at the head of the valley. If Kelly and Dog Eater were using it as their hideout, Luke couldn't just ride up there. They might see him coming and ambush him.

After he had ridden a couple miles up the valley, he stopped to rest his horse in a jumble of rocks and trees and wait until nightfall before continuing. He even got a little sleep, which showed just how cool-nerved he really was.

Once it was dark, he moved on up the valley, taking it slow and easy. His pulse quickened when he spotted a light up ahead. Out in the mountain wilderness, miles from the nearest village, he took the faint glow as a good omen. It had to be manmade, and he told himself that the men who'd made it were the ones he was after.

The light grew stronger as he got closer. Luke dismounted, drew his rifle, and left the horse in a thicket of scrubby pine trees to steal forward on foot.

After a few minutes, he was able to make out the buildings of the abandoned mine. Time and the elements had taken a toll. A long adobe building that might have served as a barracks had partially collapsed. So had a smaller, squat structure set some distance away that had probably housed the powder magazine. But a house built of stone was still standing, not far from the black hole in the side of the mountain that marked the mouth of the mine shaft. The light glowed from a window.

The superintendent of the mine must have lived in that stone house, Luke thought.

The most alarming thing he saw was a sturdy pole corral that appeared to have been built fairly recently. The corral itself wasn't what alarmed him, really, but the dozen horses inside it.

Kelly and Dog Eater had stolen horses from the ranch they had raided a day or so out of Rio Rojo, Luke recalled, but probably not that many. From the looks of it, several men besides the two outlaws were inside the house, making his job more complicated. Likely, they were the same sort of men as the ones he was after, and wouldn't allow him to just waltz in and take Kelly and the Apache.

He was pondering his next move when the sound of hoofbeats in the night made him stiffen. A lot of horses were coming, and moving fast. He pressed himself deeper into the shadows under the trees where he had been spying on the mine as a group of riders swept past him. With a clatter of hooves, they rode up to the stone house.

"Señor Kelly! Señor Creighton!" one of the newcomers called.

Two things immediately struck Luke. One was the fact that the man's voice sounded vaguely familiar. He had heard it somewhere before, although he couldn't place it. The other was a question. He wasn't surprised to hear Kelly's name, but who in blazes was Creighton?

More lights appeared as several men

stepped out of the house. Luke spotted Gunner Kelly and Dog Eater standing in the middle of the group.

The rider who had called out stepped down from his saddle and moved into the light from lanterns carried by a couple men on the porch. The yellow glow reflected off the barrels of guns held by the men on horseback.

Luke's jaw tightened as he realized why the man's voice had been familiar. He was Captain Almanzar, the renegade Rurale officer. Luke looked carefully at the new arrivals and was able to pick out the hulking form of Lopez among the group of night riders.

"I have brought you something, señors," Almanzar said in that preening, arrogant voice of his. "I came upon a patrol of my former comrades and thought you might like to question their officer. So we ambushed them."

Almanzar turned and made a flicking gesture. Lopez dismounted and hauled something down from the back of his horse. Carelessly, he tossed the burden on the ground. It was a man's body, and as he rolled onto his back so that the light shone on his face, Luke recognized the earnest features of the young lieutenant, Diego

Sanchez.

"Several more of the dogs still live," Almanzar went on. "I hope they might provide some entertainment for you, Señor Creighton."

Luke got the biggest surprise of all then. The Apache warrior known as Dog Eater looked down at the captive Lieutenant Sanchez with a fierce, bloodthirsty smile on his face and said in an accent eerily reminiscent of Milton Dietrich's, "Splendid, Captain. Absolutely splendid."

CHAPTER 25

"Have Lopez bring the lieutenant inside," Dog Eater — or rather — Creighton, as it appeared his name really was — went on. "The other prisoners can be placed in the old barracks. Part of it still has walls and a roof and is sturdy enough to contain them."

Luke's mind was reeling. Dog Eater didn't sound like any Apache he had ever encountered. But there was no doubt in Luke's mind that the man was the same one who had taken that shot at him back in Rio Rojo as the bank robbers made their escape. He never forgot the face of a man who tried to kill him.

Kelly spoke up. "What do you want with those Rurales?"

"They might have valuable information regarding how much the Mexican government knows about us," Creighton replied. "Our plans pose a threat to it, you know."

Kelly grunted. "I don't reckon anybody in

Mexico City has ever heard of us, at least not yet."

"They will," Creighton said. "When we take over all the territory along the border, they'll know who we are. They'll have to deal with us, because we'll be the rulers of this new empire. We won't be a couple two-bit bank robbers anymore."

The whole thing was loco, Luke thought, but it was starting to make a sort of cock-eyed sense. Creighton, or Dog Eater, or whatever the hell his name was, had an ambitious streak.

Like everybody else whose trail had crossed that of Gunner Kelly and Dog Eater, Luke had assumed that Kelly was the boss of the pair. Clearly, though, Dog Eater was more than just Kelly's sidekick. From the sound of it, he was the brains of the operation.

Luke wondered if he was actually an Apache.

Remaining concealed in the shadows, Luke watched as Lopez picked up Sanchez's senseless form, threw it over his shoulder, and carried the officer into the house, following behind Kelly, Creighton, and Almanzar.

Luke turned his attention to the other new arrivals and the half dozen prisoners with them. The captives had their hands tied and were roped together, with the lead rope attached to one of the horses so that they had been forced to run along behind. Their ripped, bloodstained clothing indicated that they had fallen at least once and been dragged before regaining their feet.

Luke didn't feel any real sympathy for the captive Rurales. Even Lieutenant Sanchez, who apparently was devoted to his duty, probably wasn't as innocent as he acted.

But Luke still wanted to capture or kill the two men he had pursued, and since the odds against him had gone up, he needed some allies. He didn't have to like those Rurales to get some use out of them.

The men who had ridden in with Almanzar and Lopez prodded the prisoners toward the old barracks. One of the men who had brought a lantern out of the house went with them. By its light, Luke got a look at the gang Kelly and Creighton had gathered. The outlaws were the usual motley mix of border trash from both sides of the line, some Mexican, some gringo, all hardened killers and thieves. They were plenty dangerous, all right, but not impressive in any other way.

And yet, judging by what Creighton had said, he intended to use them as an army to take over that part of Mexico. It wasn't unheard of. There was always some tinpot dictator-in-the-making stirring up trouble in Mexico.

The thing of it was, from time to time, they were successful enough to challenge the government. If Creighton gathered enough followers and financed his efforts with the proceeds of the bank job in Rio Rojo and other robberies, there was no way of knowing what he might be able to accomplish.

That was another reason to stop him, Luke thought. He would be nipping a potential revolution in the bud.

Mainly, though, he just wanted another shot at the two bank robbers.

With that in mind, he waited until the prisoners had been marched into the barracks and the outlaws returned outside. A couple didn't emerge from the building, and Luke supposed they had been left to guard the Rurales. The others unsaddled their horses and turned them into the corral. Then the men went into the stone house.

The old Don del Oro mine was quiet again.

Luke's brain worked quickly. He couldn't get to Kelly and Creighton as long as they were surrounded by nearly a dozen men.

What he needed was a distraction to draw the others out of the house. The prisoners would provide that distraction if he could set them free. They would know they would be fighting for their lives.

Already, they knew they would be lucky if the outlaws simply executed them. It was more than likely they would be tortured to death in the name of sport.

With a plan of sorts in mind, Luke set out to circle around toward the old barracks.

He used every bit of cover and shadow he could find and moved with the stealth that had become part of him during his years of man hunting. There was a good chance none of the outlaws expected trouble in their stronghold. As far as they knew, no one else was aware that the abandoned mine was their hideout.

Luke reached the far side of the partially collapsed adobe building and knelt a couple feet from a large gap where part of the wall had fallen in. He listened and heard two men talking softly in Spanish. A smell slightly sweeter than that of regular tobacco drifted to his nose. He knew they were smoking hemp as they stood guard over the prisoners.

He took off his hat and edged his head into the gap to take a look. It was too dark to see anything, but he sensed the guards were close by.

He couldn't just bust in there with guns blazing. That would alert the men in the house and ruin any chance he had of taking them by surprise. After thinking for a moment, he picked up a chunk of adobe that had been left scattered on the ground when the wall collapsed and tossed it so that it landed with a thud about a dozen feet on the other side of the gap.

The noise was loud enough to be heard inside the barracks. The soft, bored voices of the guards came to an abrupt halt. Silence reigned for a few seconds, then one man asked the other if he had heard that.

"It must have been Almanzar or one of the other men," the second guard replied in Spanish.

"They all went into the house. There is no reason for any of them to be behind the barracks."

"It was nothing," the second guard insisted. "Just one of the noises that the night makes."

Luke tossed a smaller, fist-sized piece of adobe. It bounced when it hit the ground and clattered against the wall.

"Something is back there," the first guard said.

"An animal. I'll take a look." The second guard didn't sound all that convinced there was nothing to worry about, despite his claim that an animal of some sort had caused the noises. His pride wasn't going to let him back down, though.

Luke heard wary footsteps as the man approached the opening in the wall.

A rifle barrel protruded through the opening first, followed by the rest of the weapon and the upper body of the man holding it. The guard leaned forward to peer along the wall in the direction of the sounds. He stood motionless for a long moment. Not seeing anything, he stepped over the eight inches of adobe wall that still stood at the bottom of the opening, turning his back to Luke.

The bounty hunter was ready. He had drawn the right-hand Remington and reversed it, gripping it so he could strike with the butt. He raised the gun, flipped the sombrero off the guard's head so it wouldn't cushion the blow, and brought the gun down fast and hard.

It smashed into the back of the guard's head with a crunch of bone. Without a sound, the man dropped like a shot. If he'd been startled by his hat flying off for no apparent reason, his confusion hadn't lasted long. He was either already dead from the shattered skull or soon would be.

"Paco!" The name was an urgent whisper from the other guard. He hadn't been able to tell exactly what had happened in the shadows behind the barracks, but had heard the impact of Luke's gun against the first man's head. "Paco, are you all right?"

Paco was long past being able to answer.

Several tense moments went by. Luke waited, utterly quiet. Finally he heard the soft shuffle of reluctant footsteps approaching the opening.

The other guard wasn't a fool. Without warning, his sombrero sailed out through the gap in the wall.

Luke's steely nerves kept him from reacting, but he knew that a lot of men who were keyed up for trouble would have been spooked into taking a shot at the headgear.

When the sombrero didn't draw a response, the guard stuck his head out to take a look.

Luke didn't wait for the man to step completely out of the barracks. He struck instantly. The Remington flashed down, and once again the gun butt smashed into bone with enough force to shatter it.

The guard was conscious just long enough to let out a grunt of surprise and pain before he slumped forward. Luke grabbed his collar and hauled him over what was left of the wall, letting him spill on the ground behind the barracks. He checked for a pulse on both men, but didn't find one on either.

Two of the outlaws were accounted for.

Straightening, Luke stepped over the wall into the old barracks. He turned his gun around and held it ready to fire. Enough starlight came through the big holes in the roof for him to make out a door on the other side of the room. The bar that rested in brackets across it told him the prisoners had to be on the other side.

He moved quickly and put his mouth to the tiny crack beside the door. "Anybody in there speak English?" he asked in an urgent whisper.

He heard some surprised muttering in Spanish. Then a man whispered back, "I speak some, gringo. Who are you?"

"The man Lieutenant Sanchez spoke to yesterday in the badlands. I've come to get you out of there."

Again there was silence on the other side of the door. Luke could almost see the Rurales thinking, wondering if it was some sort of trick.

At last, the man who had spoken asked, "Are you not part of the same gang as the traitors Almanzar and Lopez?"

"I am not," Luke said. "I came here to bring the leaders of that gang, the men called Kelly and Creighton, to justice."

"Then you are, how do you say, a bounty hunter?"

"That's right. I'm only interested in those two. You can have Almanzar, Lopez, and the rest."

"How?" the Rurale asked. "We have no weapons."

"There are two dead guards out here. They each had a rifle, a pistol, and a machete. That's enough to arm six of you. If you can lure the other members of the gang in here and jump them, you ought to be able to take their weapons away and use them."

"Some of us will be killed."

"That may be true. But they massacred your compadres. This is your chance for vengeance." Luke knew that would appeal to the Rurales. He heard them talking among themselves in hurried whispers on the other side of the door.

After a couple of minutes of discussion, the spokesman said, "If you let us out, what would you have us do in return?"

"Wait here for ten minutes," Luke said. "Then take one of the guns and fire several quick shots as if you are breaking out and the guards are trying to stop you. That ought to be enough to bring the others out here to see what's going on."

And if that happened, it would give him a chance to slip into the stone house and get the drop on Creighton and Kelly, he hoped.

"What about Lieutenant Sanchez?"

"I'll find him and see that he's safe," Luke promised. "I just need you men to make sure the odds aren't overwhelming against me."

Again the prisoners considered what he said. All the talk and delay that went with it were starting to get on Luke's nerves, but he made himself remain calm and cool. He needed the Rurales' help.

"Those men ambushed us," the spokesman finally said. "Shot down our amigos without mercy. And they told us while they were dragging us here that they would make us scream and beg for death. We think they are the ones who should scream."

"That sounds good to me," Luke agreed. "Do we have a deal?"

"We have a deal, gringo . . . if we can trust you to keep your word."

"We have to trust each other," Luke pointed out. "You'll find the dead guards right outside the back wall. Remember, give me ten minutes before you make your move."

"*Sí,* ten minutes."

Luke holstered his gun and took hold of the bar that kept the door closed. It was long, thick, and heavy, designed for two men to lower into place. The room on the other side of it must have been used as a stockade when the mine was operating, he thought. The workers in Mexican mines were usually treated little better than slaves. It wouldn't surprise him if some of them had been locked up for perceived violations of the superintendent's rules.

With a grunt of effort, Luke strained against the bar and felt it move. He gave another heave. The beam rasped against the door as it shifted and rose in the brackets. The muscles of Luke's arms and shoulders bulged against the black fabric of his shirt as he threw all his strength into the task.

The bar cleared the brackets. As soon as he felt it come free, he stepped back quickly and let go of it. The bar crashed to the hard-packed dirt floor. The door swung open, but only a couple inches before the bar stopped it again.

Luke didn't completely trust the Rurales. "Put your backs into it and you can shove the door open now. I have to go."

He ducked quickly through the opening in the wall and catfooted away into the night. He was out of the barracks before the Rurales were free and could double-cross him.

All he could do was hope the former prisoners would carry out their end of the bargain. He thought they would, if for no other reason than the opportunity to kill the men who had bushwhacked the patrol. But the chance to loot whatever they could find in the stone house would be a powerful incentive for men like them, too.

Luke broke into a run. He circled back to the trees where he had left his horse and untied the animal. Leading the horse, he hurried toward the back of the stone house.

He was counting off the seconds in his head as he moved. He knew he couldn't count on anything more than an approximation of the time the Rurales were supposed to wait before they fired those shots. By the time he reached 300, he was crouched next to an old shed behind the superintendent's residence. The house didn't have a back door, but there were a couple windows on that side.

Leaving the horse ground-hitched by the shed, Luke stole closer to the house. He pressed against the wall beneath one of the windows and listened. The room was dark and quiet, and after another minute had gone by, he reached up, gripped the sill, and hauled himself in.

Light came along a corridor from another room. He drew both revolvers and crept toward it, pausing outside the door.

The crackle of flames from around the corner told him there was a fireplace in the room. Someone had built a fire to ward off the chill of the mountain night. He heard voices talking in English.

Luke looked around. He was too much in plain sight. When the Rurales staged their distraction and the outlaws rushed out, he might be spotted. He eased into a doorless alcove that must have been some sort of storage area at one time. Hinges indicated that a door had closed it off once, but that panel was gone.

The only important thing was that the shadows inside the alcove were thick enough to keep him from being seen. He stood in stygian darkness and continued counting the seconds. He had reached 500 and was closing in on 600.

Three rapid shots hammered through the night, followed by two more. Shouts sounded inside the house. Swift footsteps rattled on the plank floors. A door slammed open and more shouts came from outside.

Then all hell broke loose. Gunshots, yelled curses, howls of pain . . . all the sounds of a battle going on out there.

That was his chance, Luke thought. He grasped both guns, stepped out of the alcove, and swung around the corner into the room where the light came from. Instantly, he spotted three men, leveled the Remingtons at them, and barked, "Don't move!"

CHAPTER 26

Actually there were four men in the room, Luke realized a second later — Creighton, Kelly, Almanzar, and Lieutenant Sanchez. He hadn't seen the young Rurale officer because he was lying on the floor where it appeared Almanzar had been kicking him.

The little renegade stared at Luke in amazement for a heartbeat, then exclaimed, "You!"

"You know this bastard, Almanzar?" Kelly growled. He stood tensely in front of the fireplace as if he wanted to slap leather, but he and Creighton and Almanzar were all grouped together so that Luke could cover them at the same time.

"He seems familiar to me as well," Creighton said in the voice that seemed so odd coming from an Apache warrior. "But I can't quite place — Rio Rojo! The man in the hotel window, correct?"

"That's right," Luke said. "My name's

Luke Jensen."

"And you've been on our trail ever since then? Remarkable!"

Almanzar pointed a trembling finger at Luke. "He ruined everything for me in La Farva! We should kill him!"

"Feel free to reach for your gun, Captain," Creighton said. "I'm sure Mr. Jensen would be glad to kill you . . . and that would give Gunner and me the time to kill him."

"You'd be betting that I can't get all three of you," Luke said with a ghost of a smile.

"It's a good bet," Kelly said. Like Almanzar, he was shaking a little from anger and the desire to kill.

Creighton leaned his head toward the door. "I assume you're responsible for that disturbance?"

The shooting and yelling continued outside.

Luke said, "I figured it might be a good idea to have some sort of distraction going on while I got in here and found the lieutenant."

"So you killed the guards in the barracks and freed the prisoners." Creighton nodded. "A sound strategy. It would have been wise, too, to start shooting as soon as you stepped in here. Why didn't you?"

"A couple reasons," Luke replied honestly.

"I didn't know exactly where Lieutenant Sanchez was, and I didn't want him catching a stray slug. And the other reason, mister . . . is you."

Creighton's swarthy face was as stolid as ever, but a flash of amusement twinkled in his dark eyes. "You're mystified by me, eh?"

"I heard you talk outside. I figured I had to find out how an Apache — Mescalero, right? — wound up with a Boston accent."

"I prefer to think of it as a Harvard accent, since I spent a year there. And as for your guess, yes, I am part of the Mescalero band, but only half. My father was Alexander Creighton. Have you heard of him?"

"I can't say as I have," Luke replied.

"He was a railroad man. A tycoon, some people called him. He had a mansion in Phoenix. My mother worked there as a maid. She was captured in a cavalry raid when she was just a girl and lived for years among the whites. Despite having a wife of his own, my father fancied her. . . ." Creighton shrugged. "When I came along he named me Sebastian and tried to see to it that I was educated and raised as white, even though he never officially claimed me as his own. He even sent me back east to college. Unfortunately, the other side of my heritage was stronger than he or even I realized. It came out one day during a disagreement with a fellow student. When he attacked me, I reacted instinctively."

"You killed him?"

"Actually, no. I did scalp him, but he survived. The university tends to frown on behavior like that, however, so I was expelled. I had no choice but to return west. My father disowned me and I went to live among my mother's people, but they didn't want me, either."

"So you turned outlaw," Luke guessed.

Creighton's control slipped and he showed a flash of temper as he snapped, "I'll be much more than a simple outlaw before I'm through. I'll be the lord and master of this whole part of the country."

"So you can show your father what his illegitimate son has done."

"My father died two years ago," Creighton said. "If I ever see him again, it'll be in hell."

"You called yourself Dog Eater and teamed up with Kelly so everybody would think he was the one running things. You didn't figure anybody would pay attention to a half-breed."

The shooting had stopped outside. Luke could only hope that the battle had ended with the Rurales having the upper hand. If the outlaws had won, the odds of him surviving the next five minutes were pretty slim.

"You're obviously an intelligent man, Mr. Jensen." Creighton shook his head. "It's a shame you're not going to get out of here alive."

"What makes you think that?"

Creighton nodded toward the doorway behind Luke and said, "Because you're about to be ripped limb from limb."

Luke might have thought Creighton was trying to trick him, but at that moment he heard a heavy footstep behind him, followed by a bellow of rage. He twisted around in time to see Lopez lunging at him. The giant renegade had streaks of blood on him from various wounds suffered in the battle outside, but the injuries didn't slow him down any.

From the corner of his eye Luke saw Creighton, Kelly, and Almanzar grab for their guns, but Lopez was almost right on top of him so he had to deal with that threat first.

Luke fired both Remingtons. Flame spurted from the barrels as they roared. Lopez was too big a target to miss, but the bullets seemed to have no effect on him. He crashed into Luke and drove him back against a table left there when the mine was abandoned.

The wood was rotten and splintered under the impact as Luke and Lopez landed on it. They went down amid the debris. The giant Rurale fell on top of Luke, forcing all the air out of his lungs. Luke managed to hang on to the gun in his right hand, but lost his grip on the left-hand revolver and it slipped away from him.

Lopez's weight pinned him to the floor. Luke gasped for air he couldn't get. Lopez had one huge hand wrapped around his throat and the other hand around the wrist of his gun hand. Luke couldn't breathe, nor could he bring the Remington to bear.

Lopez shifted his terrible grip on Luke's throat and twisted Luke's head to the side, almost like he was trying to rip it from his shoulders. Blood roared like a raging river inside Luke's head and a crimson haze dropped over his eyes. He knew he was only seconds away from dying.

Even if he could somehow survive Lopez's onslaught, Creighton, Kelly, and Almanzar had drawn their guns and were waiting to fill him with lead as soon as they got the chance.

Through that red haze, Luke saw something that the others couldn't. Behind them, Lieutenant Sanchez was forcing his bloody, battered form up from the floor. . . .

That glance gave Luke a glimmer of hope. He flailed out with his free hand and closed his fingers around a jagged piece of the broken table. With his head held to the side by Lopez, Luke had to thrust up blindly, but he put all the strength he could muster behind the blow.

Lopez spasmed wildly. Luke felt drops of hot rain spray across his face. It wasn't rain, though. It was blood, and it came from the hideous wound the sharp piece of wood had torn in the giant's throat. Lopez's grip suddenly weakened, allowing Luke to tear free.

The huge Rurale had lost quite a bit of blood already from his other wounds, and his massive body had finally reached its limit. His big hands pawed feebly at the piece of wood stuck in his ravaged throat as Luke shoved him aside and rolled away from him.

A gun roared, but when Luke came up on one knee, gasping for air, he saw flame geyser again from the muzzle of the revolver in Almanzar's hand as the captain struggled with Sanchez over the weapon.

Almanzar was occupied for the moment, leaving Creighton and Kelly to try to kill Luke. Both fired as Luke threw himself flat on the floor. The slugs whipped through the air above him. He triggered the Remington he still held and put two bullets into Gunner Kelly's chest. The redheaded outlaw rocked back as his eyes widened in pain and shock.

Almanzar and Sanchez reeled into Creighton, upsetting the aim of the half-breed Apache. Luke fired and saw Creighton jerk around as the bullet clipped him on the right arm. Creighton's gun fell from suddenly nerveless fingers.

The face of the bank robber and would-be emperor twisted in hate and insane rage as he jerked a machete with his left hand from behind the sash around his waist and leaped at Luke, savagely swinging the big blade.

Luke rolled aside desperately.

The machete hit the plank floor and stuck for a second before Creighton could rip it free. He swung a backhand at Luke as the bounty hunter came up. Luke went over backward to avoid it.

From the floor, Luke fired his last two rounds. The slugs punched into Creighton's belly and doubled him over. Screaming in pain, Creighton dropped the machete, clutched at himself, and stumbled forward a step before falling on his face. He lay there, huddled in a ball, as a pool of blood spread around him.

Across the room, Almanzar broke free of

Sanchez and struck him across the face, causing him to fall down. Panting, with his back to Luke, Almanzar raised the pistol he still held and aimed it at the fallen Sanchez.

Luke saw that, but the gun in his hand was empty. He spotted the other Remington, well out of reach.

He snatched up the machete Creighton had dropped, drew back his arm, and whipped it forward in a last-ditch throw. The machete struck Almanzar with such force that the blade drove all the way through his body and stuck its bloody tip a few inches out from his chest.

Almanzar stiffened. His head tipped forward as he looked down at what he could see of the machete. Then the gun slipped from his fingers, his eyes rolled up in their sockets, and he pitched forward onto the floor.

Luke scrambled to his feet. A quick step took him to the loaded Remington. He scooped it up and turned to cover the outlaws if any of them still wanted to fight.

They were going to have a hard time doing that, however. All four of them appeared to be dead.

"Sanchez," Luke rasped. "How bad are you hurt?"

"I . . . I will be all right, señor," the young

officer panted. "What about you?"

"I think so. If you can stand up, you'd better grab a gun so we can check on what happened outside."

"Sí. My men . . ."

"They jumped the rest of this bunch. I don't reckon you and I would be alive if they hadn't."

Sanchez armed himself with a couple pistols from the dead men, and Luke picked up one of the guns as well, not taking the time to reload his empty Remington. They stepped out of the house to look across a scene of carnage.

Bodies lay sprawled under the moonlight from the risen moon. Rurales and renegades alike, none of them were moving. No one moaned or made a sound.

It was a field of death, Luke realized. The two groups had wiped each other out.

"Go get a burning branch from the fireplace," Luke said. "We'll see if we can find any survivors."

The search turned out to be futile. Everyone at the abandoned mine was dead except for Luke and Sanchez. The young officer muttered horrified prayers as he realized the rest of his patrol had been killed.

"What am I going to do now?" he asked, seeming to direct the question to the universe at large as much as to Luke.

"Go back to your superior officers and report that you and your men valiantly did battle with a gang of outlaws and killed them," Luke answered. "Your men all died as heroes." He added grimly, "Maybe they'll get medals . . . posthumously."

Sanchez shook his head. "Not in the Rurales. There will be no medals for them, or for me."

"You get your life," Luke said. "That's the best reward."

And speaking of rewards, he thought. He went back into the house and walked over to Almanzar's body. Reaching down, he grasped the handle of the machete and pulled it free.

Sanchez came into the room after him and asked, "What are you going to do, Señor Jensen?"

"I came down here below the border looking for a couple things," Luke said as he tested the keenness of the blade with a thumb and eyed the necks of Creighton and Kelly. "I intend to take them back with me."

Two weeks later, Luke rode into Rio Rojo. He no longer had the heads of Sebastian Creighton, alias Dog Eater, and Gunner Kelly with him, and he was thankful for that. They had smelled bad enough by the time he'd gotten to Tucson and had the sheriff there identify them. The lawman had sent the necessary wires, and Luke's reward was waiting for him.

He did have the money stolen from the bank in Rio Rojo with him in his saddlebags, but no one knew that except him. He had found it cached in the stone house at the abandoned mine and was able to pack it away without Lieutenant Sanchez being aware of it. Since then, Luke hadn't told anyone about the money because he hadn't wanted to have to guard it from would-be thieves all the way back to Rio Rojo. Word of such things had a way of getting around.

He had taken his leave of Sanchez at the Don del Oro after shaking the young officer's hand and thanking him for helping to save his life.

"I will be disgraced when I go back," Sanchez had said, hanging his head. "I lost all my men."

"You might be surprised," Luke told him. "Your superior officers won't care about that as much as they will that you succeeded in wiping out those deserters, along with a bunch of other outlaws."

Sanchez had frowned. "But you and your friends killed many of the deserters at that town called La Farva."

"Well . . . nobody in Mexico knows that except you and me, now do they?"

Sanchez had been frowning in thought as Luke rode away.

As Luke rode past the livery stable, Cyril Dunbar came out of the barn and called, "Luke Jensen! Didn't know if we'd ever see you again in these parts."

"How are you, Mr. Dunbar?" Luke asked.

"Oh, I'm fine. Middlin' fair, I reckon, considerin' I don't have any help anymore. That boy Hobie done ran off!"

Luke grinned. "I know. He decided he wanted to be a bounty hunter. Then he changed his mind, took up with a beautiful redhead, and headed off to California . . . to go into the ranching business, I expect."

Dunbar stared at him for a couple seconds before asking, "How in blazes do you know all that?"

"It's a long story," Luke told him. "How's your brother doing? Is he up and around yet?"

"Gettin' there, gettin' there. He goes into his office an hour or so a day. Think he's there now, in fact."

"I'm glad to hear he's recuperating. Maybe it'll make him feel even better to know that the two men who shot him and robbed the bank are both dead."

The liveryman nodded solemnly and said, "Caught up to 'em, did you? Have much trouble along the way?"

"Not that much," Luke said wryly. He lifted a hand in farewell and rode on to the marshal's office.

When he went in, Marshal Cyrus Dunbar looked up from the desk where he was drinking coffee and sorting through some papers. "Jensen! Good Lord, man, you been gone so long nobody figured you were comin' back."

"That's sort of what your brother told me." Luke set his saddlebags on the desk in front of the marshal. "There's the bank's money. I didn't bring the heads of Kelly and Dog Eater with me, but they're dead, too."

"I know. Got a wire from the sheriff in Tucson. It didn't say anything about the money, though."

"Figured I'd play those cards pretty close to my vest."

The lawman nodded in understanding. "That was probably smart of you. You got a nice payday comin'. Of course, you could've just kept ridin' with that money and nobody would've ever knowed the difference."

"That's not the way I do business, Marshal," Luke said with a shake of his head. "I want what's coming to me for Monroe Epps, Kelly and Dog Eater, and recovering the money. That's all."

"You'll have it," Dunbar swore. "I'll see to that, and so will Mrs. Vanderslice. She'll be mighty pleased to see you."

"I've been on the trail for a long time. I ought to get some of this dust off me first. You'll take care of those saddlebags for me?"

Dunbar stood up, moving carefully. "I'll take 'em over to the bank right now and see that they're locked up in the safe."

"Then I'll go pay a visit to Felipe's."

"Oh, yeah, that reminds me," Dunbar said. "Remember that fella who busted in on you while you were takin' a bath and dallyin' with that little Philomena gal? The one you had to shoot?"

"I wasn't *dallying* with Philomena," Luke protested. "In fact, I was doing my damnedest *not* to dally. But what about that hombre?"

"Turns out he was wanted, all right, just like we suspected. Had a two thousand dollar reward on his head. So I reckon you've got that comin' to you, too."

Luke threw back his head and laughed at that unexpected stroke of good fortune. "I'll take it. I'll sure take it."

CPSIA information can be obtained
at www.ICGtesting.com
Printed in the USA
FFOW04n1842091113